Easton at the Forks
A Novel

Endorsements

"A heartwarming read full of memorable characters. If you loved the Mitford series, you'll love this."

Bill Myers, Bestselling author of *Eli*

"*Easton at the Forks* allows you to share the voyage of discovery and rediscovery of its heroine through her pain in loss and pride in the revelation of her family's deep Easton roots and contribution of her ancestors, including Peter Kichline, to the formation of our country."

Christyn Olmstead, Editor, PSSDAR Newsletter

"What fun! A fantastic representation of the fascinating stories one can uncover when they dive into their genealogy while also capturing the energy and adventure of the search. I wish everyone took the time to tell their story this way."

D. Joshua Taylor, Nationally known and recognized genealogical author, lecturer, researcher, and TV personality featured in *Who Do You Think You Are?* and *Genealogy Roadshow*.

"Rebecca's delightful book paints the landscape for a living, breathing Easton of the 1760s. Names we have only read in dry history books come to life. *Easton at the Forks* is a treat!"

Christopher Black, Artistic Director of the Bachmann Players

"Lovers of American history will especially enjoy this delightful new offering from author Rebecca Price Janney. Filled with both historical and modern details, *Easton at the Forks* brims with Rebecca's love for her topic and her joy in bringing this story to readers. Grab this book and snuggle in for a warm and wonderful read!"

Marlo Schalesky, award-winning and multi-published author of *Waiting for Wonder*

"In her book, *Easton at the Forks,* Rebecca Price Janney captures a story that is both historical and entertaining as her main character, Erin, strives to learn everything about her ancestral family lineage. Rebecca takes you from the present quest to search the family tree back to the 18th century with actual happenings of Erin's ancestor's role in the establishment of this great country we call America. The book is thoroughly enjoyable reading and presents an interesting format between then and now."

Salvatore J. Panto, Jr., Mayor, City of Easton, PA

"Rebecca Price Janney weaves a delightful tale of two families intertwined throughout history for all time. This absorbing story traces the heroine's search for a Revolutionary War patriot. I couldn't put it down until I finished—an enjoyable read!"

Sara Jane McCurdy, Southeast District Director, Pennsylvania State Society Daughters of the American Revolution

Easton at the Forks
A Novel

Rebecca Price Janney

Elk Lake
PUBLISHING™

Plymouth, Massachusetts

Cover Design: Jeff Gifford
Interior Design: Vanessa Moore
Editor: Deb Haggerty
Published in Association with WordWise Media Services

PUBLISHED BY: Elk Lake Publishing, Inc., 35 Dogwood Dr., Plymouth, MA 02360

Library Cataloging Data
Names: Janney, Rebecca Price (Rebecca Price Janney)
Title: Easton at the Forks; A Novel / Rebecca Price Janney
226 p. 23cm × 15cm (9 in. × 6 in.)
Description: Elk Lake Publishing, Inc. digital eBook edition | Elk Lake Publishing, Inc.
Trade paperback edition | Massachusetts: Elk Lake Publishing, Inc., 2016.
Summary: Two people connected through time …
Identifiers: ISBN-13: 978-1-944430-18-4 (trade) | 978-1-944430-16-0 (POD) | 978-1-944430-17-7 (ebk.)
1. Christian 2. Genealogy 3. Easton PA 4. Historical Fiction 5. Ancestral History 6. Coping with Death 7. Purpose in Life

Dedication

"For all the saints, who from their labors rest"—
especially my grandmothers.

Acknowledgments

You've heard of labors of love? Well, *Easton at the Forks* has been one of them. Just as I treasure my real visits to Easton, so have I reveled in going there every time I sat down to write this story. I'd like to thank all the dear people who have encouraged and inspired me, including my personal cheerleaders Sandra Allen, Marlo Schalesky, my husband, Scott, my mother, and my father, who believes this should be a *New York Times* bestseller. Thanks, Dad! Here's hoping you're right. Thanks also to my son, David, who always encourages people to buy his mom's books and who loves a good story himself. Then there's my intrepid agent and friend, Dave Fessenden, who always listens to my stories.

I'd also like to recognize and thank Sharon Gothard of the Easton Area Public Library's Marx Room, Kim Rose and Nancy O'Hanlon of the Sigal Museum, the Rev. Michael Dowd, Christopher Black, Paul Strikwerda, Richard Hope, and the late great Jane Moyer. All of you have inspired me so very much.

I want to pay tribute to four dear friends whose husbands died when those friends were quite young—Janet Anderson, Mary Ann Knox, Karen Lyman, and Marlene Ciranowicz. Your faith and fortitude have inspired me, and I wish each of you the brightest of futures.

Finally, huzzahs and kudos to some of the nicest, most fun ladies I've ever known, with whom I share membership in the Daughters of the American Revolution, Valley Forge Chapter, especially our past regent, Christyn Olmstead.

One generation will commend your works to another;
they will tell of your mighty acts.

—Psalm 145:4

❧ • ❧

CHAPTER ONE

E rin savored her South Korean students' interest in immigrant stories from the early 1900s. This particular American history class had always brought out their talkativeness, ever since she'd starting teaching the unit almost ten years ago. These students knew what leaving home for a strange new place was like, even if they'd done so in a matter of hours by air rather than taking several days to cross an ocean in a crowded steerage section. She wandered around the college classroom, pausing over their desks, listening to their small group discussions, feeling her eyes mist as they talked. Afterward, she walked to the front and sat on the edge of the table, glancing up at the Eisenhower-era wall clock, which always ran six minutes slow. Four minutes left.

"I really enjoyed hearing your stories. Do you have any comments?" Erin looked from one student to another. "Do you have any questions?"

"I do, Professor Miles."

"Yes, Kang." Kang, which Erin had learned was pronounced "Kong," as in "King Kong," not only kept conversations going, but he also acted as a translator when she or one of the students didn't understand each other—a frequent occurrence.

"When did your family come to America?" the student asked.

She took a deep breath, then slipped into default mode. "Well, the first Miles who came to America was James. You know how we've talked about William Penn, the founder of Pennsylvania?"

"Yes." Kang nodded.

"Good! By way of review, he was a Quaker, who wanted to establish a new kind of colony where people of all religions could live together peacefully, very much unlike Europe at the time. That's why Philadelphia means—"

"City of Brotherly Love."

"That's right. James Miles was a Quaker, who came here two years after Penn in 1683, and he owned land which is now part of the Independence Hall area."

Their eyes lit with admiration. This was her identity now.

"James Miles' grandson, Samuel, was a colonel in the American Revolution, and afterward, he served as a mayor of Philadelphia. Actually, I'm doing my doctoral dissertation about him."

"Did you say sixteen hundred eighty-three?" Kang asked.

"Yes, that's right."

"That was a long time ago," he said.

She remembered how she'd felt shopping in a women's store on Philadelphia's tony Main Line when the salesclerk had looked at her in admiration upon seeing the name Miles on Erin's credit card. "Are you related to *the* Miles family?" the clerk had asked.

"Yes, but the money ran out a long time ago," was her plucky answer.

"Don't worry, honey," the clerk had whispered after leaning over the counter. "We get some poor DuPonts in here too."

Sarah now spoke up. "That is most impressive, Professor. But that is your husband's family, yes?"

"That's correct, Sarah."

"What about yours? When did they come to America?"

She uncrossed her legs, then crossed them again. Two minutes left on the clock. "I'm afraid I don't know much about my mother's side of the family." A cement truck rumbled past on the street, rattling the open windows.

"What about your father's people?" Sarah asked, persistent.

"They came here in the 1920s."

"Where were they from?" Kang asked.

"Italy."

"Ah, you are Eye-talian, then!" Sarah said.

The word hung suspended like a piñata, which Erin half expected someone to take a swing at, just like old times. "Well, that's all for today. For our next class, please read the chapter about the 1920s and answer the questions on your syllabus."

The students rose and pushed their books into colorful backpacks while she gathered her notes, tossed her empty coffee cup in the trash, and cleaned the white board. "*Anyoung hee gyeseyo!*" they called out as they left.

Even after teaching Koreans all these years, Erin wasn't exactly sure about the nuances of saying good-bye in their language, so she stuck with English. She then turned out the light and walked down the hall to the main faculty office to hand in her attendance sheet. The bulletin board now contained the fall course lists, and she smiled when she saw the names next to several history classes blank. Once she got the full-time professorship, her name would be there. Hatfield College was no Lafayette, where she'd gone, or Villanova, her husband Jim's alma mater and where she'd gotten her master's and was finishing her doctorate. However, according to *U.S. News and World Report*, the college was "up-and-coming," in no small measure due to the generosity of her husband's parents and grandparents. Now she and Jim were making significant contributions.

"You're a shoo-in," her best friend, Melissa, had said over lunch the previous week after the last set of interviews. "You've taught there part-time for years. The students give you high evaluations every semester, not to mention your family. You've earned that position!"

Erin's one doubt emerged. "Hatfield's getting more selective, and I don't have my doctorate."

"You've been moving in that direction, though."

She'd been stalled in the "ABD"—all-but-dissertation—time warp for three years, but if she secured the position, she'd have all summer to finish.

◈ • ◈

Erin could hear the TV from the garage and feeling addled, wondered if she'd left the set on before running out the door to class, which she'd done twice before. Oh, well, at least she hadn't left the iron or the oven on—or had she? Anxiety bubbled up inside her as she entered the house. Erin stopped so suddenly when she saw Jim sitting on the sofa she almost fell over her dog. *Why is he watching Ina Garten making kale and sausage soup? Jim never watches the Food Network, and he's never home in the middle of the day.*

Without removing her coat, she moved toward him. "Hi honey. What are you doing home so early?" She waited for him to turn his face in her direction so she could kiss him, and hesitated when she saw the strange look on his face. Then, she remembered his doctor's appointment, how she'd urged him to go since he'd been so sluggish, practically making the phone call herself until he finally gave in. She fully expected him to say something about needing to work less and relax more, maybe take a vitamin or join the gym. If that had been the case, though, why wouldn't he have just gone back to work and texted her? "How did you make out at the doctor's?"

She was still standing when he said, "I have cancer."

Erin looked up at the sign reading "Adams Cancer Center" wondering how such words could in any way apply to her virile husband or their lives. The sight of them affected her like a sharp blow straight to her middle, and her stomach wrenched, not for the first time that day. She straightened her shoulders and pressed toward the entrance, holding Jim's hand. They would get through this. They would battle this thing together, and once they came out on the other side of this experience, they'd inspire other people going through the same thing.

She continued holding Jim's hand when the gray-haired oncologist spewed forth unfamiliar words, rapidly—hepatocellular carcinoma, metastasize, hemochromatosis, hepatic. Erin's mind swirled like a pot of rice boiling over onto the stove. The doctor must've seen her bewildered expression because he slowed down and said, "I know this is all very new." He pushed a brochure with a picture of smiling people in bike helmets across his desk. "This will go into further detail, and you can always call me with any questions."

That's it? A medical dictionary full of words? We're being dismissed already?

"So, what's the treatment plan? What are my options?" Jim asked.

The doctor pursed his lips, and Erin focused on a tiny freckle at the left corner of his mouth, making the specialist look almost boyish. "With this kind of aggressive cancer we can try chemo, but in most cases, it isn't very effective, and the side effects can be difficult to manage."

Erin felt the blow, which left her sprawling emotionally all over the green carpeting. She wanted to say something, but she was mute. If she opened her mouth, she might just lose her breakfast.

"Maybe if we'd caught it earlier …" Jim's voice was quiet as he bowed his head.

Erin squeezed his hand until her knuckles went pale. *How helpless he must feel!*

The doctor folded his hands on his lab-coated lap. Outside the window, a construction worker in a yellow hard hat ascended scaffolding. "This kind of cancer is difficult to detect in the early stages because it mimics other conditions, such as flu. It tends to have a rapid onset and progress just as quickly."

Erin tried wrapping her mind around this while tiny specks swam before her eyes. She took a deep breath so she wouldn't faint. *If I'd just pushed Jim to get a checkup two months ago, maybe we wouldn't be living through this nightmare.* "Isn't there anything you can do?" Her tiny voice sounded like a five-year-old who'd just discovered a mortally wounded bird in her yard.

"We'll do everything we can to make Jim comfortable and, of course, you can decide about pursuing some treatments, which could prolong life." The doctor leaned back in his chair, his mouth a straight line, his brown eyes as soulful as Erin and Jim's basset hound.

The words "prolong life" sliced through her thoughts, cutting to the heart of the matter.

"By how much?" Jim asked, his hand grasping Erin's so tightly her circulation was getting cut off. "A year? Two years?"

"I'm afraid not that much." The doctor cleared his throat. "A month. Perhaps two."

A month? I'll only have Jim another month? She hadn't seen this train wreck coming, but now the blast of the engine's whistle throbbed in her ears.

The doctor threw them a bone. "This is one of the less painful forms of cancer. My patients actually have an ongoing sense of well-being."

A Bible verse came to Erin out of the blue—*Though he slay me, yet will I trust in him.* She, Ethan, and Jim were about to be slain. As for trust, that remained to be seen. When they got home, she scarfed down her own brand of comfort food—a salami and Nutella sandwich on cinnamon raisin bread.

≈ • ≈

Jim spent most of the time in the bathroom after his first treatment and though he returned to work for a week, at night he came home looking like a puddle about to evaporate in the heat. When he could no longer venture beyond the house, the Miles home became a place of visiting nurses, relatives, and friends. Erin wanted her family to come, too, but at first, she wasn't sure they would.

"Erin, you know I don't drive that far," her mom told her over the phone.

"We live less than an hour away." Her teeth clenched. "Didn't you tell me your friend offered to bring you here?"

"Yes, but I can't impose on her."

Erin knew better than to argue the point with Audrey Pelleriti. *She always does this. She wouldn't even come visit me when I was in the hospital in grad school. She won't drive a stupid hour from home, and she won't let anyone else bring her either!*

This time, however, Erin's brother, Allen, and his wife, Tanya, ferried Audrey to Lansdale. Tanya brought a chicken casserole and said, "I'm sure you don't have a lot of time to cook." Allen lingered along the sidelines, offering tentative conversation when prompted.

Allen's never been comfortable around illness. But having them here seems so normal, the way things are supposed to be, the way they are with the Miles.

Her nieces, Alana and Kate, arrived with their kids the following weekend, and Erin watched as Ethan bounced on the trampoline with his cousins in the backyard while Toby stood guard.

"Honestly, Aunt Erin, if there's anything I can do, please call," Alana said, squeezing her arm. "I have time now that I'm not working."

"That goes for me as well," Kate said.

Everyone within a reasonable distance came, except Erin's father. They spoke a few times a week on the phone, but she hesitated every time she came close to inviting him. Tony had never been to her home and having him here now felt awkward. Finally, she stopped trying to convince herself.

Jim's remaining days flowed like the Lehigh River on its steady, unhurried course toward its rendezvous with the Delaware. Rather than suffer, he experienced a sense of well-being, as if he'd just walked a couple of miles and was bathed in endorphins. He told corny jokes to Ethan—"Why did the chicken cross the road? To show the squirrels, it could be done," and quoted passages from T.S. Eliot to Erin, who was surprised Jim knew them in the first place. He especially liked to say, "What we call the beginning is often the end. And to make an end is to make a beginning. The end is where we start from." *I know in my heart Jim isn't just cheerful because of some strange twist of his disease—he's a man at peace with God.*

One day while she sat with him on their bed looking through an old photo album, Jim gazed at her and smiled. "You know, Erin, I'm not angry about this, just disappointed I won't get to see Ethan grow up or hold hands with you when we're old and gray and tottering through the park on walkers." When he squeezed her hand, she felt its cold thinness, almost as if he needed mittens to stay warm.

I wish I had his peace. I bounce between hope and despair, but I can't let Jim know how I feel. And poor Ethan's being such a soldier, but he gives way to tears when he doesn't get the key hit on his baseball team or can't answer a math question. He seems to want to be with Jim, to hole himself up in our room like a hermit.

"Everything's going to be okay," Jim kept assuring her. "You won't have financial worries. I've taken care of that. You have Ethan, and your friends, and teaching. My family will be there for you and your family too." His amber eyes stared into hers. "Be sure to spend time with them." She felt an ache in the pit of her heart. "Someday, when the time comes, I hope you'll find someone new to pour your love into."

"I can't imagine that ever happening," she said through a veil of tears, for once unable to hold them back.

He stroked the side of her damp face and pushed her hair behind her ear. "They say when people are happily married, they're more likely to remarry when a spouse dies. I like to think we've been very happily married."

She felt like her throat was stuffed with dry cotton. "Yes, we have."

"Of course," he said, sounding like his old self, "no one could ever replace me."

There were no words.

∾ • ∾

At the beginning of May, the river of Jim's life spilled over the dam, just like the Lehigh at the Forks of the Delaware, but his flowed in the direction of eternity. Erin, who lay next to him, felt her husband let go.

∾ • ∾

Although noon was long past and she felt hungry, Erin didn't want to eat. There were just so many people to greet and thank for coming to the funeral and the luncheon, including Jim's best friend from college who'd driven all the way from North Carolina to be there. *I bet I smell like a fruit salad after hugging so many people with all these different perfumes and aftershaves.* She also spotted guys from the garage band Jim had formed back in high school.

"We thought we were going to be the next REO Speedwagon, but in the end, we just enjoyed being together," Brad, their lead singer, said. His thinning blonde hair was now longer than hers.

The Kiwanis was there too, and dozens of employees from the family's meat packing plant, some in uniforms because they'd come over the lunch hour. Every student from her two classes at Hatfield College had shown up, along with most of the professors and administrators. One of her own childhood friends had driven down from the Lehigh Valley for the service, including someone Erin hadn't seen since her and Jim's wedding. Karen looked like her youthful self, although age had started to carve her features more deeply.

"Do you remember me?"

"Oh, Karen, I could never forget you." Erin hugged her.

"I brought my mother too."

Sure enough, there was Yvette, who'd been Audrey's best friend during Erin's childhood. Erin went to find her mother, feeling almost happy when the old friends embraced through tears, smiles, and a multitude of staccato expressions like, "I can't believe it! I haven't seen you in years!" They didn't say much about Erin's loss—their very presence spoke to that—but they did reminisce.

"Do you remember when we sat up all night on New Year's Eve in your room listening to the radio?" Karen asked.

Erin laughed. "Yes, and we kept trying to get through on the contest line."

"Oh, you kids and that radio!" Audrey's tone conveyed mock disgust. "You drove me crazy."

"Didn't you win passes to Dorney Park once?" Karen asked.

"I did, but …"

"I couldn't go. I came down with mono." She looked like a contestant on *Wheel of Fortune,* who'd just completed the puzzle.

Erin's expression went roguish. "And the time your mom made chicken cacciatore and forgot to peel the onions?"

Karen laughed out loud. "Oh, I know! We sat there sliding the skins off our teeth."

Yvette rolled her eyes. "Oh, please, don't remind me of that!"

Her delicate laugh was like a sweet chime, and Erin smiled as she remembered how Yvette had always reminded her of Jackie Onassis.

"Speaking of teeth … remember when you fell on a pile of boards my dad was cutting and had to be rushed to the dentist?" Karen asked. "Whatever happened?"

Erin pointed to her mouth. "Braces." She'd paid for them herself after she got married. Her father had refused—*If God wanted you to have straight teeth, you'd have been born with them*—and her mother never had enough money for so-called extras. "Wait here while I get Allen. He'll love seeing you again."

For a few minutes, Erin felt like she was at a party, not her husband's funeral luncheon.

❧ • ☙

"Erin, dear. I think you should try to eat something."

She looked up from a conversation with her neighbors, Todd and Julia, into the benevolent face of her mother-in-law, Pat Miles. She loved that face. She was one of the fortunate women who got along well with their husband's mothers.

"You've been going hard all day." Pat pressed a plate into Erin's hands. "If you'll excuse us, Erin needs to eat lunch."

"Actually, we have to go," Todd said. "Annie has a pee-wee softball game in an hour."

"Thanks for coming, you two," Erin said and obediently followed Pat to a table where Melissa and her husband, Tim, sat. Erin kept looking over her shoulder at all the people she hadn't spoken to yet. Jim had had so many friends.

"Make sure she eats, Melissa," Pat said.

"I will, Mrs. Miles."

"Where's Ethan?" Erin looked around the table.

"I saw him a while ago with your niece's children. Don't worry, he's doing fine," Melissa said.

She noticed the chicken wrap on her plate for the first time and frowned. Something was missing. She opened up the tortilla part and sprinkled a heaping teaspoon of sugar on the contents. Better, but still not right.

Tim seemed to read Erin's mind. "I'll take that." He snatched the plate, went up to the buffet, and returned in a few minutes. "There you go."

Erin examined Tim's handiwork. He'd added pickled beets, a slab of Jello salad, and a handful of French fries to the wrap, which had been transformed into a culinary Battle of the Bulge.

Melissa frowned at the plate. "What in the world is that?"

Tim puffed out his chest, his green eyes twinkling. "This is my version of a Primanti sandwich."

"Huh?" Erin stared at the food. *This looks really good.*

"Primanti Brothers. I'm from Pittsburgh, remember? At their restaurants, they put everything that normally goes on the side of a sandwich inside the sandwich. Besides, I know all about your strange concoctions."

"Sounds like my kind of place." Erin picked up the wrap and took a bite, nodding with satisfaction as she caught a drop of mayo with her napkin.

As she ate, her eyes continued searching the packed hall until she saw her son at a table with her father, Bridget, and one of her nieces, Ethan looking very much at home with them. He was probably regaling them with stories about Minecraft, and to their credit, they managed to appear deeply interested. Bridget was even asking him questions, and Ethan was enthusiastically answering. She just hoped her mother didn't see this. Perhaps with Audrey's diminishing eyesight, she wouldn't notice Bridget was even in the room. Erin couldn't stand the thought of a scene. She imagined herself intervening, yelling at them for being inappropriate, shuddering at the thought of something like that spilling onto her carefully cultivated life and relationships.

She saw Pat and Al move toward her Dad and Bridget, wrapping their smiles around them. They'd never actually met Erin's father and stepmother before. Was a clearer path opening to her family now? Were these new encounters cutting through the barbed wire? She wasn't sure what to expect, especially since people at funerals tended to be on their best behavior.

Melissa followed Erin's eyes to that table and back. "Ethan seems to be enjoying your dad."

"I like seeing them together." She bit into a pickle she'd dipped into a chocolate fountain then sprinkled with pepper.

"I'm glad you're okay with that." She pressed her warm hand over Erin's. "I introduced myself to him and his wife. They were very nice."

"That's good to know." *I should say something else, but I'm not up to small talk right now.*

Melissa started talking about her nephew's son's girlfriend's daughter in Oregon, but Erin wasn't able to follow the story past the opening scene. She was okay with that, though. Erin ate strange things when she was stressed or excited, and Melissa got off on tangents. They understood each other.

She watched as her dad produced a coin from a pocket and handed the quarter to Ethan, whose face lit up. When he hugged his grandfather and didn't let go, Erin froze. Her father had never been much for hugging, always breaking free of her as quickly as possible. Her mama bear instincts filled her with strength she knew would propel her straight across that room if he hurt her son. She let out big breath when Tony embraced Ethan tightly, for a long time, as tears ran down both their cheeks.

CHAPTER TWO

Easton, Pennsylvania, April 1766

He was so eager to read the weekly news from Philadelphia he didn't notice the breakfast Greta had put before him until the scent finally caught his attention. *Something is definitely wrong.* He put the paper aside, careful not to get food stains on it because the periodical would be making the rounds at the courthouse. Few people in the village could afford such a luxury, and he was only too glad to share his paper with them. He realized something else was amiss.

Where are my children, and why aren't they ever at meals anymore? He stared at the clock on the mantel without actually seeing the time as he made a quick mental inventory. *Peter and Andrew might be at the mill with Jacob tagging along, but then again, they won't be there until after school.* Susannah was normally at home being taught, but since Margaretta's death, the six-year-old didn't seem to be around much either. Alarm prickled his scalp, along with a dose of shame because he didn't know where his own children were.

Since that harsh day in February when Margaretta's body was lowered into the frosty ground, Sheriff Peter Kichline had wandered around in a half dream. He was just now awakening to the routines of a home he'd never had to manage, not with his capable wife in charge. The only one running things at this point seemed to be his indentured servant, and he had his doubts about her abilities.

He looked down at the contents of his plate. *Is that bacon?* The meat bore the slightest smell of bacon, yet resembled chunks of scorched wood. He glanced toward what he thought was a fried egg, but when he dipped in his fork, he discovered porridge instead. *How strange. Why didn't Greta put the cereal in a porringer? At least the bread looks edible.* He brightened at the prospect until he lifted the small loaf. That's when he noticed the bread bore a striking resemblance to Assemblyman Benjamin Franklin of Philadelphia, whom he'd met during the Indian troubles several years ago. He studied the likeness, mystified by how that had happened and not wanting to deprive that good fellow of his head, pushed the plate aside. When had Greta's cooking failed so utterly? He became aware of the roominess of his breeches, but hadn't Mr. Chatterfield just taken in the waist? If he didn't tighten them just right, his fellow citizens would see a lot more of their sheriff than they'd bargained for.

He glanced about the dining room where cobwebs had gathered in the corners of the deep windowsills. Margaretta would never have allowed that. *What is wrong with Greta anyway? Is she taking unfair advantage of her and her father's upcoming release?* He pushed the thought aside. *No, Greta has never been a wastrel before; she's always been a hard and conscientious young woman and a decent cook.* Something else was afoot, yet he was baffled to know how to begin dealing with it, a feeling he fervently disliked.

The young fräulein entered the room with her usual quick movements as if she were being chased. Although she looked like she wanted to cluck her tongue at him for not eating, she seemed to remember her place. A wife could get away with that, not a servant.

"You haven't touched your food, Sheriff."

He tried to keep a civil tongue in his head. "I regret to say, Fräulein Greta, there was nothing I could eat."

She lifted the plate and tears leaked from her perpetually startled-looking brown eyes. "*Es tut mir Leid*, Herr Kichline. I am, well … preoccupied."

"Well, then. Is everything all right?" he asked, not knowing what he would say if she did tell him.

She hesitated. "I … wouldn't trouble you with it, sir."

Her response came as a relief, not because he didn't care but because he wasn't especially good with feminine troubles. "Do you know if my boys are at school?"

In a voice so quiet he had to lean forward to catch her words, Greta admitted, "They were gone before I rose."

"And Susannah?" His voice was a low growl. Greta might be forgiven for burning the bacon, but not knowing where his little girl was?

"I am so sorry, sir."

He let out a puff of air through his nose and shook his head. Greta was truly repentant, but he was still irritated, not to mention alarmed. He got up and walked to the hall for his hat, deciding to visit the Great Square, the school, and the mill in search of his children. He was far better at running Northampton County than this household, at dealing with wars and rumors of wars, horse thieves, and people who couldn't pay their taxes than with flustered servants and children who needed their mother.

ఌ • ఔ

He tucked the newspaper under his left arm and stepped out onto Northampton Street, heading east toward the Great Square. The Delaware River shimmered in the near distance a few blocks past the center of town, flanked by the edge of New Jersey on one side and joined at the forks by the Lehigh River just downstream. In the morning sun, the windows in the new court-house's cupola glimmered, a crowning jewel in the county seat. Peter smiled as he looked upon the building, happy the courts were running more efficiently than in the early years of Northampton County when sessions were held in local taverns. The courthouse added a certain panache to Easton, a visual respite in the nascent village of log cabins and shops, sprinkled with a few stone houses occupied by the better-off, including himself.

Back in 1752, before he'd begun noticing silver threads in his light auburn hair, Peter and his wife Margaretta had thrown in their lot with the new town of Easton. At first, they helped by running a tavern and working to build a new school. They'd seen the place through Indian wars and treaties, epidemics, and floods, and they had prospered. When Peter had to give up the tavern to serve as Northampton County's Sheriff, he'd turned to milling. That profession led to a generous livelihood for his family which, as of February 20, consisted of two nearly adult sons, a younger boy, and a sweet six-year-old daughter.

As he walked, he came upon two men, one so engrossed in a rant he didn't notice the sheriff—until too late.

"If you put all their brains together, you'd still have nothing but a half-wit." The man spat on the ground. "Them and that stuttering Jew, Michael Hart."

The other man wore a trapped, panicked look when he saw Peter coming.

"The cursed Germans think they own this place!"

As soon as the last word had fallen from his lips, Robert Bell noticed Peter, closed his eyes and turned away.

The sheriff tipped his cap, looking down at the much shorter Bell. "Good day, Mr. Bell." Turning to one of the town's two tailors he said, "And a good day to you, Mr. Chatterfield."

"Oh, good morning, good morning, Sheriff."

"Sheriff." Bell nodded, his face flaming under his hat.

Peter thought Bell was probably more ashamed of getting caught than because of actual remorse. The man was known for voicing his opinions in Easton's taverns about the German populace, especially after a few tankards of ale. He would always shut up, though, when the sheriff was around. Peter Kichline was, after all, a force to be reckoned with—wealthy, Heidelberg-educated, influential. Bell hadn't been to any university here or abroad, but he seemed to think his English pedigree made him superior to everyone else.

"Good day." Bell turned to leave, walked straight into a pile of sheep dung, which emitted a loud squish. He stomped off, muttering an oath under his breath.

Chatterfield put a hand to his mouth as if to stifle a laugh.

Peter winked at the tailor, who was a good enough fellow. Since he kept a public business, he had to deal with all sorts, including the Bells of Easton, of which there were more than a few.

"I hope you don't think, Sheriff, that I … I …"

Peter clapped him on the back. "Never, my friend."

Chatterfield stood a little straighter. "Well, then, good day to you."

"And a good day to you as well."

Like the rest of Pennsylvania, Easton was a place where people from all over Europe were learning to live together in what William Penn had foreseen as a place of brotherly love. The founder's ideal was not always reality, however, especially since his worldlier sons had assumed the colony's proprietorship after he died. The English-Scottish contingent, although a minority in Easton, tended to malign the Germans, who far outnumbered them. Though the Germans were poorer and handicapped by their lack of English-speaking skills, they were generally hardworking and honest, and they very much looked up to Peter Kichline, whom they regarded as a protector.

There was also the Indian population, which had diminished after the last decade's brutal massacres of European settlers. Some of the Lenape had mixed in with the Europeans as farmers and craftsmen, a few had intermarried with the whites, but many more had pushed further west.

Walking another block, he paused before the door of his friend, Lewis Gordon. Peter hoped Lewis' sister might have some knowledge of Susannah's whereabouts and might be able to advise him about finding a new servant once Greta finished her indenture. Before he could knock, the door opened, and he was faced with the imposing figure of Frau Neuss, the Gordons' housekeeper, holding a rug and a paddle to beat the carpet into submission.

"*Ach, Guten Morgen, Herr Kichline!*" Her smile revealed an almost toothless condition.

"*Guten Morgen, Frau Neuss.*" He tipped his hat and stated his business. "*Ich bin gekommen, um Herr Gordon zu sehen.*" Whenever he spoke his native language, his accent deepened, although he had been polishing it to a softer shine since he came to America when he was twenty.

"*Ja, ja!*" She opened the door wide and motioned for him to step inside. There wasn't much room for him to pass, considering her bulk, but he slid his six-foot-two frame through and removed his hat, which she gladly accepted. She could never seem to do enough for him.

"Is that you, Sheriff?" Gordon called from the next room.

"Yes, it is."

"Come in, my friend, come in."

Gordon rose from his desk and shook Peter's hand while clapping him on the back. "How are you this fine morning?"

"I'm well, thank you. How is your health?"

"Hale and hearty." When the housekeeper continued standing there, staring at the sheriff with open admiration, her employer spoke up. "That is all, Frau Neuss."

"*Ja, ja.*" She bowed her way out the door, still holding the rug.

"Come inside."

He entered the front room, which served as the lawyer's office and couldn't help but notice the remains of eggs and sausages at the far end of the table. When Mrs. Gordon was alive, she constantly tried to get her husband to take meals with her in the dining room, but he preferred eating as he applied himself to legal cases. Peter sat opposite his friend, appreciating the orderliness and serenity of this home. When Gordon's older sister, Naomi Kleet, entered, he rose. "Good morning, Mrs. Kleet."

"Well, good morning. What a nice surprise!" She gave her brother a sideways look. "We were actually just talking about you, Sheriff Kichline."

"Would you care to join us, Naomi?" Lewis asked.

"If the sheriff doesn't mind." Her eyes shone with eagerness.

"I would be honored, madam." Peter offered her a seat. "I was hoping to speak with both of you."

He was heartened that Gordon had recovered from his own wife's death three years earlier. Most people he knew had lost loved ones to diseases, accidents, and childbirth. There was grief, but there was also acceptance of the way things were in life, and recovery had always followed. Surely, the lines would once again fall in pleasant places for his family. He just needed time to figure things out, to settle down. He had, however, no widowed sister, only two younger brothers and a stepbrother living with their own families in Bedminster. His relief wouldn't come in exactly the same way Lewis' had.

"How are you, Sheriff?" she asked.

Unlike her brother, Mrs. Kleet had grown homely with age, which Peter figured to be about the mid-fifties. Her own husband had passed away shortly after Gordon's wife, and together she and her brother had made a new life for themselves.

"I am quite well," he said. To his consternation, his stomach growled, and there was no covering the sound, although he tried to by lifting his hand to his mouth and clearing his throat.

"My good man, have you breakfasted yet?" Gordon asked.

"Why yes, yes, I have."

Naomi Kleet grimaced. "Posh! If I know that scatterbrained Greta, you've had nothing but burnt toast." Once again, he could see that strange image of Benjamin Franklin embedded in his daily bread. "I'll get coffee and rolls." She was up before he could stop her. In truth, he didn't much want to stop her.

"I'm afraid Greta has been scatterbrained, as your good sister has just said." He hoped this comment could help him transition into a conversation about Susannah and getting a new housekeeper.

Within a few minutes, his hostess reappeared with a silver tray, setting the viands before him on an end table. This was one of the few homes in Easton with such fineries, but the late Mrs. Gordon had been from Philadelphia, the daughter of a prosperous merchant, a woman who knew her way around silver and mahogany. He smiled at the thought of the many times his Margaretta and Mary Gordon had spent in this home talking about things that occupy women's minds.

Mrs. Kleet poured cups of coffee for everyone, and Peter began to eat after Gordon helped himself to a roll.

"You look as if you've lost some weight, my friend," the lawyer observed.

He chewed and swallowed a bite of the warm, yeasty bread before responding, "Yes, I believe I have."

"I regret your Greta is not taking better care of you." Gordon's sister looked as if she wanted to delve further into the matter.

"She appears to have something on her mind," Peter said.

She sniffed. "I'll say—the form of a certain British captain."

This is new. "British captain?"

She regarded him as if he were as dumb as a post, which anyone clearly knew a Heidelberg man was not, except perhaps in the ways of women and servants. "Why, yes, Captain Hough—"

Peter tried to wrap his mind around this tidbit of information as he took another bite of roll with its delectable hints of cinnamon and nutmeg. Now *this* was food. "Captain Hough has been to see me a few times with reports about conditions in the upper Bushkill and Wyoming areas."

"Precisely, Sheriff Kichline, and as honest a fellow as the captain is, he seems to have stolen Greta's heart." Naomi Kleet lifted her chin, looking smug. "I hear they plan to marry as soon as her indenture is up."

Greta and Captain Hough? He had difficulty imagining those two together, one so stalwart and proper, the other a servant. And German. "But her English is lacking."

"My dear sir, that hardly matters when hearts are drawn together," his hostess said.

He put down the empty plate. "Does he return her affections?"

"It would seem so."

How haven't I noticed? Since Margaretta's death, time and routines had taken on such a strange effect, as if hours and days were regulated according to some other standard of measurement. One only saw the most immediate tasks, like making sure the county was safe, and the town and mills running smoothly, things he knew how to do. He came to the subject that had brought him here in the first place, although he would have loved to have eaten another roll, maybe two.

"Well, Mrs. Kleet, whatever may come of this infatuation, I must come to terms with the fact of Greta and her father leaving me when their indenture ends in a month. I need to find house help. The mill isn't a problem with Peter and Andrew assisting me, and I can hire men from town. I find, however, running mills and protecting the county are easier for me than running a house."

Her lips formed a smile, making Lewis's sister seem girlish—no mean feat. "Don't you worry about a thing, Sheriff Kichline. I'm sure I can help you find someone." She looked sideways at her brother.

"It matters little to me if the person is indentured or an employee. I just want someone to run my home efficiently and to provide companionship for Susannah, who is"—he cleared his throat—"missing her mother."

"Must she be German?" Gordon asked. "I know you enjoy assisting your kinsmen."

Peter considered correcting his friend. The fact was, the Kichlines were a good bit Swiss as well. He decided not to mention his heritage. "Yes, well, I'm more concerned about a good fit between her and my family."

As Naomi Kleet spoke about her experiences with housekeepers, he reached for another roll and washed it down with dark, bracing coffee, feeling much more like his old self.

When their visit came to an end, Peter rose. There was still one embarrassing matter he hadn't raised. "I'm deeply grateful for your friendship and your hospitality."

"As we are for yours," Gordon said.

Frau Neuss seemed to appear out of nowhere and handed the sheriff his hat, and he bowed. "*Danke schoen.*" Then he lowered his voice and asked, "Mrs. Kleet, might you know where my Susannah spends her time?"

She drew nearer, taking him by the arm, and as he felt the softness and warmth of her hand, he realized he hadn't been touched by a woman since Margaretta had reached for him that one last time. He found the sensation both comforting and unsettling.

"She is often with the Dolls, especially since the school has not been meeting."

Now he spoke in a more normal tone to include Gordon in the conversation. "What is this about the school?"

"Why, my good man, Mr. Humstead took ill two weeks ago and has resigned his post," the lawyer said. "The search is on for a replacement." He regarded Peter sympathetically.

"How is it I've been unaware of this?" He had helped start the school over ten years ago and had stayed closely involved ever since, except for the past two months.

Mrs. Kleet spoke up. "You have much on your mind these days, Sheriff. We did not see fit to trouble you."

"But my children go there. I'm a trustee." He looked at Gordon for an answer.

"Perhaps now you can come on board. We hope to have a candidate very soon. We've been getting the word out to neighboring communities about our need."

Peter mentally wandered through a maze as he wondered what else he might have missed.

"Sheriff, before you go," Mrs. Kleet said, "I would like to invite you to dinner next Tuesday evening. My widowed daughter will be paying her first visit here from Philadelphia, and we'll be having some people over for her to meet."

"Why, thank you. That is most kind of you."

As he left, he thought he saw Gordon and his sister share a wink.

CHAPTER THREE

Dean Sanders asked her to come to his office after her class, and for the first time since Jim's death a month ago, Erin shook away the numbness that had been her persistent companion. She conjured up the familiar image of herself sitting behind her own desk in her own office with "Professor Erin Miles" on a brass door sign, students lined up in the hallway to see her. When the nights had grown too long and her thoughts too dark, she'd clung to that vision of her future.

She approached the opened door and caught Ed Sanders's eye before she had a chance to announce herself.

"Erin." He rose, always the gentleman. "Please come in and have a seat." The lanky dean waved to a chair across from his desk. "How did today go?"

"Class was good. They've been a wonderful group." She thought about their many kindnesses—the flowers, cards, and Korean food, which Ethan refused to eat but whose unfamiliar flavors Erin happened to enjoy.

"I'm so glad." Sanders looked at her closely over his reading glasses, which he wore at all times. "How are you doing?"

"I'm getting along, focusing on what's ahead." She hoped he understood her deeper meaning.

When he smiled, Erin noticed a piece of what appeared to be spinach stuck between his two front teeth. Whenever this had happened with her and Jim, they'd subtly point to the area requiring attention, but she didn't feel she could take such liberties with a colleague.

"I'm glad you're looking ahead because that's why I want to talk to you. You were a strong candidate for the assistant professor of history position, Erin."

"I've dreamed about the job for a really long time." She normally wouldn't have been so out there with her deepest desires, but she felt that confident about the outcome.

"We're going to offer you a different opportunity, though, one we think uniquely suits your talents."

What was that?

"We'd like you to teach introductory English composition." He smiled as if he'd just handed her the keys to a brand-new Porsche.

Her wits deserted her. The room was upended. "Excuse me?"

Sanders repeated himself, but the words didn't make any more sense the second time around.

"But I'm a history professor," she said.

"Yes, and you brought many good qualities to those classes."

Brought? What was this brought?

"We had a very strong applicant pool. Over a hundred CVs, people from all over the country." He pushed his shoulders back, looking greatly pleased about that. "We ended up choosing someone from Mississippi who's published widely on pre-Columbian America."

"I … I don't understand." A breeze from his open window lifted some hair around her temples, but she was too numb to notice.

"As you know, Erin, Hatfield is an up-and-coming institution, and the professional consultant we hired this year strongly suggested all new tenure-track professors have their PhDs."

"But I'll have mine in a few months." Her voice sounded much smaller than she would have liked.

He leaned forward. "We also need to diversify, and our new guy is Hispanic."

She was out of words.

"Erin, you're an important part of Hatfield, and since you do some writing, we believe you'll make an excellent English composition adjunct." He grinned. "If all goes well and you do get your doctorate, we can talk about full time next year … with benefits."

She looked past the intrusive spinach in his teeth and imagined herself sitting at the kitchen table grading stacks of poorly written papers. There she sat, writing in red *then, not than,* and *awkward* repeatedly, hunched over, her eyesight giving out like her mom's. "But I'm a history professor," she repeated. *Didn't he hear me the first time? What is wrong with him?*

"Believe me, Erin, we'd let you continue teaching history if we could. Your students love you, but so will your new ones." He was talking as if she'd accepted his offer.

"Are you saying I can't teach history at all, even part-time?" she was clawing at the air, trying to find something to hang onto as she went off the ledge.

"The new professor will be teaching all those classes." He stood. "We know you'll understand. In a perfect world, things would've been different."

This obviously wasn't a perfect world.

❧ • ☙

She drove straight to Melissa's house. As the friends sat at the kitchen table, Erin cradled a mug of Darjeeling.

"I'm sorry my house is such a mess," Melissa said.

"I've seen worse." Erin was astonished at her ability to crack a joke when a lead weight dragged down her spirit. "Believe me, your house is not a mess, and even if it were, I wouldn't notice."

"What's up, hon'?" Melissa covered Erin's hand with hers for a few seconds by the ticking kitchen clock. Jim had hated the sound of ticking clocks.

"I thought I had everything worked out, you know? This being a widow— oh, I hate that word! I've been coping alright, though. I kept thinking as long as I had that teaching position, everything would be okay." She hoped she was making sense.

Melissa frowned. "Did you hear something?"

"Uh-huh." Erin sipped her tea and put the mug down on the table, clinging to its warmth. "I met the dean after class, and I was all ready for the formal offer, but … well, it wasn't what I thought it would be." She paused, grateful Melissa wasn't the kind of person who needed to fill every silence. "He said there's a new policy at Hatfield, and they're only hiring tenure-track professors who have PhDs. Since I haven't finished my dissertation, they picked somebody else."

"What?" Melissa's jaw dropped.

She nodded. "Yup."

"But you were planning to finish the dissertation this summer. You could have your doctorate by early or mid-fall!"

Erin sat up straighter and assumed an official tone. "According to the administration, it wouldn't be the same as hiring someone who's already a doctor. Besides, the dean said they needed more diversity, and the guy they hired is a Hispanic whose specialty is pre-Columbian America."

21

"I can't believe this, Erin! Oh, honey, you had your heart set on this." She balled up her hands and clenched them. "After all you and your family have done for that school, they couldn't cut you this one break? They could've given you a deadline to finish the dissertation."

Normally her friend was the very essence of calm—her outburst felt satisfying to Erin. *Melissa "gets" this. I wonder how Jim would've reacted to this news.* She resisted the thought of how practical he'd always been. Sure, he would've felt her pain, but then he would've said something like, "Why not teach those English classes? At least you'll still be in the classroom." What would Pat and Al say? Would they be at all incensed? Even if they were, it wasn't like them to use their beefy gifts to Hatfield for personal leverage, not that Erin would want them to.

"Actually, they did offer me a job, Melissa."

Her friend squinted. "I'm confused."

"The dean wants me to continue on an adjunct basis teaching freshman composition, and once I get my doctorate, they might make it full time."

Melissa slammed down her mug, and tea splashed onto the table. "Are you kidding? Freshman comp? Is he out of his mind?"

"He thinks because I do some writing, I can teach freshman how to. Honestly, I can't see myself grading freshman comp papers 'til the cows come home." Erin shuddered.

"Neither can I. I mean, how deadly boring would that be!" The buzzer from the dryer sounded in the laundry room. "So, what are you going to do?" Melissa asked.

"I know this much—I'm not about to take that offer. But beyond that, I don't know." Tears rose to the surface, and she sniffed them back, reaching in her purse for a tissue.

"How about just teaching your history courses part-time, like you've been doing?"

"The new guy is going to teach them." Erin already disliked him, seeing him as her nemesis. She groaned, "I feel like there's this hole in my life, Melissa—like some of the most basic things I counted on—Jim most of all, then my career—are gone, and I just don't know how to fill those places." She paused. "Or if I ever will."

Again, the comforting hand closed over Erin's, which was trembling. "I think a lot of new things are ahead for you. You're having a hard time now, but you will be filled again. I promise. God promises."

Her voice wavered. "I just want my old life back."

❧ • ❧

22

Erin was glad to see the evening empty its pockets so there were no more surprises to deal with. After her time with Melissa, there'd been a mix-up with the insurance company over one of Jim's hospital bills. That had taken two hours and a bevy of frustrating telephone calls with people who barely spoke English or kept disconnecting her so she had to go back to the beginning of the hellish queue. Then the principal called because Ethan pushed a teacher after they had words about his refusal to do an assignment. Considering the Miles's current situation and what Ethan was dealing with, the school had decided to issue a warning rather than suspend him.

They'd eaten supper quietly, each lost in their own thoughts, and following homework and the bedtime routine, she tucked her son under the covers and padded downstairs in her frumpiest pajama pants and Jim's 2009 Philadelphia Folk Festival tee shirt. Turning off the parenting channel and being alone with her thoughts felt good. She sank onto the leather sofa in the family room with her dog, Toby, feeling a need to be mothered herself. Pat was just a phone call and a few blocks away. She would listen and encourage her, but for once, Erin just wanted her own mom, in part because she wasn't ready to tell her in-laws about the situation at Hatfield. There was another reason as well. Erin wanted to connect with her mom if at all possible. She glanced at her cell phone, wondering whether or not to make the call, reasoning that her mom would say all the right things, for a while at least. The ringing of the phone startled her, and when she saw the caller ID, she was even more surprised. "Can you believe it, Toby?" she said to the basset hound.

"Mom, I was just thinking about you."

"Well, you're constantly on my mind, and I wanted to see how you are," Audrey said.

"Actually, not so hot tonight," she blurted, pulling a throw over her legs. "I had a bad day."

"What happened?"

Erin recognized the how-dare-anything-bad-happen tone, but she took a risk and told her mother everything anyway—the teaching position, the insurance fiasco, even Ethan's rough patch at school.

"I can't imagine what those people are thinking! Don't they know they're lucky to have you teaching there in the first place?" Audrey snorted. "And Jim's people give them a lot of money. How could they pull something like that? What's wrong with people?"

"I know," Erin said.

"So, what are you going to do about it?"

"I'm not about to teach freshman composition, that's for sure." She stroked Toby's back, feeling comforted by the rhythmic motion.

"Good for you! Maybe you should finish your doctorate, then something else will come up somewhere else, some place a lot better than that old school. Any place would be proud to have you teach there."

"Actually, that's not a bad idea, Mom."

"And I wouldn't worry too much about Ethan. You're both having a hard time, but he's a good boy, and you're a good mother, and you have your faith."

So far, so good. "Thanks."

"You'll be okay. You'll get through this."

There was nothing about Audrey in the remarks, just a clear focus on Erin. Amazing. After Audrey promised to keep them in her prayers, Erin hung up feeling a lot like she had as a child when her mother had soothed her fears away after a bad dream. *Maybe Mom's not so hard to talk to after, all, at least not always.* She felt like watching TV and started flipping through the channels for something light, definitely not *Finding Bigfoot,* which Ethan used to watch with his father for laughs, or *Dog with a Blog,* her son's number one show.

She stopped when she spotted Rob Lowe talking to the camera. Erin had had a big crush on him during middle and high school, practically wallpapering her room with his pictures and buying all the celebrity magazines about him. Memories from that era came floating back like driftwood, including a bittersweet one of Sean O'Malley, who'd been a junior when she was a freshman. He'd flirted with and teased her all during play practices until one golden afternoon at a dress rehearsal, he'd bent over and kissed her backstage. Erin just knew he was going to ask her to the junior prom, until a spiteful girl in Spanish class whispered, "Sean's taking Pamela Case." Pamela, who was all bleached white teeth and Louis Vuitton.

Erin had cried over her disappointment to her mother and could still hear Audrey's response. "It figures he'd ask her. Sean's father is Dr. O'Malley, and the Cases have money." Erin got the encrypted message that her family wasn't good enough for the likes of Sean O'Malley. Someday she'd get out of this stifling town where she felt so limited because her parents didn't have money or position. In the meantime, she imagined what walking into the prom with Rob Lowe would be like, while every head in the place turned in envy.

Over the years, Erin had followed the actor's career from a distance, picking up a magazine every now and then to see what he was up to. Just now revisiting an innocent crush from a time before cancer and widowhood would be comforting. The clock on the cable box read 9:02, so the show was just starting.

"Tonight, actor Rob Lowe explores his mother's heritage, finding roots in the American Revolution."

The camera panned to Lowe saying, "My guy's out there trying to kill George Washington."

The opening scenes played for *Who Do You Think You Are?* about the family histories of various celebrities whose pictures popped up during the intro. The show looked promising, just the kind of story she could lose herself in. She learned Lowe had grown up in Dayton, Ohio, but after a divorce, his mother moved him and his siblings to the West Coast. He spoke about his life-long love for American politics and history and how he'd been delighted to end up playing a top aide to the President of the United States on "The West Wing."

"My mother's death has left me wishing I'd asked her more questions about her family, who they were and where they came from," he said.

Lowe and his brother started looking through their mother's scrapbook for bits of information and came upon a wedding photo of relatives named "Oran Hepler and Bessie May East." There was also a 1906 Lima, Ohio, newspaper clipping about a family reunion for descendants of a Christopher East.

Erin was intrigued when they pulled out a laptop and went to a website, Ancestry.com, something she'd seen advertised on TV. The brothers put their ancestor's name in the correct search fields, along with where he'd lived, and they came up with a John Christopher East, whose name appeared in an abstract of Revolutionary War patriots. *That's hitting the history jackpot!* Erin thought. She remembered how, as a small child, she would put on a hat and gloves and pretend she was a Daughter of the American Revolution sipping tea in the Orr's restaurant with the town's leading ladies. She'd always loved that era of history best, but her dream would never come true. She was just a "Dago" girl on her dad's side, and her mom's family had come from Germany after the Civil War. No Revolutionary patriots for her.

At this point in the show, Lowe left California for Washington, DC, where he worked with a DAR genealogist, Joshua Taylor, to help him find out if Bessie May East was related to the John Christopher they'd found on Ancestry. They discovered the actor was, in fact, connected to him. Taylor found a document listing East as a Private in the Revolutionary Army, but when he pulled that application, there was no documentation to support that Lowe's "five times great-grandfather" had in any way supported the cause.

Lowe went to the Library of Congress to search further for information about his ancestor with the help of a Revolutionary War historian, who uncovered disturbing news. East actually had been on the other side of the conflict, a Hessian soldier who'd served at Trenton when General Washington made his famous Christmas crossing of the Delaware. East's commander was killed in the fighting, and the young German became a prisoner of war. When Washington offered the

Hessians an opportunity to throw in their lot with the Americans, East accepted. *What a ride! First, he thinks he has a patriot ancestor, then finds out the guy was trying to kill George Washington, then East ends up becoming an American!*

To more fully appreciate his ancestor's life before he came to America, Lowe traveled to the stunning medieval town of Marburg, Germany, which East had never seen again once he left his homeland to serve in the army. Christopher was one of a large number of siblings and only twelve when their father died. Because the boy wouldn't inherit any property as a younger son, his choices were to work on someone else's farm, become a day laborer, or join the army. Christopher East chose the life of a soldier and ended up fighting alongside the British forces in America.

While at his German hotel sitting before a fireplace, Rob Lowe received a letter from Joshua Taylor with more information he'd uncovered about East. New research had compelled the DAR to accept him as a patriot because East had, in fact, paid taxes specifically raised to support the war effort. Lowe was qualified to become a member of the Sons of the American Revolution. Tears filled the actor's eyes, as well as Erin's, as he read his letter of acceptance. She could only imagine the joy he felt.

She considered something he'd said earlier in the program, how he regretted his mother had died before he had a chance to ask about their family's background. Erin remembered how one of Jim's friends had been estranged from his father for several years in spite of his father's attempts at reconciliation. Jim had encouraged him to make amends before it was too late. "You'll always regret it if you don't," he'd said. The guy finally relented, and his father ended up dying two months later.

You just never know how much time you have with your loved ones. I know that now. Erin's mind often worked like a connect-the-dots puzzle, and she thought back to the visit her nieces had made before Jim died when their kids and Ethan had hit it off. That night when she tucked Ethan in bed, he'd asked her, "Why don't we ever see them? I want to."

Her dog looked up with soulful eyes as Erin absently rubbed his ears. She still had time to go deeper with her parents, her brother and his family, her aunts and uncles. She smiled. When she was young and had that crush on Lowe, her fantasies about meeting him had carried her through some gritty episodes in her own life. They'd given her the ability to run away from home, at least in her mind, to a life of peace and happiness. How odd now, at this moment in her life, Lowe had shown up again. The actor's story of family discovery seemed like an invitation to know her own.

CHAPTER FOUR

Erin let Toby out while she put water on for tea, watching his shadowy form slip into the darkness as he located his favorite spot. When she heard him bounding up the steps to the deck a few minutes later, she opened the door and gave him a dog biscuit, something he seemed to regard as his God-given right. He lumbered over to the garage door and stood there looking—waiting, she knew, for Jim to come home. This had been Toby's time-honored ritual in the evenings just before Jim arrived from work, and the dog hadn't stopped watching for his master. Erin's chest clenched. "He's not here, Toby. It's just you, me, and Ethan now."

The dog apparently wasn't buying her explanation because he made a couple of circles before settling on the rug by the door. She wondered how long this would go on. "Come here, Toby," she called, patting her thighs with the palms of her hands and a throb in her voice. "I need you. Come on, boy."

He rose, stretched and came to her. Together, they settled on the family room sofa where he snuggled against her as she drank her tea and reached back into her family memories. The distant origins of Rob Lowe's many times great-grandfather reminded Erin of a conversation she'd had with her Grammy Ott years ago.

"Really, Grammy? Indians? I don't believe it."

"Well, that's what my mother always said, we were part Indian."

Erin was about thirteen at the time, incredulous her family might be part Native American, wishing it to be true so she actually could have a stake in American colonial history. How could she prove it, though?

"How did Grammy Smith know?" she had asked.

"Well, she did teach us how to count in Delaware Indian."

"Really! Do you remember any of it?"

"Let me see." Grammy Ott looked up at the ceiling. "It was something like een, teen, tether, feather, fipp, latta, datta, satta, double bow bip."

As Erin recalled that incident, she felt the same fascination she'd known as an adolescent. From what her mother had told her years ago, Great-grandmother Smith had been a notorious joker, and it would've been just like her to make up such a story about Indians just to get a rise out of people. What Erin did know about her mom's side of the family was their German origins and how they'd probably come to America after the Civil War. Grammy Ott had often expressed herself in "Pennsylvania Dutch," saying things like, "Slow as molasses in January," "Outen the lights," and "We grow too soon old and too late smart." She also made a mean dessert called "funny" cake and shoofly pie. When her grandmother had died in the late 1980s, Erin remembered the mind-boggling array of shoofly pies, cakes, muffins, and even cookies neighbors brought to the little white house on Lewis Street.

She reached for a legal tablet and started jotting down names and dates, anything she could remember about her mom's family, things she could enter on Ancestry.com like Rob Lowe had done. The process had seemed so easy—who knew what she'd be able to uncover with even a small amount of information? For starters, she knew her mother was born in February 1935; her grandmother in May of 1903. Although Erin didn't know her great-grandmother Smith's birth year, she figured it would've been some time in the 1870s to early 1880s, based on Grammy Ott's dates. She also knew her grandmother had had a sister who died young, but she didn't know which of them had been born first. She'd met her great-uncle Keith a few times and knew he was her grandmother's younger sibling but by how many years, Erin didn't know. *So, Grammy Smith would've been born considerably after the Civil War. I know a lot of Germans came to America back then. Why she told stories about Indians, I haven't a clue.*

Because Grammy Ott was born in Easton, Erin guessed that's where her German family had settled once they came to America, but she didn't know if Grammy Smith was born there too, or back in the Old Country. Of course, if they actually did have some Native American roots, at least part of their family had been in this country a lot longer. That was one family mystery she hoped to solve along the way, although she wasn't counting on a dramatic outcome.

As for her Pappy Ott, when Erin was very young, she'd thought he was her grandfather until her mother corrected her. Her real grandfather was a man named Thomas Owen, who'd died at the age of fifty when Audrey was a freshman in high school.

"When we went on our first date," Grammy Ott had told Erin years before, "Thomas took off his hat in the movie theater, and don't you know, he was completely bald!"

He'd been married once before, but his first wife had died delivering their second child, who also didn't survive. Their little girl had gone to live with single aunts until Thomas married Erin's grandmother. She paused from her note taking. *Mom always said her father's family was Welsh because Owen was a Welsh name.* Erin laughed. *She also thought her dad was a "Welsh tenor." Somehow I doubt his singing abilities had anything to do with his ancestry.*

On top of one column on her notepad, Erin wrote "Thomas Owen." If her mom were about fourteen when he died, and Thomas had been fifty, his birth date would've been around 1898. She knew he was from the tiny town of Stewartsville, New Jersey, next to Phillipsburg, which was across the Delaware River from Easton. When she was little, Erin hadn't realized at first that Easton and Phillipsburg were two separate towns because the meandering river just seemed like a big street going right down the middle. When she found out they were distinct, Erin had wished she'd been born in Easton instead because she liked the city so much better, the parks, stores, playgrounds—the energy. She envied her cousins who lived there and considered their home on McCartney Street to be far superior to hers.

As for Stewartsville, she didn't know much about the town except the Owens had lived there—how long, she didn't know. Assuming her Grandfather Owen was born there, however, she wrote, "Thomas Owen, born about 1898, Stewartsville, New Jersey." She had no idea what his parents' names were or if they were also from that town. What she had wasn't a lot to go on, not like Rob Lowe's 1906 newspaper article, or the mention of his ancestor in Abstracts of Revolutionary War Soldiers from the DAR, but she had a start.

Erin had one of those nights when her over-stimulated mind continued pouring forth stories while she slept. She dreamed vignettes of childhood experiences, ones she'd put behind years ago, ones she refused to admit to consciousness in the light of day. Although she was her present age in the dream, she happened to be standing in a convenience store with a junior high friend looking at magazines when her Uncle Ben came through the door, filling the place with his strange laughter. Erin's heart pounded as he started grabbing candy bars and

Tastykakes. Her friend pointed and giggled, "Get a load of that!" Everyone's eyes were riveted on the spectacle, all except for hers. Erin couldn't bear to look at her mother's brother. Nor could she bear her friend knowing they were related. She ran out the door to safety.

She tossed from that dream to another, to the apartment she'd shared with her mother during Erin's high school years. Audrey came home from work looking like people did after seeing Casper the Friendly Ghost in those old cartoons.

"What happened, Mom?"

"That woman came to the store today," Audrey said.

Erin knew instinctively who she meant—Bridget, the woman she could never think of as a stepmother.

In a courtroom, a judge issued a restraining order. Erin noticed he was wearing a white wig.

The dreams wouldn't quit. She was in her room, the walls covered with posters of Rob Lowe. In one of them, he was wearing a tricorn hat and a sash that said "Sons of the American Revolution."

The next thing she knew, she was talking with her Chinese friend, Meggie, from graduate school, who was convinced Erin had grown up with "big potatoes."

"What's that?"

"You, know, important people," Meggie said. "Was your father a lawyer?"

"No"

"A doctor."

"No."

"A teacher? He was an intellectual, right?"

"My dad worked in a factory." Erin looked away.

Finally, her dreams took her back to Lewis Street where she stood outside her grandmother's house looking around, stunned by what had happened to the block where both sets of grandparents had lived for fifty years. The working class neighborhood had always been tidy, and the homes and lawns well maintained, a source of pride to their owners. Now they were just plain rundown, with graffiti and litter, blistered sidewalks, and peeling paint. Erin wondered how the residents could tolerate living like that. There were signs on several boarded-up houses reading, "Condemned for habitation." Only one or two little stragglers of respectability remained. Then suddenly, a renaissance! Erin stood amazed as new buildings, sleek and modern with optimal views of the Delaware River and Easton rose up. "Wow," she thought, "what a transformation!"

As she began to awaken in the stillness of a new day, Erin *heard* a quiet voice—*I will restore the years the locusts have eaten.*

CHAPTER FIVE

The smell of pigs and cows reached him before he arrived at the courthouse, the animals having taken up residence at a nearby pond awaiting further instructions from their owners. Ziba Wiggins stood sentinel over the scene and, spotting Peter, walked over with a big smile. A loose-jointed carpenter with droopy cheeks in the shape of an upside-down triangle, he'd helped build the two-story limestone courthouse with its distinctive cupola, the kind you'd expect to see in a much bigger and more sophisticated city, like Philadelphia. Upon its completion, Wiggins decided to stay in Easton. He appointed himself gatekeeper of the courthouse, opening its doors each morning and putting it to bed at night as if it were his child, which in a way, it had become. Wiggins did this labor of love *gratis* until Sheriff Kichline suggested he receive at least a small stipend, which the trustees approved after deliberating for a total of two minutes. Even in Easton where the residents weren't averse to quibbling over a few pence, no one had questioned the arrangement because as far as Wiggins and the courthouse went, you couldn't have one without the other.

Some tongues suggested Mrs. Wiggins might be a tad jealous of the affection her husband felt for the edifice, but even if she did, she never let on. She went right along with Ziba and even became part of the courthouse routine herself. Every day promptly at noon, she showed up with a basket containing three pickled eggs, a wedge of cheese, half a loaf of bread, and a tankard of cider for his dinner. Residents without the benefit of clocks oriented their weekday schedules around this appearance. When she showed up at the courthouse, it was time to put the kettle on.

"Good morning, Sheriff Kichline!" Wiggins said.

He tipped his hat to Wiggins and a few others, who stood more erect in his presence. He only planned to stay a few minutes before checking in on the Dolls'. "A beautiful morning it is, Mr. Wiggins," he said, feeling the welcome sun caress his face. The winter had been so hard.

Wiggins made a show of inhaling deeply, then puffing his breath out. "I think spring is finally here to stay. Before long the shad will be running."

Grunting and bleating animals had their say about the matter. There was something incongruous about the presence of animals outside a temple of justice, and more than a few locals had begun to complain, suggesting the creatures stay at a more respectable distance. Then again, others pointed out at least the pigs kept the roads, such as they were, free of rubbish.

"I see you brought the *Gazette*." Wiggins nodded toward the newspaper, and the sheriff handed it to him. "I guess nothing can beat the news from last time, about the King revoking that wretched Stamp Act."

"There's nothing so momentous this time," Peter said.

As carefully as he kept watch over the courthouse, Wiggins also handled the doling out of the sheriff's personal newspaper. He had a rule as binding as those of the Medes and the Persians—no one reading the paper was allowed to fold its pages or eat or drink anything around it or, heaven forbid, cut anything out of it. Everyone in town knew if that happened, the miscreant might just spend an afternoon in the stocks and be banished forever from reading Kichline's paper. Each person who desired to peruse the *Gazette* was given an hour on the premises before handing it off to the next person. Peter wasn't the only man in Easton who subscribed to the newspaper, but he was the only one who shared publicly, hoping to give residents ample opportunities to know what was happening in the world beyond their small village at the Forks of the Delaware. When everyone who wanted to read the courthouse edition had a go at it, Ziba filed it with the others under lock and key.

"Sheriff!"

Peter turned in the direction of the voice. He saw Anthony Esser, the butcher, who hadn't bothered to change his apron after what appeared to have been a full morning's work. Peter could never understand why Esser didn't exercise more discretion, but then the butcher didn't have issues with the untidiness of his profession, nor did he much care what others thought. He had an annoying way of steering the sheriff in the direction of any work Esser thought he should be doing because Peter was, after all, a public servant.

"Good morning, Mr. Esser,"

A low grumble passed for a greeting. "Did you hear about the Widow Eckert, Sheriff?"

"I have not."

"Seems she's been missing some things and coming up short at the tavern."

"She hasn't mentioned this to me."

"Better look into it."

Peter was as tall as Esser was wide and when he stepped closer, the butcher took a step back. "Thank you for the information."

Another grunt, then Esser, having performed his duty, returned to his shop off the square. The matter didn't seem urgent, so Peter decided he would pay a visit to Frau Eckert after calling on the Dolls to check on Susannah. As he turned to go, he noticed a recent newcomer to Easton, Egbert Weed, who was always dressed as if it were Sunday morning. He seemed far better suited to the life of a shopkeeper than the farmer he was in the process of trying to become. His shoulders slumped as he absently poked a walking stick into the pond while several of the thinnest pigs Peter had ever seen wallowed languidly near him.

"Good morning, Sheriff Kichline."

"Good morning, Mr. Weed. And how might you be getting along these days?"

A frown crossed his face, adding to the wrinkles wreathing his eyes. "I hate to admit it, but my pigs aren't doing very well. I can't figure it out for the life of me." He nodded toward the animals, whose ribs had begun to show.

"They do look rather thin," Peter said.

"They keep losing weight. They were healthy when I bought them."

Peter reached inside himself for a solution, wanting to help Weed solve his problem. "What are you feeding them?"

"Let me see." He looked up to the sky and stroked his chin while two robins flew past them on their way to building a nest under one of the courthouse gables. "Mostly cabbage and potatoes."

Although Peter wasn't a farmer, he knew enough about animal husbandry to know pigs needed a wide variety of foods to thrive. Raw potatoes tended not to be the best thing to feed them anyway. "How much are you giving them?"

"Well, I fill a bowl, yea big"—he gestured with his hands—"then I take each pig and hold it next to me while I feed it."

Peter had excellent hearing, but he was sure he'd got that right. "Excuse me?"

"I feed each pig in turn so they get the attention they need."

"Mr. Weed, I'm afraid I don't understand. What do you mean you feed each one?"

Weed looked at Peter as if to say, "What is so hard about that? Aren't you supposed to be an intelligent man?" What he said was, "I have a wooden spoon, a good-sized one, and I put each pig on my lap and feed it."

Peter arched his eyebrows and shook his head. "Mr. Weed, are you saying you spoon feed your pigs?"

"Why, yes, sir, I do. I want only the best for them."

"Let me explain a few things to you …"

❧ • ❧

One of Caspar Doll's four girls—he could never quite keep them all straight—answered his knock at the log cabin door.

"Sheriff Kichline! Mama, the sheriff is here!" The freckle-faced child, a couple years older than Susannah, opened the door wide and motioned for him to enter.

He stooped so he wouldn't knock his head against the top, having learned his lesson the hard way on a previous visit, and removed his hat. A fire blazed on the open hearth and the smell of bread baking permeated the small dwelling.

"Your papa is here!" the same girl cried, and Susannah rushed forward, casting herself into his arms. Although he wasn't averse to hugging her in the privacy of their home, this took him by surprise. He embraced her a bit stiffly, patting her on the back while noting with relief how pink-cheeked she appeared, how cheerful.

"Papa! We're making bread and pies. Anna is the best baker in the world, and she is showing me how."

"Come in, come in." Frau Doll greeted him with flour-coated hands. She guided him to a rustic table, which was at this hour the center of the home's activity. "If you've come to see my husband, he and the boys are out with the animals. This is baking day." A row of fragrant loaves lined a table under an open window, bearing evidence to the morning's hard labor.

Margaretha Doll was an average-built woman whose thick chestnut-colored hair hadn't surrendered to gray, and her dark eyes, the startling color of turquoise, gave her a compelling appearance. The only thing detracting from her comeliness was a mustache, twice as dark and almost as thick as Peter's facial hair, when he let it grow. Fortunately, three of her daughters had inherited their mother's creamy complexion and striking eyes while only the fourth showed signs of her mother's upper lip. Considering how nice looking Frau Doll was

34

overall, one could overlook the whiskers. Besides, their families went way back together, to the early days of their American sojourn, in Bedminster, Bucks County.

She had him sit at the table with a cup of hot tea and a thick slice of warm bread slathered in butter while Susannah hovered at his side.

"I helped make this bread, Papa. Do you like it?" She was bright-eyed and eager, her dark blonde hair in contrast to the brown locks of the Dolls.

"She did indeed, Herr Kichline," Margaretha said. "Your daughter is quite the little baker."

He took a bite, allowing the melted butter to liven his taste buds, wanting to wolf it down in short order but holding back for the sake of propriety. Like Mr. Weed's pigs, Peter Kichline had gone too long without decent fare. "This is very good, Susannah."

She beamed at him, looking ready to burst. "Anna showed me," she repeated, and when Peter turned to face the Doll's nineteen-year-old daughter, she blushed.

"She's easy to teach," Anna said.

"Papa, I've also made an apple pie!"

"Apples, is it?"

"Uh-huh. I know your favorite is any kind of berry pie, but all we have left from winter is apples."

"Are apples," the youngest Doll girl corrected.

Peter noticed how his daughter referred to the Dolls' foodstuffs as if they were her own. "When do you think you'll be finished here, Susannah?" he asked when he finished a second piece of bread.

"Oh, not for a long while yet, Papa. There's still so much to do." She left his side to sit next to Sarah, who was peeling apples. "I see." He looked over at Mrs. Doll to try to read her thoughts. "I hope she's no bother."

"Bother? Of course not! She's like one of my own daughters. Susannah is always welcome here."

He made small talk while he drank the robust tea, then he rose. "I must be going. Susannah, I expect you home this afternoon since Fräulein Greta could use some help too."

"She sure could," Susannah muttered under her breath but loud enough for him to hear. He telegraphed Mrs. Doll a look that communicated his desire to speak privately. At the door, he said, "Frau Doll, I want to thank you for looking after Susannah." He felt awkward, an emotion with which he was not well acquainted. "I must confess I didn't realize until now how often she's been coming here."

"Herr Kichline, may I speak frankly?"

"Of course."

"Susannah has lost her mother, and she is in need of guidance and affection. As I said at the table, she's like one of my own daughters. She's pleasant and helpful, and my children adore her. I think we've been able to help her through her loss, and she's welcome here as long as you allow it."

He turned his hat in his hands. "I thank you deeply, Frau Doll. My own home has been somewhat disordered these last two months, and I regret Fräulein Greta has not kept pace with my family's needs." He couldn't bring himself to admit he hadn't either, but he knew Margaretha Doll knew.

She snorted, "She has one foot out of your door, Herr Kichline."

"Yes, yes she does." He was still coming to terms with the idea of her and the English captain. "I'm in need of another housekeeper—"

She cut him off. "I'll be glad to assist you."

"Yes, well, that's very kind. Mrs. Kleet also is looking out for someone."

"I'll bet she is," she mumbled. Peter said nothing. "Yes, well then, Herr Kichline, you and your sons are also welcome to sit at our table and around our hearth whenever you like. Actually, they already do, especially Jacob." She broke into a big smile.

Fortunately, there was no condemnation here. "*Ich bin ihnen sehr dankbar.*"

"*Ich bin dankbar.*"

CHAPTER SIX

After walking Ethan to the bus stop, Erin hopped into the minivan she called "Mr. Scott" because of Jim's favorite Star Trek character and headed toward the Pennsylvania Turnpike's Northeast Extension. She was going to spend the morning with her mother looking through her grandmother's photo albums, gathering information about their family history, and she felt equal parts anticipation and dread. Rob Lowe had found a patriot in his ancestry; Erin expected the usual stories of disappointment and heartache, but just possibly, there could be more to her family than that.

"You never know," Melissa had texted her the night before. "There might be some pleasant surprises."

The day was good for a road trip, sunny with a projected high of sixty-eight degrees. She debated whether to go up to the Lehigh Valley Exit and across Route 22 to Easton and Phillipsburg or to take the way Jim had always favored. He liked to get off at Quakertown, travel northeast on John Fries Highway for two miles, taking picturesque back roads to Pennsburg, then Pennsylvania 309 and Route 78 East. There the interstate wound through breathtaking views of the Lehigh Valley. Since it was a beautiful spring day and his route would help her feel closer to Jim, Erin decided that was the way to go. She put on the Philadelphia oldies station, pleased the radio host was playing a lot of 70s and early 80s songs. Music always put her in a particular mood, and Erin knew titles from her youth would help her get in touch with the best parts of her younger self and experiences.

Thirty minutes into the trip, she had to keep tearing her attention away from the view so she didn't wander off into the wrong lane. Route 78 perched high above the Valley, opening up a vista that swept east to west and north to south across miles of small cities and boroughs from Allentown and Bethlehem to Easton at the edge of Pennsylvania, onto her hometown of Phillipsburg just across the river. A trail of white clouds hovered over the idyllic scene, pulling her eyes to the northern edge, to Bangor, Bath, Pen Argyl, and the meandering Pocono Mountains where she'd learned to ski in college. Wealthier students who belonged to the ski club didn't always use their weekly passes, and Erin was given permission by the school to take advantage of the unused vouchers. She could make out the Wind Gap just above Nazareth and laughed out loud as she recalled a story her grandmother had told her as a child.

"I used to take the train to Jim Thorpe when I was a girl, and the conductor had a thick accent." Mimicking the man's Pennsylvania German dialect, she'd recite, "Bangor, Bass, and Nassarass, and don't forget your packagesass, car stops as bose ends!"

Erin never tired of asking her grandmother to repeat the spiel, and her grandmother never tired of doing it.

The Lehigh Valley had never seemed of much importance to Erin when she was growing up, with the possible exception of the largest city, Allentown, which boasted an airport, Hess's Department Store, and Yocco's hot dogs. Rather, this was a place she planned to escape when she was old enough and could put its confines behind her. Gazing at the scenery now, flowing below the highway, placid and beckoning, she'd never realized just how beautiful the region was, how the Creator had positioned the Valley between rolling hills, earnest mountains, and lovely rivers, the Delaware running north-south, the Lehigh meandering along an east-west path. Maybe it wasn't such a bad place after all.

As she approached Easton's outer limits, she considered whether to enter the city by the newer Route 33 to 22 and across the toll bridge, or along 611 into the heart of the small city, down Northampton Street and over the free bridge. She opted for the former, following its twisty turns around "Cemetery Curve," which her mother had always navigated with white knuckles as semis whizzed by, heedless of the thirty-five-mile-per-hour speed limit. Every local knew stories about cocky truck drivers who'd been put firmly in their place by underestimating the power of that curve. There was the Northampton County Courthouse on a hill to the south, cupola shimmering in the sun, while the campus of her alma mater, Lafayette College, balanced on the cliffs at her left. The lanes narrowed even further as she approached the toll bridge, which residents still referred to as "the new bridge" in spite of its having been built in the 1930s.

Its sister span just to the south had been conveying people and vehicles back and forth across the state line since the 1890s, forever making the toll bridge the new kid on the block.

Recent heavy rains had swollen the Delaware River, reminding Erin of stories her mother had told her about the great flood that had wiped out the Northampton Street Bridge way back in 1955. It had stood strong as the uncontrolled waters spilled over its roadway, only to succumb to the impact of large pieces of a covered bridge that had broken loose upstream, snapping the structure in half, leaving the center parts dangling like concrete icicles. For many years during especially stressful times in her life, Erin had dreamed of being caught in the swirling, unyielding waters, waking up just before she went under. She could never understand the affection her parents had for the Delaware, their fond memories of learning to swim in it, how they'd spent endless summer hours with their friends on what they called "Sloppy Beach." To her, the river had always seemed sinister.

Audrey Pelleriti had lived in the senior citizens' apartment building for twenty years, ever since she'd sold her mother's home on Lewis Street shortly after Grammy Ott's death. When Erin arrived, she called her mother's number from an enclosed vestibule so Audrey could buzz her in. Erin checked the time—9:30. They would have two hours before Audrey would have to leave for her part-time job as a receptionist in a state employment office on South Main Street. Erin was glad her mother was plucky enough to continue working at eighty, but she worried about Audrey's poor eyesight and her insistence that she still drive. "I'll give up driving when I'm not safe anymore," her mother said, but Erin knew that boat had floated a long time ago.

"Hi, Mom, I'm here," she said when Audrey answered the phone.

"Okay! Come on up."

The buzzer activated a switch, and Erin entered the lobby with its comfortable couch, wing chairs, and potted trees. She greeted a handful of residents who sat watching younger people come and go, vigilant lest some visitor happened to park in a resident's spot. She took the elevator to the second floor and walked down the hall to her mother's corner apartment.

"Oh, Erin, it is so good to see you!" Audrey threw her arms around her and hung on.

"Hi, Mom, I'm glad to see you, too."

"Let me see you." She held Erin at arm's length. "Your hair is getting long." She gently stroked it.

"Do you like it?" She couldn't tell. Her mom had always been of the opinion women over twenty-five should keep their hair short.

"I do. You look beautiful." Her fading eyes searched Erin's face. "How are you getting along?"

"I'm doing pretty well." She didn't want her mother's pity, which tended toward the maudlin.

Erin noticed Audrey had dyed her hair again, a shade of yellow not found in nature. The apartment was a good ten degrees hotter than Erin preferred, but her aging, slender mother required the warmth. Erin removed her cardigan and placed the sweater on the recliner near the hutch, seeing her mother had cleared the kitchen table of all but two old photograph albums.

"I see you found Grammy's albums."

"Yes, I did, and it sure took me awhile. They were buried in one of my closets. I'm so glad you want to see them. Can I get you a cup of tea?"

"Uh, okay. Thanks." Erin never liked the way her mom mashed several varieties into a can, making plain black tea taste like Earl Grey and giving the latter a hint of cloves from Constant Comment, not to mention since Audrey didn't drink the stuff, they were who knew how old.

As her mother fished out two chipped mugs, one which Erin had given her twenty years ago, and put the water on to boil she asked, "Now, why do you want to see them again?"

"I'm curious, Mom. We know so little about our family history before your grandmother, and I'd really like to know where we come from." She pulled a notebook out of her handbag. "I want to look through the albums and ask you some questions. There's a website that helps you find information about your family tree, and the more I have to begin with, the better are my chances of finding answers."

"I guess there's not too much you can't find on computers these days. Are they going to steal your identity, though? You have to be careful, you know."

"I'm pretty sure the website is safe."

"Well, alright. You know these things better than I do." She brought out the tea bags, and Erin searched for a bag not of Vietnam War vintage.

"Do you want a pecan twirl or some Ho Hos?" Audrey asked.

"Uh, no thanks." Nutrition was another subject she and her mother diverged on.

"I know there are some old newspaper articles in there, and I think I have Grammy's death certificate somewhere. Maybe those will help."

"Oh, they will!" She couldn't wait to see them.

The first album was brown and rectangular with gilding around the edges, held together with a cord that looked like a heavy shoelace. Erin opened the book to black and white photos of her grandmother holding a toddler in what appeared to be someone's backyard. Grammy Ott had always been gray-haired and chubby to Erin, so it was fun to see her young and-almost-slim.

"Who's this baby with Grammy?"

Audrey looked over her shoulder, squinting until she got the angle just right.

"I think that's your Uncle Thomas. He was a good-looking boy."

"He was the firstborn, right?"

"Well, yes and no," Audrey said. "You know my dad was married before?"

"Yes. He had Aunt Barbara with his first wife."

"I forget her name now, let's see." Audrey pursed her lips and stared out the window. "It was something like Emma, and she was Dutch."

"Were her people from Holland?"

"Oh, I guess so."

"I mean, were they actually from Holland and came here before she was born?" Erin asked.

"Heck, I don't know. I just always heard she was Dutch. Anyway, my dad's first wife died in childbirth, and Barbara was just a baby herself. She went to live with two or three maiden aunts until my dad married my mother."

The story was just as Erin had always heard it. "When was that?"

"Oh, let me see. I was born in 1935, and Barbara was about ten years older than me. Thomas was five years older than me, so I'd say around 1930. Barbara used to take care of me while my mother worked, but then she married young."

"How young?"

"Oh, right after high school, I think. I didn't like her husband. He was kind of creepy, but they had three nice kids."

Erin recited their names. "Ken, Steve, and Nancy."

"They were so beautiful. When Barbara and her husband divorced, he took them to California. I always blamed him for Steve's death." It was obvious she hadn't forgiven him to this day.

"What happened?" Erin asked.

"He bought Steve a car, an old junker, and he was killed in an accident driving it. Then, of course, Ken had polio and had to use crutches and braces afterward. Nancy was going to be in the movies, but she ended up marrying a trucker from Oklahoma. Her father was not pleased. Heck, Barbara wasn't either, but they still have a good marriage all these years later."

Erin scribbled the names and dates on her notepad, thinking, this time, her mother might actually be getting things right. She could never figure out how she had such a good mind for dates when her mother's memory for them was notoriously dubious.

On the first few pages were more photos of her Grammy Ott and small children, whom Audrey identified as Erin's aunts and uncles. Since they looked enough like their older selves, Erin figured her mom was being accurate.

"Who's this charming little guy?" She pointed to a photo of a smiling boy on a pony.

"That's your Uncle Ben."

"That's Uncle Ben?" she exclaimed. She'd only ever known him as bald and loopy, but here he was, a normal-looking child with a huge smile.

"He was a good-looking boy. It's such a shame."

"What was a shame? What happened to him?"

Her mother shook her head. "I'm not exactly sure, but he was always a little slow. He went to a Catholic school, and the nuns were good to him, but my mother insisted the work was too much for him, and she made him quit."

"Where did he go after that?" Erin asked.

"He didn't. Mom kept him home. I took care of him until I got married so she could work, then she married Harold."

"I don't get it," Erin said. She sipped the lukewarm tea tasting of rancid oranges and managed not to grimace.

"Well, I don't get it either. I'm not sure anyone does."

Wanting to change the subject, Erin turned to the next page featuring her mother's high school graduation. In one photo, Audrey was in a 1950s-era skirt and sweater, smiling along with three of her friends as they stood with their arms around each other in front of the red brick high school. The building looked exactly the same as when Erin had gone there thirty-some years later. In another picture, Grammy Ott stood next to Audrey, who was in her cap and gown. Grammy wore a light-colored suit, hat, white gloves, and a slight smile, but she was several inches away from Audrey, who was no longer smiling. Next, there was a picture of Audrey with Grammy Ott and a tiny, elderly, well-dressed woman.

"Mom, this page is about your graduation. You're with Grammy and an older lady."

"Well, let me see now." She looked at it up, down, and sideways. "That's Grammy Smith."

"Your grandmother?"

"Uh-huh."

Erin noticed the woman's no-nonsense expression, but which betrayed a certain impishness. "She was really short."

"And feisty." Audrey curled her hands around her mug. "She always said exactly what she thought, and she had a wicked sense of humor."

"How so?"

"I remember she'd go around singing high opera—'I smell a stink. I smell a stink! I smell a stink. Someboday f-ar-ted!'"

"Oh, Mom! That's terrible." Erin felt embarrassed just hearing about it. She hoped her mother would never tell that story to Ethan, who would most certainly never forget it.

"That was Grammy Smith for you."

"I remember hearing her husband died tragically. What happened?"

"He worked on the railroad as a conductor, and there was a terrible accident." She shuddered. "I think his head was cut off."

"That's just horrible! Poor Grammy Ott! Poor Grammy Smith!"

"I know. My mother was used to having a lot of nice things when she was young, like that diamond ring she got for confirmation, the one she gave you a long time ago, and she had furs and went on trips, but after my grandfather died, times got hard for them."

These were some of the hard-luck stories Erin had grown up knowing about her hard-luck family. She wished wholeheartedly there were better ones to find.

"How old was Grammy's brother?"

"Uncle Keith was a lot younger," Audrey said. "There was also a little sister, Mae, but I'm not sure when she died."

"Grammy told me a long time ago her sister pulled down a pan of boiling water from the stove." She closed her eyes, the mother in her unable to imagine such calamity.

Audrey let out a puff of air. "That's what she told me, too."

Erin paused, feeling the weight of all that sadness. "What did Grammy Smith do after her husband died?"

"Well, my mother had to go to work to help out—Uncle Keith was still young, but as he got older, he started drinking. Then Mom married my dad. Grammy Smith lived with them for a while, but I don't remember it, so it must've been before I was born."

"How did Grammy meet your father?"

"I'm not exactly sure."

She wanted to know more about her great-grandmother Smith's background. "Do you know the names of your great-grandparents, Mom?"

"Only their last names. They died before I was born. Grandmother Smith was a Brotz before she was married."

"And you think her parents were from Germany?"

"That's what I've always thought when I gave it any thought."

"What was her father's name?"

"Oh, let's see." Audrey looked down at the tablecloth. "Daniel. Daniel Brotz."

Erin wrote all of it down. "Do you think there was anything to the story that we were part Native American?"

Audrey shrugged her shoulders. "Who knows? My grandmother always said we were, but she was a great kidder."

They looked at more photos, circa mid-century, and Erin guessed some of the more unfamiliar faces might belong to the Brotz or Smith families. Unfortunately, there was no writing on the backs of the pictures, and her mother couldn't see them clearly enough to tell. Audrey guessed they were her mother's uncles. "I remember one of them was a barber with thick white hair, and he always wore a white suit."

"This guy looks just like that," Erin said.

"That would be Uncle Emmanuel then. My father didn't like it when the Brotzes came because they drank. He finally told them to keep the alcohol outside the house."

"That must've been awkward." Erin paused. "How about your dad's side of the family, the Owens? Do you remember anything about those grandparents?"

"Just that my mom said my father's father was afraid I would die when I was born because I was so little, so he told her to keep me in the oven."

"The oven!" Erin was appalled. "Whatever for?"

"I guess to keep me warm. It worked anyway." Audrey grinned, and they both laughed.

"What was he like?"

"I don't know. He died when I was really little. You know my father died young." Audrey had jumped from one death to the next. "I was twelve, and I'd just started high school. I remember sitting in one classroom and looking out the window toward the cemetery where he was buried. I hated that class."

Her mother had told this story many times and each time, Erin caught the discrepancy. If Audrey had just started high school, she would've been at least fourteen. She wrote down, "Grandfather Owen, died around 1949."

"What did he die of?"

"He had ulcers, and they got worse and worse." A cloud seemed to pass over her face. "I wasn't there when he died. I was at Sloppy Beach with my friends."

44

Erin had heard about that as well, and she'd never known how to ease her mother's obvious guilt and regret. She recalled how that memory had flooded back to her mom the day her Uncle Thomas died suddenly of a heart attack while Erin and her mother had been on a picnic at Audrey's friend's house in Tatamy, near Easton. To Erin, they'd done nothing wrong, but she didn't know how to speak to her mother's pain.

For the next hour and a half, Erin combed through both albums with her mother pointing out various aunts, uncles, and cousins, whose names, fortunately, did appear on the backs of photos, sharing memories about them, many of them happy, fortunately. Erin also found newspaper articles about her Uncle Thomas's service in the Navy during the Korean War, and her Aunt Jane's triumphs on the dog show circuit. There were wedding photos of Audrey and Tony from the early 1960s, her father beaming, her mother wearing a tentative expression. In fact, in most of Audrey's photos, she looked like she was nursing a hidden wound.

By the time Erin had to leave, she felt she was a little further along in her family search. She also had a copy of her Grammy Ott's death certificate from 1994, which listed her parents' names and her birth place, Easton. She was still eager to find out when her great-great-grandparents had come from Germany, as well as to investigate the Owens side of the family, all which would have to wait for another day. *When I get home, I'm going to sign up for Ancestry.com and start filling out those search boxes, just like Rob Lowe. Of course, I don't expect to find someone as illustrious as Christopher East, but maybe there's some beauty for all these ashes.*

❧ • ❧

CHAPTER SEVEN

When he opened the door and felt the tavern's coolness, a slew of memories greeted Peter. He and Margaretta had built this place in Easton's early days, creating one of the more genteel public establishments. High and low all knew better than to break the peace here. In those days, Peter had become a confidante to many in the town, especially the German residents who regarded him as a champion. Those in difficulty knew they could trust him with their problems, that he would give advice when solicited, and tangible help whenever he could. They kept the tavern going until four years ago when Peter accepted his appointment as High Sheriff of Northampton County, and he could no longer serve spirits at a public house. He and Margaretta had sold the business to Eduard and Elena Echkert, who pledged to keep it going in the manner Eastonians had come to expect. When Edward died two years later, Elena started running an even tighter ship, a formidable presence in spite of her shortness—her tongue made up for her size.

Her voice carried from a back room as Peter closed the door behind him, removing his hat and nodding at a handful of male patrons talking over steins of beer.

"I told you, no *Spinnwebe*! I will not tolerate it. *Verstehe?*"

Peter saw the slender form of Martin Lutz retreat up the stairs as if pursued by wild boars. Frau Eckert noticed the sheriff and scurried over to greet him, straightening her apron over her generous middle, her expression abruptly switching from the frowns of a scolding mistress to the smile of an amiable hostess. "*Guten morgen*, Herr Kichline! *Wie geht es ihnen?*"

"*Es geht mir gut.*" When she extended her hand with not a fair amount of eagerness he took it, bowing politely.

"Please excuse me for not seeing you when you came in. I was detained." She cast a withering expression over her left shoulder. "May I offer you something?"

"No, thank you very much."

She led him to a table away from the other men, and they sat.

"How is Martin working out for you?" he asked, hoping for a favorable report.

The youth had recently become orphaned and was trying to make a living for himself and his four younger brothers and sisters. He was only fourteen, the same age as Peter's son, Andrew, but without the privileges. Peter was the one who had suggested Frau Eckert take the boy on after her daughter's marriage to a man from Bethlehem and her son's decision to farm a little to the north in Plainfield. Each of them had invited their mother to sell the tavern and live with them, but she preferred to stay in Easton where she could keep an eye on things.

She put her right hand on her chest. "He is a lovely boy, Herr Kichline, and I thank you for bringing him to me. He is just slow sometimes, mainly about the housekeeping. I want our guest quarters to be spotless, but he does not yet understand what this means." She smiled, looking directly into the sheriff's eyes. "He is quite good at the heavy chores, though, and I will teach him the rest. He's only been here a week."

Peter looked toward the fireplace where lunch was cooking in a cast iron pot, a delectable aroma wafting through the tavern. Some sort of stew he thought. That was one thing about Frau Eckert, she could cook. "I'm certain you will." He cleared his throat.

"Are you sure I can't get you something?" She appeared eager to perform some service for him.

"I'm quite sure, thank you. Actually, I came to ask about a report you're missing some items."

"I was trying to keep that quiet! Who told you?" She glowered, but Peter could tell her anger wasn't aimed at him.

"Herr Esser mentioned it to me this morning."

"That man! He pokes his nose into everyone's business, does he not?"

He thought it best not to respond to such a question. "What are you missing?"

She threw up her hands. "Oh, just a few spoons. I've searched high and low but have not found them."

Anthony Esser was known for making mountains of molehills. "When did this happen?" Peter asked.

"Over the last week."

He felt a lump in his throat. "Have you questioned Martin?"

"Actually, he was the one who told me they were gone. He has quite a head for numbers, and when he was putting away the cutlery one night, he noticed some of it was missing." She leaned closer and when she spoke, Peter felt her breath, smelling like cinders, on his face. "Martin may not clean like a *frau*, but that boy is honest." She stabbed the table with her right forefinger for emphasis. "I'll tell you who I suspect." Again, the leaning toward the sheriff. "You know, that strange Old Pig Drover is back in town."

This was one more indication since Margaretta's death, he'd been walking about in a kind of stupor. It was a good thing he'd begun to climb back into the light of day, or this town might start going to the dogs. "He's never been known to do any harm before," he said. "Why do you suspect him?"

She shrugged her shoulders. "He's odd, and we know so little about him, just that he comes, then he goes, just as he pleases."

That wasn't enough to pin a crime to a man. "Has he been in here?"

"Yes, for a few meals."

"And did the items go missing while he was here?"

"I can't say for sure," she admitted, "but I still think it could be him. If not, then that Indian, Nicholas Tatamy." She spat out the name. "He's been around here a lot lately."

He stiffened. "Here as in the tavern, or here as in the town?"

She didn't answer right away, apparently considering her words carefully. "Well, just around."

Although the late Moses Tatamy had become a Christian and raised his children in the faith, and although young Nicholas had married a German girl and was generally regarded as an upstanding citizen, there were still those in Easton who weren't about to accept him on equal terms. Because Frau Eckert was one of these, Peter couldn't take her accusation seriously.

"Would you please investigate, Herr Kichline?" she asked, fluttering her eyelashes. Peter didn't notice when two men sitting across the room elbowed each other and sniggered.

"Yes, of course. Please let me know right away if anything else appears to be lost or stolen." He rose.

"Oh, thank you, and if there's ever anything I can do for you, please just say the word." Frau Eckert squeezed his arm and grinned. "I know I can count on you. Whatever would this town do without you? What would I do without you?"

Peter's grist mill was on the edge of town along the Bushkill Creek. Just across the narrow stream and a little to the east stood his newer saw mill, both businesses prospering in the growing village. A sharp cliff rose above the first mill and on its crest German Eastonians buried their dead, just a few blocks northwest of the courthouse. The last time the Old Pig Drover had come to Easton on his way to market, he'd camped in that vicinity. He really didn't suspect the odd man of thievery, but to lay certain suspicions to rest, Peter decided to look into the matter.

To get to the cemetery faster, he avoided Northampton Street, heading instead down Hamilton, with a left onto Spring Garden, his hands clasped behind his back. He was tempted to visit his boys at the mills first, eager to see their faces, concerned he may have left too many things undone in the stupor of his grief, but he'd do that after searching for the Pig Drover.

He noticed just ahead of him and unaware of his presence, the familiar figure of his oldest child, head bent, hands clasped behind him, the shoulders a little stooped. Peter's namesake reminded him of himself as a youth, tall and lean as in the days before he filled out, with a hint of impending manhood. Peter quickened his pace. When his son heard footsteps, turned and noticed him, Peter enjoyed seeing pleasant recognition in his eldest's brown eyes.

"Good morning, Father." He smiled, but a stronger emotion lay behind the façade.

"Good morning to you, Peter. It certainly is a fine day."

"Yes, it is."

"I missed seeing you at breakfast."

"I wanted to get to the mill early."

"And did you?"

"Yes, sir."

"Is everything in order?"

"It is." Peter Jr. gave a small laugh. "Mr. Becker came for his bakery flour first thing, and he told me once more about the early days of Easton when there were no roads …"

"And I walked the old Indian trails all the way to Bethlehem to get flour at the only mill in the area …" Peter Sr. continued.

"Then walked back to Easton with a heavy sack of flour on my back," his son completed.

They laughed easily at their telling of the oft-repeated story in tandem, just as they were walking.

"Doesn't he realize he's told me the same thing over and over again?" young Peter asked with a roll of his eyes and a lightening of his spirit.

"I think he just enjoys the telling of it."

"He's our best customer, so I make the most of it."

"That's a good fellow."

"Oh, and Frau Schultz came in," Peter Jr. said. "She asked for such a small amount of flour, and I could tell she didn't have enough to pay even for that."

"What did you do?"

"I took what she offered and gave her more than she asked for. It must be hard to have your husband and son both die and be alone, except for your daughter-in-law."

This young man was even thinking like himself. "Whenever you can, be generous with them. They're good and decent people who need the benefit of kindness."

"I will, Father."

Peter knew he couldn't put off collecting their taxes much longer. They'd barely been able to make the payments in the three years since their men had passed away during Easton's smallpox epidemic. He couldn't imagine where they'd get the money now. Something would have to be done about it. "How do you think we'll manage once Hans completes his indenture?" he asked, changing the subject.

Peter Jr. pursed his lips. "I've been wondering about that too, Father." They stopped in front of an ancient oak tree showing off its early spring clothing as robins competed with grackles in a raucous chirping contest from its limbs. "Hans has told me he'd like to stay as an employee when his term ends. What do you think?"

The sheriff crossed his arms against his chest, considering this bit of good news. "He's a hard worker. I don't want you boys so tied to the mills your education suffers." He cocked his head. "I regret you won't have the opportunity I had to study at a place like Heidelberg."

"I'm fine with that, Father. You've taught us well, and the school here is decent."

"And we'll get a new schoolmaster soon, hopefully, someone especially intelligent who can keep up with my boys." He smiled.

"Yes, at least as good as Mr. Humstead. I liked him. Too bad he got sick."

"Where has he gone?"

"To his sister's home in Worcester."

Out of the blue, Peter heard himself say, "You're a good son."

"And you're a good father."

They stood awkwardly for a moment, then Peter cleared his throat. "I'm not averse to keeping Hans, but Greta is another matter."

"You've noticed."

"Yes, finally, I've noticed. She did well under Mother's guidance but now … Where, by the way, have you been eating your meals?" He thought he knew but wanted to hear it from Peter Jr. just the same.

He looked down again. "Well, mostly at the Dolls or one of the taverns. Frau Eckert is always trying to feed me. Sometimes I make my own food, or Hans fixes something at the mill for Andrew, Jacob, and me. He's actually quite a good cook."

"Is that so? Maybe he and Greta can switch places then." He and his son laughed, but Peter was feeling serious about bringing his family back together. "We're going to need a new housekeeper."

"Yes, one way or the other. I think Greta may be on the verge of marrying after the indenture," Peter Jr. said.

There it was again. "That captain?"

"Yes, sir."

"Does he return her affections?" He was still more than a little dubious about the match and wanted to make sure.

"From what I've seen, yes."

Peter's eyebrows rose as he wondered just what his boy had seen.

"Well, then, I'll get someone else as quickly as possible." After a moment, he asked, "Where were you headed?"

"Uh, I was just going to the cemetery."

"May I join you?" He'd look up the Old Pig Drover afterward.

The young man nodded, and they walked in comfortable silence to the place where wife and mother lay under a stone reading *Sie ruht in Gott*—You rest in God. After some moments, Peter asked, "Do you come here often?"

"About once a week."

"So do I," he admitted

"You do?" His son searched Peter's face with a look of combined surprise and relief.

"She doesn't seem as far away here."

"Father, do you, are you, I mean this hurts you, right, I mean her leaving us?"

"Yes, right here." He placed his hand over his heart.

"Do you ever, well, struggle?"

"How do you mean, exactly?" Peter cocked his head in a listening gesture.

"Well, there's the part about just plain missing her, and there's the part about, well, God. I mean, I believe in Him, of course, and I believe in heaven, but … I guess I'm having trouble trusting Him." He kicked at a tree root with his right foot.

Peter knew what he said would carry a lot of weight, and he chose his words carefully. "I remember feeling that way after my father died."

"You did?" His son looked up, surprised.

"Yes. Of course, I was a lot younger than you are now, not quite six. I wondered what would happen to us, that if God hadn't stopped my father from dying, how could I trust Him with other things?"

"That's exactly what I mean, Father." Peter Jr. looked relieved. "What did you do?"

"I carried that with me for a long time, and then I started living as if I did trust Him. Afterward, everything just started falling into place in my spirit, and in our lives."

"Grandmother remarried, and you moved here."

"Yes, not right away, but over time." Peter stopped to let the noisy birds fill a moment of silence, then he repeated, *Obwohl er mich tötet, will ich ihm vertrauen.* He gazed at his son, expecting him to know one or two of the words, but not all of them or their meaning. "This is from the book of Job, about someone who also knew great loss. In the midst of his pain he affirmed his faith—*Though he slay me, yet will I trust him.*"

Peter Jr. closed his eyes and nodded. "Thank you, Father."

He put a hand on the young man's right shoulder.

❧ • ❧

CHAPTER EIGHT

Greta stood at the hearth cooking the noonday meal, and he noticed the room had been swept clean. On the table sat hearty loaves of rye bread along with a tray of his favorite iced apple dumplings. Early into Greta's indenture, Margaretta had taught her how to make them, not too sweet and with a melt-in-your-mouth consistency.

"Good day, Greta."

"Good day, Herr Kichline." She gave the pot another stir. "Good day, Meister Peter."

"Hello, Greta," Peter Jr. said.

"This smells good," the sheriff said, pleased by her efforts.

"Danke." She gave a small curtsy. "I wonder if I may speak with you, sir," she said. There was that startled look again. Had she always appeared that way? He was embarrassed he couldn't remember, hadn't paid that much attention to her.

"Of course."

"If you'll excuse me," Peter Jr. said, and he headed upstairs.

She twisted her apron. "I'm very sorry for the way I've let you down." Peter sensed she had more to say so he waited to respond. "If you'll forgive me for saying so, I felt lost when Frau Kichline died, just like I did when my own mother left me." She stopped, sniffed, collected herself. "Frau Kichline taught me well, and I'll do my best to honor her."

Peter's throat felt as if he'd swallowed a fish head. "Thank you, Greta. And I ask your pardon for not realizing how my wife's death would affect you."

"Oh, Herr Kichline, that's not necessary!" Her eyes opened wider, but she appeared more relieved than she'd initially been.

"I believe it is. Each of us has retreated into ourselves to nurse our wounds, and now is the time to come together." He looked around. "I would say from the appearance of this room and these wonderful aromas, you're back in form."

"Thank you, sir." A tear slipped down her cheek, and she wiped it with the edge of her apron.

He smiled at her. "I also understand you have something else happening in your life, a certain British captain, I believe?"

Greta blushed to the roots of her dark brown hair. "Captain Hough is an honorable man, like yourself. Be assured, though, I won't leave until you find someone to replace me."

"Thank you. I happen to be working on that. Frau Kichline would be very happy for you." He wondered if his wife had known about the captain, then he smiled to himself—Margaretta had never been one to miss a trick.

Peter filled his lungs with the mild spring air, enjoying the flutter of leaves in their exuberant state of youth and the darting of rabbits and squirrels across Spring Garden Street. In the near distance, the Bushkill meandered along Easton's north side, powering his mills. He stayed on the dirt road for a half mile until the path ended in a meadow shaded by oak trees and filled with clover, where the smell of an open fire and the sound of a fife drew him straight to the Old Pig Drover. The man, who seemed to be in possession of no other name, stopped playing when he saw Peter approach.

"Well, well, hello there, Sheriff! How nice of you to stop by. Draw up a seat." He pointed to a well-placed stone just across from him, greeting Peter as if he were welcoming the lawman into a formal parlor. A few dozen piglets snorted, foraging the lush ground.

Except for the man's vivid blue eyes, his grizzled face and hair color were roughly the same shade of off-white. Peter had difficulty seeing where one feature ended and the next began under the man's encroaching beard. *How old is he anyway? Not elderly, but then again, definitely not young.*

"I'm sorry I don't have a bigger rock to offer," the Old Pig Drover said. "Those long legs of your'n don't be fitting it so well."

"Not to worry. I heard you were back in town."

"Yes, sir. I've been here nigh two days now. I come from upwards, 'round Nazareth, gatherin' my shoats fer market." He looked over the herd with satisfaction. "These'll fetch a goodly price in Philadelphia." He pointed to a battered pot. "Kin I git you a cup o' coffee?"

"Yes, thank you. So, business is good these days then?"

"Yes, Sheriff, mighty good, I'm pleased to say. I've developed some reg'lars along my route, and I give 'em a fair price fer their shoats." He laughed as he handed a chipped cup to Peter, revealing the full extent of his nearly toothless condition. "Of course, you have one feller in town who don't know you aren't supposed to feed pigs with a spoon!"

"I see you've met our Mr. Weed." He sipped the coffee and finding the taste to be something like tree bark, decided not to drink any more. Out of courtesy, he held onto the cup.

The Old Pig Drover slapped his right hand on his thigh and laughed, accompanied by the squealing of pigs as if they, too, enjoyed the joke. "Imagine trying to feed a pig with a spoon!"

Peter smiled. "Mr. Weed is new to farming."

"That's puttin' it mild-like. Well, once he gits the hang of it, I'll be back to buy some of his shoats, too." One of the small herd nudged his leg, and the Pig Drover patted its head.

He studied the curious man whose appearance and words were those of a transient with little means of support other than his shoats. Peter could tell, however, the man's old-fashioned and threadbare suit of clothes had once been a finely tailored outfit woven of expensive cloth. The same could be said for his battered hat, which lay on the ground next to him just now. Although shabby, the Old Pig Drover wasn't dirty in the least. Except for his hirsute face, he was actually well-groomed, his fingernails trim and clean, his body emitting no unpleasant odors, which was more than could be said about many of Easton's residents. Peter wondered if the man might even be literate.

"Say, Sheriff, did ye hear about the artist who painted beautiful faces in his pictures but had homely children?"

"I can't say I have."

"Someone asked him why this was so, and the artist said, 'Because I make the pictures by daylight and the children in the dark.'"

Peter cracked a smile as the Old Pig Drover rocked back and forth with laughter.

"I got more where that'n come from. A farmer was out in his fields when he come upon a young man and his lass, quite busy-like near a gate. Says the farmer, 'What are you up to?' Replies the young man, 'No harm, farmer, we are only going to prop-a-gate.'" He slapped his leg again and howled, sounding oddly like his pigs.

The man was on a roll, but Peter thought it best to leave once he gathered a little information. He rose and discreetly poured out the contents of his cup when the Old Pig Drover wasn't looking. "Thank you for your hospitality. How long do you think you'll be with us in Easton this time?"

"Oh, not more'n a day or two, Sheriff. There's a few more farms to visit, then I'll be headin' on me merry way. Before you go," he said, reaching into a leather pouch as worn as everything else he owned, "I'm afraid I did somethin' th' other day that might have been misconstrued." He pulled out a pewter spoon. "I was takin' my victuals at the Widow Eckert's tavern and, absent-minded-like, I put this in my pouch when I left." He handed the spoon to the sheriff. "I meant no harm. I jest warn't thinking. Would you please give this to her and maybe smooth things over so I can go back? She's a fine cook, you know." He shook his head. "It's jest too bad she hasn't a tongue to match."

"I'll be happy to," Peter said. This was just one spoon, though. What had become of the others Frau Eckert was missing? Tipping his hat, he bid the Old Pig Drover good day.

Peter walked back to the grist mill to talk with Hans Schmidt about staying on after the indenture.

"Yes, I'd sure like to continue working for you, Sheriff," Hans said in his native language. "If that would be agreeable."

The sound of the waterwheel on its circuit played out in the background.

"You've been a good worker, Hans. I'd be happy to keep you as an employee." Peter mentioned a sum, and the forty-year-old German nodded.

"That would be very nice, sir. *Danke.*"

"Where will you live?"

"I have a plot of land in mind over this way." He pointed in the general direction while speaking the exact coordinates. "If I could continue living at the mill for a few months, I might be able to buy the ground and build a small house."

Peter pursed his lips in his typical thinking gesture. "I own that land, Hans. You've worked hard for me these seven years, and I'll gladly give the land to you as one of the terms of fulfilling your indenture. As for living here until you build the house, by all means stay."

"Oh, thank you, sir." He shook Peter's hand with gusto. "As for Greta …"

"I spoke with her a little while ago, and she told me about her captain. Congratulations."

"Thank you, sir, but I find it necessary to say something else about her. She adored Frau Kichline, so when she died, Greta had a difficult time. I understand she hasn't been performing her duties well, and this is not to excuse her, but ..."

"Please, don't give it another thought, Hans. She's spoken to me, and all is well." Hans had also gone through the loss of a wife. They were part of the same fraternity. Many people had known grief and lived beyond the pain. Hardship was the way of the world, after all, and if you had faith in God, you rose to the occasion.

Naomi Kleet had outdone herself. When Peter and his children arrived at her dinner party Tuesday evening, they found the house aglow with candles and ringing with conversation. There were at least a dozen adults and several children dressed in their finest to dine at the home of Easton's esteemed lawyer. Peter had done his best to dress nicely without the guidance Margaretta had always provided, and he was feeling ill at ease. His cravat itched, and his breeches felt too loose, although he'd tied them securely at the top.

"Sheriff Kichline, do come in. Hello, children. The young people are in the parlor."

Before Peter could say anything, Naomi pointed Peter, Jr., Andrew, Jacob, and Susannah in that direction and, taking him by the arm, escorted him to her brother's office where the adults had gathered around a bowl of shrub. Lewis spotted him and waved, and Peter walked over, Naomi clinging to his arm. Her brother was speaking with Easton's young scrivener, Robert Traill, who reached out to shake the sheriff's hand.

"We have a fine night for a gathering," Gordon observed.

Peter agreed. "The weather is just right, and what a sunset there was!"

"Any night is good to dine with friends," Traill said in his native Scottish brogue, and they laughed, knowing his fondness for good food. He turned to Peter. "I'll bet you're happy about the Stamp Act being revoked."

"I'm glad the King saw the wisdom of eliminating it."

"Maybe the retraction will calm down those firebrands in Boston," Gordon added.

"Perhaps, Mr. Lewis, but they do have a point after all," Traill said.

Naomi looked up at the ceiling and shook her head. "Men and their politics! Let's forget about the King tonight. Sheriff, Mr. Traill, I'd like to introduce you to my daughter." Taking each man by the elbow, she steered them toward a blonde woman who was talking with the minister and his wife. "Mr. and Mrs. Henop, I see you've met my daughter."

Mr. Henop smiled, "Yes, and what a fine lady she is."

Although Mrs. Henop barely spoke English, having recently arrived in America, her expression spoke volumes—one part impressed, the other, scandalized.

The blonde lady dipped her chin as a sign of humility, though she obviously looked like she expected such compliments. Nor was she especially modest, wearing a gown whose neckline plunged considerably lower than those of any Easton women.

"Deborah, I'd like you to meet our good sheriff, Peter Kichline, and our scrivener, Mr. Robert Traill."

As Naomi released his arm, Peter bowed over her daughter's proffered hand. "It's a pleasure to meet you, Mrs. King." He was careful to look in the direction of her face.

"The pleasure is mine, sir." Her voice was as smooth as the powder clinging to her cheeks, and her gray eyes smiled at the sheriff as she curtsied. She went through the same motions for Robert Traill but with less enthusiasm.

"I understand you're visiting from Philadelphia," Traill said.

"Yes, sir."

"I hope you have found us welcoming," Traill said.

She turned her gaze toward Peter. "I have." Her expensive gown in shades of light green and gold brocade, along with the elaborate way she'd piled up her hair like European royalty had a diminishing effect on everyone else. "Have you been to my city, Sheriff?" she asked just as Susannah rushed up to her father, waving a piece of cloth.

"Papa! Oh, Papa! Look what Isabella Gordon made for me!"

Peter was surprised by his daughter's intrusion. "My dear, you've interrupted us," he said quietly.

"Oh, Papa, I'm sorry." Her small face twisted, her lip quivering as she seemed to notice the grown-ups for the first time.

"Is this your daughter?" Mrs. King asked.

"Yes. Susannah, I'd like you to meet Mrs. King. You know Mr. Traill and the Henops."

"I am pleased to make your acquaintance." Susannah curtsied. "Please forgive me."

Deborah King leaned over toward her. "Do not give it another thought, my dear. What do you have to show us?" Recovering her composure, Susannah showed the lady a sampler featuring the alphabet and a childlike rendering of the new courthouse. "Why, that is lovely." Mrs. King placed a smooth hand over her heart. "I'm glad to see the children of Easton learning some of the finer things."

Susannah curtsied again, clearly dazzled. "Thank you, madam. You're very beautiful." Turning to her father, "I'll return to the parlor now." She mouthed, "I'm sorry."

He patted her shoulder and watched her slim form retreat.

"Oh, Sheriff, she's charming! How old is she?"

"Six." He paused. "Do you have children?"

She closed her eyes. "I'm afraid my husband and I did not."

Naomi spoke up. "Well, then, Frau Neuss tells me dinner is served. Let's go to the dining room."

The party followed its hostess to a burnished mahogany table groaning under the weight of platters piled with roast beef and Yorkshire pudding, roast goose, a large ham studded with cloves, bowls of creamed celery, plump lima beans, and various relishes and breads. "You sit right here, Sheriff." Naomi pointed to a chair near the head of the table. "Deborah, you sit beside him with Mr. Traill on the other side."

During the meal, Naomi's daughter ate only the smallest amounts of the lavish spread, while Robert Traill made up for her lack of appetite. Peter helped himself to some of everything, reminding himself to slow down and enjoy it, although if he'd been alone, he would have gulped the food down as quickly as possible and relished every bite—maybe even licked his fingers into the bargain.

"My mother tells me you own the mills in town, in addition to being sheriff, and you're from Germany," Deborah King said. "You must have come a long time ago because your accent isn't very heavy."

Peter chewed a bite of beef and swallowed, wishing he could have another before answering. "I was born in Germany, but my father was Swiss."

"Why did he leave Switzerland?"

"He wanted his children to be educated in Germany, so he moved there as a young man."

"Well, isn't that refreshing! Most Germans here can barely speak English."

If Mrs. King had been a man, Peter would've had something to say about that.

She looked directly into his eyes, and he squirmed. "Mother tells me you're a man of great learning."

"Thank you, Mrs. King. I went to Heidelberg."

"Heidelberg! Why that is impressive." She pressed her hand to her chest. "I'll bet your father is proud of you."

"Actually, he died when I was a boy." Normally he enjoyed meeting new people, high, low, and everyone in between, but this woman was in another category altogether, self-absorbed and self-important. For the sake of his hosts and good manners, he employed as much courtesy as he could muster.

"So, when did you come to America?" She leaned forward, a little too close, and he backed away slightly.

"Twenty-four years ago, but Mr. and Mrs. Henop have arrived much more recently." He tried to steer the conversation away from himself, but Mrs. King was having none of it.

"Did you come alone?"

"I came with my mother, stepfather, and siblings." He eyed the beef on his plate.

"Do they live in Easton as well?"

"They settled in Bedminster, in Bucks County." When she paused for a long moment, he took up his fork again.

"So, how does a man of great learning enjoy living in this backwater? I should think a man like you would thrive in a place like Philadelphia with its many cultural opportunities."

Peter's shoulders stiffened. "Easton is my home. My family and I are proud to live here."

She gave a laugh and waved her hand. "As they say, 'To each his own.'"

Peter looked past the scrivener toward a line of plump pies lined up on the sideboard, wondering which he would try first.

On Wednesday afternoon, Naomi Kleet sent word via Frau Neuss that Peter was invited to tea Thursday afternoon. Since he was scheduled to meet with the new schoolmaster then, he sent his regrets via Greta. In fact, he didn't regret not going at all.

CHAPTER NINE

E rin wanted to go online right away to research her family, but Ethan's base-ball practice and homework, along with her class preparation for teaching the following morning got in the way. Bursting with anticipation, she neverthe-less had trouble thinking about anything else. Finally, she got out the laptop after putting Ethan to bed, just herself and Toby in the family room. She found Ancestry.com where the opening screen offered a free two-week trial. Although Erin could afford the membership fee, she wanted to try the site first. It had all looked so simple on TV, but who knew what the process would be like in real life without a professional genealogist looking over her shoulder? She'd been taken in more than once by alluring infomercials, like the time she'd purchased a new hair system promising a smooth, straight mane with just one product, and she'd ended up with hair looking like Albert Einstein's, with a strange hint of purple.

"M-o-m!" Her son called from the second-floor hallway.

She hadn't had a moment to herself the past two days, but she took a deep breath, trying to keep her voice even. "Yes, Ethan?"

"I can't find my flashlight."

"Look under your bed."

"I did."

This had happened before, a lot in fact, and rather than prolonging the issue, she cut to the chase. "There's one on my dresser. You may borrow it."

"Okay. Thanks." He paused. "Mom?"

"Yes, Ethan?"

"I love you."

"I love you, too."

Toby looked up from his place at her feet, and she scratched him behind the ears. "Okay, where was I?"

Erin looked at the Ancestry home page and created a username and password, then arrived at the main menu, looking at a host of links. Under a tab marked "Learning Center," there were video workshops. *One of these might help me get started.* Erin clicked on one only to discover the download would take an hour to watch. *Maybe I'll try watching, and if the lesson gets boring or too involved, I'll stop.* When she tried to open the link, nothing happened. After five unsuccessful attempts, she gave up and returned to the home page, clicked on "Search," and found spaces for a person's name and things like when and where they were born and who their relatives were. This was a lot more promising than the video, and although she might not know how the system worked, she'd figure out what to do as she went along. She started with her Grammy Ott since she had the most information about her.

"Well, here goes, Toby."

She started filling in the spaces, including her grandmother's birth year and place, then the names of Erin's great-grandmother and great-grandfather. The next screen revealed a number of categories, including things like census and voter lists, tax, church, and school records, military, immigration, and family trees. On the right, a "Matching Persons" box came up and underneath, "Matching Records," including a church and town record about her Grammy Ott's marriage, and some census lists starting with 1910. *This is like finding an old trunk, and here I sit holding the key!* She was fascinated to see her family member listed in such a public, dispassionate way. "Let's try this one first," she told her dog.

According to that census, Irene Smith was seven years old, living with her father and mother in Easton's Ward 6. No one else resided in the household, so her Uncle Keith hadn't been born yet, and their sister Mae had probably died by then. For mother's and father's birthplaces, the record listed Pennsylvania but didn't provide any place names. Erin wanted very much to know that information.

Next, she clicked on the family trees link and found three containing her grandmother's name. These were likely posted by relatives she'd never heard of, yet suddenly felt strangely connected to. *Do they live in the Lehigh Valley? Are they cousins, or maybe distant aunts or uncles?* Her Grandfather Owen's name appeared in the box for spouse, then the names of her great-grandparents on the Smith side. Erin couldn't wait to find out who they were and where they'd been born.

According to the first family tree, her great-grandmother, Emmaline Smith, had been born in Easton in 1876, and Erin's great-grandfather, Daniel Smith, was born there four years earlier. *Okay, so they were born in the United States, not Germany. My family goes back further in American history than I ever thought.* "How about that Toby?" Her dog yawned and rested his head on his forepaws. Undaunted, Erin said, "Let's see, my great-grandparents were married in 1900 in Easton." She spoke again to her dog. "I like having these Easton connections. You know, I used to wish my mom had gone into labor in Easton so I could say I was from Pennsylvania instead of New Jersey, which many consider to be 'the armpit of the nation.'"

Emmaline Smith's maiden name was Brotz, and her father was David. Erin was eager to see where he'd been born, expecting to see Germany. "What's this? He was also born in Pennsylvania, Easton to be exact, and way back in 1835." *Wow, that's going really far back, way before the Civil War. So, he didn't come from Germany. What about his wife?*

She clicked on the box for her great-great-grandmother, Catherine Anna, but the person who'd created that particular family tree hadn't supplied a maiden name and had only guessed her birth date to be around 1836. As far as where Catherine had been born, Pennsylvania was listed. Erin wondered if either of the other two family trees posted on Ancestry had more information, but they just ended up echoing the first one. She returned to the original tree and began looking into her great-grandfather, Daniel Smith's, lineage. "His parents were Thomas Daniel and Ann Marie, and Thomas was born in 1811 in Pennsylvania. Ann Marie's maiden name was Fritz, and she was also from Pennsylvania."

"That's funny," Erin spoke aloud, "I went all through grade school and high school with a girl named Jennifer Fritz. I wonder if there's a connection?" She'd caught up with Jennifer on Facebook a few years earlier, and the thought of being related to such an old friend filled her with joy. "Okay, let's see, Ann Marie was born ten years later than her husband, in Northampton County, Pennsylvania. There's no specific town listed. I can't believe how far back they go!" She looked at Toby and told him, "So far, no one's been born in Germany, so my family was actually in America a lot longer than my mom or grandmother ever knew. Isn't that so cool?"

Toby looked up, stared at her for a moment, then flopped his head back onto his paws. Erin had a sudden impulse to call out "Come here, Jim! You can't believe what I just found!" The reality of his death jolted her like the time a minivan had rear-ended her vehicle. She took a deep breath and tried to focus on the computer, but her eyes were blurry with tears. This had happened before when she'd heard a Whitney Houston song on the radio, another time at church, when she'd seen a car just like Jim's Acura at the grocery store, and when she'd found one of his shirt buttons under the bathroom sink. She wondered how long she would keep feeling this gnawing pain that felt like half of herself had been ripped away.

She blinked back her tears and continued her cyber-journey through history, distracting herself with names and dates. Finding out her great-great-great-grandfather, Jacob Fritz, was born in the 1700s put her in a much better frame of mind. His birth date was listed as 1793 to be exact, and his wife, Elizabeth Grohman, was born in 1795, both of them in Bucks County. Erin sat up a little taller. *My family has been in America since the eighteenth century! I wonder what their lives were like, if they knew more triumph than tragedy, if they were shopkeepers or farmers, iron smiths or bakers.*

Eager to know just how far back they really went, she climbed various family tree branches, so she could find out just when these German relatives had come to America. Her heart leaped at the thought they might have actually been here during the Revolutionary War. She glanced at a vase on the mantel and smiled, remembering when she'd bought the replica with Jim at Jamestown, Virginia. They'd spent several days there and in Williamsburg shortly after they were married, and she'd felt completely and totally in her element there. She'd run around buying pottery, textiles, and pewter from the shops on Duke of Gloucester Street. As she and Jim went in and out of the restored eighteenth-century buildings, she'd thought, "I could've lived back here and been perfectly happy." Jim had taken her back at least once every year since then, except for this year.

She kept scribbling the names she found in her notebook, trying to focus on the main players and not get sidetracked., "Woo hoo!" she shouted, and Toby almost perked up. "Jacob Fritz's father was also called Jacob, and he was born in 1732, in Bucks County, before the Revolution. This is incredible!" Suddenly her joy mingled with utter confusion. Another family tree said Jacob had been born in 1748, also in Bucks County. Erin felt like she was swimming through an obstacle course as she tried to figure out which tree had the facts straight. Then she saw something that caused her to yell again.

"Oh, Toby! This tree says Jacob Senior's father was Johannes, and he was born in 1704 in Germany, and his son, Abraham, served as a "teamster" in the Revolution! I can't believe one of *my* relatives was a patriot" A sudden hope sprang up in Erin—*Could I actually become a Daughter of the American Revolution?*

❧ • ☙

"So, what did you discover?" Melissa asked at Starbucks the next morning.

If not for the joy of sharing her findings, Erin would've begged off their weekly get-together so she could go back on Ancestry.com.

"The process is amazing. There are so many people in my family tree—in anyone's family tree, actually—people I've never heard of, never even knew existed, and there they all are, related to me. Have you ever done anything like this?"

"No. My aunt has all the family information, and I'm only now becoming interested, mostly because of you."

"Well, I always thought my great-great-grandparents came from Germany around the mid-nineteenth century, and I was hoping they might've been here at least by the Civil War. So far, though, all the ones I've found were born in Pennsylvania way before then—in fact, one side went all the way back to 1704 in Germany!"

"Wow!"

"Their last name was Fritz," Erin said, "and the first guy to come to America got here between 1710 and 1720—I'm not sure exactly when yet."

"That's so amazing!" Melissa's face lit up.

Erin loved how her friend was always so happy for her when good things happened. "I know. I can hardly believe what I'm finding. Knowing these things really changes my perception of my family."

"How so?" Melissa sipped her latte, then licked some stray foam from her upper lip.

"They were pioneers, people who came here when the country was really young. I don't know. I have trouble explaining this. You know how much I adore early American history, always have, so finding out these things means a lot to me."

"I think I understand," Melissa said. "The closest I ever got to that was being a Pioneer Girl when I was a kid. We used to meet at this tiny church in my neighborhood, and I wore a little blue cap I still have …"

There she goes off on a tangent, but Erin was sure in a few minutes Melissa would circle back around to the topic. When she did, Erin picked up her story about the Fritzes. "Anyway, I was amazed because I knew a Jennifer Fritz all through school when I was growing up, plus I found an Abraham Fritz who served as a teamster during the Revolution!" She broke into a big smile.

"That is so cool, Erin! You might actually be able to be a Daughter of the American Revolution!" She squeezed Erin's hand.

"I know!" Not wanting to hog all the attention, she asked, "Do you have any ancestors who go back that far?"

"I don't, but Tim's grandmother was a DAR. Both my mother's and father's families came from Germany in the 1890s." She paused. "I think you should check this out, you know, contact someone from the DAR. Maybe they can help you."

"I think I'll do just that," Erin said. "I honestly can't believe this."

"Believe it, my friend!" Melissa paused. "I'm so glad this is helping you just now. I have a feeling some very good things are about to happen."

Erin wasted no time when she got home and immediately looked up the Daughters of the American Revolution website where she found an "Interested in Becoming a Member" portal. There was a "Chapter Locator," and Erin typed in her zip code. Next, there was a form to fill out with her personal information and the name of her patriot ancestor, which she listed as Abraham Fritz. She clicked on the "submit" button and leaned back in her chair, wondering what might happen next. Toby ambled over and laid himself on top of her feet, which always gave Erin a feeling of contentment. "Imagine, Toby, I, Erin Pelleriti Miles, might actually become a Daughter of the American Revolution!"

Audrey called the next day, and Erin told her mom what she'd discovered.

"I never knew anything about those people you mentioned. I never even heard of their names," Audrey said.

"I know; I never did either."

"Are you sure this information is true, Erin? I hear a lot of bad things about the Internet."

"This website is fine, Mom." She didn't want her mother raining on her parade.

"Well, imagine our family going that far back."

"I know, I almost can't."

"Well, I'm calling about a family thing, too."

"Really? What?" Erin asked.

"After you left the other day, I realized I have a lot more things in drawers and closets, so I went looking. I found a marriage certificate my cousin Edith— you know, my father's sister's daughter—gave me a long time ago. I'm not sure why, but I have it."

Erin's heart pounded. "Whose is it?"

"Like I said, she gave the certificate to me."

"No, I mean whose names are written there?"

"Oh. I think my grandfather's, my dad's dad, and my grandmother's," Audrey said. "I can hardly read it anymore, because the writing is pretty faded, and you know about my eyes."

Erin knew. She wished her mother could be more at peace with her situation. "So, you can't see what's on it?"

"Not really, just a little here and there, words like Stewartsville, and I think 1870-something."

"Oh, Mom, that's super!"

"When do you think you'll be coming up to see it? I miss you."

Erin gave a quick mental rundown of her schedule for the next few days. "Maybe Ethan and I can drive up after his game Saturday morning."

"That would be nice. I never get to see him."

She ignored the last comment.

꧁ • ꧂

CHAPTER TEN

The following day her mother called just after Ethan went to school while she was sitting at the kitchen table with her second cup of coffee and a leftover taco.

"Hi, Erin, it's Mom." Audrey still didn't understand the concept of caller ID.

"Hi, Mom. How are you?"

"Oh, pretty good. You know my cousin Edith?"

"Uh-huh. You mentioned her last night."

"Well, I talked to her a few minutes ago about your interest in family history, and we started talking about that marriage certificate she gave me."

Erin grabbed an electric bill and a pen so she could take notes.

Her mom said, "All I can make out is 'Marriage Certificate.' She put it in a nice frame. My cousin always did things right. She and Fred always had money, even if they never had children."

"So, what did your cousin tell you?" Erin asked.

"Oh, let's see, that our grandfather's name was John, and our grandmother was Louisa."

"Do you know what her maiden name was?"

"We think it was something like Rickline. My dad said she used to smoke a pipe."

Erin burst out laughing as she scribbled the names. "Are you serious, Mom?"

"Yes."

"She must've been something else. Do you remember her?"

"Oh, no. She died before I was born."

Besides her grandfather's death in his fifties, Erin wondered if maybe this other side of the family had known more happiness than her maternal grandmother's people. The thing about researching your family was that one tree branch led to another, spreading out far and wide until you weren't sure which one to perch on first. She had trouble focusing on just one line when all the others were out there waving to get her attention. Rather than be frustrated by the process, however, Erin welcomed every bit. It was giving her something else to think about besides missing Jim and worrying about what was going to happen next with her teaching career.

"I can't wait for you to see this," Audrey said.

"Well, we're coming up on Saturday."

"What time are you planning to be here?"

"Ethan's game should be over by eleven."

"I have a hair appointment at eleven-thirty. I've been waiting for too long. I'm a bush. Could you come after lunch?"

Erin wished her mom would let her stylist do her color, as well as a cut. Then she had an idea. Maybe she could take Ethan to see his grandfather first, then they'd go over to her mom's. Of course, she wouldn't mention that to Audrey. "Sure. We'll come around, say one-thirty-ish."

"Okay. Just be careful."

Her mother always told her to be careful, even if she were just going out to the mailbox. She wasn't sure what Audrey was afraid of, but on second thought, her mom seemed to fear just about everything.

"Sit down, sit down," Bridget said.

Erin wasn't exactly sure where. She'd never actually eaten at her dad's apartment, and the table was on the small side, nestled at the edge of the galley kitchen with Reagan-era appliances and scuffed linoleum that appeared to have been green at one time. She waited for instructions while Ethan stood there examining the cast iron truck her dad had just given to him. When Ethan shook the toy, coins rattled inside. She liked that her dad had done this, the way grandfathers were supposed to.

"You sit right here." Bridget pointed to one of the chairs. "Ethan, you sit by me."

Erin had watched her dad's wife make the food, too uncertain of her relationship with the woman to say Ethan probably wouldn't go for olive loaf. The meal wasn't kid friendly, but then Bridget had never been around children much.

"What is this?" Ethan asked when Bridget put the plate in front of him.

"Olive loaf," Bridget said.

"Don't you like baloney?" Tony asked.

"Uh, I never had it," Ethan said.

"You've never had baloney?" Tony laughed. "What about olives?" Ethan shook his head. "What kid doesn't eat baloney? Well, try it, you might like it." He turned to Erin. "Do you remember that old commercial? What was that for?"

"Life cereal," Erin said.

"That's right."

"The boy's name was Mikey," Bridget added.

Ethan took a tentative bite, which apparently was quite enough. At least he didn't fuss, Erin thought. As for herself, she managed to get half the sandwich down without trying to think about the strange textures. When her dad urged her to eat up, she made excuses—she'd had a big breakfast. She wasn't hungry.

Bridget offered Ethan a package of chocolate Tastykakes. "I know cupcakes aren't the best thing to give him, but then, don't grandparents like to spoil their grandchildren?"

Something began spreading inside Erin, a kind of warmth, a sense of things falling into a much more pleasant place.

Her great-grandparents' marriage certificate was old all right, the script faded. The glass was also cloudy from sitting in a drawer since Bill Clinton was in office, so Erin gently wiped the object clean with one of her mother's wash cloths with a faded Philadelphia Flyers logo. She remembered when her best friend had bought her a set of towels for Christmas when Erin was going through an ice hockey phase. Audrey had clung to other relics, a framed jigsaw puzzle of an old school hanging crookedly on one wall, Erin and Allen's fading high school photos, a stack of Mr. Peanut coasters, knickknacks from garage sales, an ashtray from the Trump Taj Mahal. To Erin, this was junk and clutter, to her mother, treasures she'd bought with her own money.

Erin studied the Victorian Era document with its touch of gilding around the edge, curlicue lettering, and a romantic drawing of a bride and groom gazing at each other—from a respectable distance, of course.

"Wow, that's really old," Ethan said, leaning over his mom's shoulder for a better look.

"This is your grandparents' marriage certificate," Audrey said, then she quickly corrected herself. "I mean, this is my grandparents'; they'd be your, let's see …"

"Great-great-grandparents," Ethan said.

Erin copied the information she found written on it in her notebook. "They were married at the Lutheran Church in Stewartsville in, let's see, 1878."

"That's right," Audrey said. "I remember my father's people went to that church."

Erin continued reading. "His name was Thomas Owen and hers was Louisa. Let's see, her maiden name was Kichline."

"That's funny. I always thought her name was Rickline."

"You were close."

"Kichline," her mother repeated. "It seems I've heard that name before."

When she finished writing down the information, Erin spent another hour with her mom until the weariness of the day began catching up with her. At the door, Audrey handed the framed document to her daughter.

"I want you to have this."

"Really! Are you sure?"

"I'm sure. I don't think Allen would care, and I know you'll appreciate it."

Erin got home and went directly to her computer, filling in more spaces on Ancestry.com. She'd decided to subscribe after all so she'd have full access, plus she'd start a family tree page to keep track of her discoveries. Her favorite method of finding information was looking at other people's family trees, and she was learning how to export them to the one she was creating. She added the names of John Owen and his bride, Louisa Kichline, along with the wedding date, guessing at their approximate birthdates since Ancestry gave you up to ten years of wiggle room. Right away, Erin found six other related family trees and prepared to settle in for a long session while Ethan played Minecraft.

Over the next two hours, she traveled down the Owen line, which led her to a certain John Sharp, whose information included a citing in Abstract Graves of Revolutionary Patriots. Erin munched on cashews and freeze dried kale as she became increasingly confused. "How can there be so many John Sharps living in New Jersey at the same time?" she asked out loud. "I don't know how to figure out which one was which."

"Did you say something, Mom?" Ethan called from the sun room.

"Just talking to myself," she said.

When that search became too bewildering, she began looking into her Great-grandmother Louisa's line. Louisa' father, Joseph, had been born in the 1820s in Forks Township, just above the city of Easton. Louisa's mother was an Everhart, also from Forks Township. Erin decided to follow the Kichlines and save the other side for later. *There are so many possibilities!*

Joseph's father, Samuel, was listed in most of the available family trees as being born in Northampton County, Pennsylvania in 1798. *There's the eighteenth century again!* Every time Erin saw a 17—something date, joy rushed through her spirit, liked she'd finally snatched the brass ring on a carousel. When she clicked on a link to find Samuel's parents, she discovered a Joseph Kachlein—slightly different spelling—born in 1775 in Bedminster, Bucks County. *I don't know where that is. I wonder why the last names were spelled differently.* Erin became even more befuddled when she came upon Joseph's father's name, Keichline. In her earlier research, she'd come across a similar name and reached across her desk for her notes where she found a story about colonial Easton. A Swiss pastor, the Rev. Michael Schlatter, had come to America in 1752 with Bibles and money to start German Reformed churches and schools. On July 31, 1755, several of Easton's leading townsmen signed a document pledging their financial support and labor to build a school. *I wonder what Easton was like during the colonial era.* She imagined men in tricorn hats and women in puffy dresses walking up and down Northampton Street accompanied by the sound of fifes and drums. Among the names of the trustees was a Peter Kichline. *Could he be related to my Great-grandmother Louisa?*

"Mom, I'm hungry." Ethan's voice brought Erin back to the present. "It's almost seven."

"Holy cow!" She realized he'd only eaten Tasty Kakes and peanut butter pretzels at her mom's, since lunch. This boy needed to be fed. She made pizza, and while it baked, Erin checked her email. There was one whose address she didn't recognize—an automated response from the DAR. Her heart beat faster as she read it.

> *Thank you! Your request is being processed. Your information is being added to our database. The State Membership Chairman in your state is also being contacted. She will notify a local chapter, who will contact you.*

Chapters meet once a month, September thru May, so please allow up to two months for chapter contact. Your reference number is 161357. Thank you for your interest, Membership Information Department, NSDAR. ProspectiveMembers@dar.org

Much to her son's amusement, Erin started belting out an old song, "Something tells me I'm into something good."

CHAPTER ELEVEN

Frau Eckert examined the spoon, her head bobbing up and down. "That's it alright! Oh, Sheriff Kichline, how did you find it so quickly?" She went from a smile to a growl in an instant. "That Old Pig Drover took it, didn't he?"

"He's the one who gave the spoon to me," Peter said.

"He gave it to you?" She rubbed the spoon over her apron.

"He took it from your tavern a few days ago, but he didn't mean to—just a bit of absentmindedness."

By the sour look on her face, she clearly wasn't impressed. "Humpf!"

"Now, Frau Eckert, I have no reason not to believe him."

Her hands went to her hips. "Then why didn't he return it?"

"He was embarrassed. He hoped I'd be able to clear things up because he enjoys your cooking so much." Peter hoped that would soften her up.

"Well, I guess we all make mistakes."

"That's the spirit." He paused. "I'm afraid we still don't know who took the other missing spoons, though."

"Actually, there's no mystery about that, Sheriff," she said, lowering her voice. "There were some spoons I'd put aside for a special cleaning, and I plum forgot about them."

"Well, then, that problem seems to be solved." He turned toward the door, but she detained him by grabbing his right forearm.

"There's something else, Sheriff Kichline." He wanted to shake off her hand but didn't want to be rude. "I'm short this week by two pounds, and Herr

Rinker told me he was too." Once again she leaned closer, her breath like week-old cream filling the space between them. "You can't trust those Indians."

He tried not to lose his patience with her. "Have any of them been in here?"

"Well, not exactly," she said, backing up, "but they're sneaky, they are."

"I'll tell you what, you and Martin keep a close watch on your money box and other valuables, and let me know if you see anyone acting out of the ordinary."

"I will, Sheriff." She put her hand back on his arm. "I'm so thankful for your help."

"It's my pleasure." Although he said the words only out of courtesy, she blushed, her face going all blotchy.

Peter stepped into the street, seeing the daily stage coach to Philadelphia departing and waving to the driver, noticed Naomi Kleet's daughter inside. He didn't realize she was leaving Easton so soon. He raised his hat to her and with curled lips and an upturned face, she nodded. "I wonder what that's all about," he muttered, watching as the vehicle disappeared down Pomfret Street.

✍ • ✍

He visited the half dozen other taverns in town, in addition to Meyer Hart's store, to see if they'd experienced any thefts. John Rinker, William Craig, and Jacob Opp reported the loss of pewter pitchers, flatware, and tankards, as well as small amounts of currency. Meyer hadn't arrived at his store yet but his son, Michael, was there. Peter took the interview nice and slow because Michael always spoke better when people didn't rush him.

"S-s-s-someone st-st-st-stole s-s-s-some l-l-l-linens."

"About how many?" Peter asked.

Michael scratched the side of his head with his right forefinger. "About t-t-t-ten p-p-p-pounds' w-w-w-worth."

"That's a lot of lost merchandise." Michael nodded in agreement. "Do you suspect anyone in particular?"

"N-n-n-no, b-b-b-but F-F-F-Father is upset."

"I imagine he would be. There seems to be an outbreak of thefts just now, and I assure you, I'm going to find out who is behind them."

"*D-d-d-danke*," Michael said.

"I've lost a few blown crystal glasses and a good-sized ham," said George Taylor, who ran the Bachmann Publick House. "I thought I was losing my mind."

"I'm happy to report you are not, my friend," Peter said. "The other tavern keepers are reporting similar instances."

"Do you have any idea who's doing this?"

"Not yet. This seems to be a recent development." He took comfort in that. Otherwise, he would've felt derelict in his duties.

"Well, I'm sure you'll be able to find out who it is and bring the criminal to justice." Taylor shook his head. "I just don't know what's the matter with people nowadays."

"Please let me know if you see anyone or anything suspicious."

"That I will do."

A slight drizzle began falling as Peter walked down the tavern's steps. He paused for a moment on Northampton Street to gaze at the river a good-sized block to the east, watching as the ferry crossed from Pennsylvania to New Jersey. The placid scene calmed him, and after taking his fill, he turned and walked toward the courthouse. Ziba Wiggins stood there waving at him.

"Sheriff Kichline, there's someone here for you."

"Hello, Mr. Wiggins," Peter said and then nodded at the tall, lanky stranger.

"This is Mr. William Hanlon, the teacher who's hoping to take the school."

"It's a pleasure to meet you, sir." The youth shook Peter's hand.

"The pleasure is mine. Welcome to Easton."

"Thank you."

"He just got here and told me he was supposed to ask for you," Wiggins said.

Peter wondered who'd given that instruction, but he didn't mind. He liked getting back into the rhythms of everyday life. Although the teacher's coat was dusty from travel and his face pale, there was an underlying strength about him, which manifested itself in a square jaw and erect posture. Just then, the rain started to pick up, accompanied by a gusty wind, and Wiggins was looking toward the shelter of the courthouse.

"I think you should get out of this rain, Mr. Wiggins. Mr. Hanlon, my home is just up this street, if you'd care to join me."

The teacher smiled, "Yes, thank you, sir."

They matched each other's swift strides up Northampton Street to Peter's stone residence where Greta and Susannah helped them with their coats. Andrew and Jacob came downstairs to see what was happening, and Peter made introductions. Then he asked, "Is young Peter here?"

"No, sir. He's at the mill. Do you want me to get him?" Andrew asked.

"Let's wait until the storm lifts." He brushed wet drops from his breeches with the palms of his hands. "I'd like you to spend some time with our guest. Greta, would you please prepare some food for Mr. Hanlon?"

"Yes, sir. There's pepper pot. Will that do?"

"That sounds wonderful," the teacher said. "Thank you."

Peter led them to the dining room where they sat down to the perfect lunch for such a day. Hanlon ate three bowls of the thick soup and a loaf of bread, apologizing more than once for his appetite. "I assure you, Sheriff, I'm not given to gluttony, but I hadn't eaten today, and this is the finest soup I have ever tasted."

Peter saw Greta's face blush from the compliment. He was just glad she was back in form.

"Will you have some shoofly pie, Mr. Hanlon?" she asked.

"Oh, if I may, yes. I enjoy German food very much."

"Do you like the pie wet or dry?" Andrew asked.

"Either way, but I slightly favor the wet kind."

"Well, that's just what I made," Greta said, then she headed toward the kitchen.

After eating two generous pieces, Hanlon followed the sheriff and his children into the parlor where they sat around a fire, which was cozy in contrast to the slashing rains outside.

"Are you going to be our new teacher?" Susannah asked. There was no mistaking the stars in the girl's eyes.

"I hope to, Miss Kichline." His eyes traveled the length and breadth of a bookshelf dominating one wall.

"Where are you from, Mr. Hanlon?" Peter asked, detecting from the youth's accent he was from somewhere in the southern colonies. He lit a pipe and relaxed into his wingback chair.

"I'm from North Carolina, sir."

"North Carolina!" Jacob's eyebrows raised.

The teacher paused for a low, rumbling belch which he seemed to keep inside only with great effort. Susannah put her hand over her mouth, apparently to stifle her giggles. "I beg your pardon!" His face reddened, and he quickly made an effort to put the unseemly noise behind them. "You see, I've always had a hankering for education, but there aren't many opportunities in the backcountry. Whenever my father could spare me, I went to the nearest school, which was ten miles away."

Jacob spoke up. "How did you get there?"

"Mostly, I walked, Master Kichline. When I couldn't make it, the teachers let me borrow a book here and there, and an esquire allowed me to use his personal library." Once again his eyes roamed the bookshelf. "Your collection, sir, is even more impressive than his."

"Thank you, Mr. Hanlon. I cherish my books above all my worldly possessions."

"Papa went to Heidelberg," Jacob said, not a little proudly.

"Is that so?" Hanlon's admiration showed in his brown eyes.

"Yes, but let's hear about you for now." He shot Jacob a look. His son knew better than to brag. Peter had always believed having privileges meant greater responsibility, not an excuse for arrogance.

"Well, sir, my goal is to study at Yale College, and I've been teaching a quarter here, a quarter there as I make my way north to Connecticut."

"That's a worthy ambition," Peter said, admiring the young man's aim.

"Thank you, sir. I got as far as Bedminster when your brother, Mr. Charles Kichline, told me Easton needed a teacher. Since they already had one, he encouraged me to come here."

Peter wondered how Charles knew all this, although word traveled relatively quickly between the two communities in spite of their being twenty-four miles apart. "Is that satchel all you have with you?" He took note of the worn condition.

"Yes, sir. I travel lightly."

"Andrew, would you please take Mr. Hanlon to your room? You, Jacob, and Peter can share with him."

The boys both jumped up to help.

"Oh, but sir, I can stay at one of the taverns," Hanlon said.

Peter doubted the youth had enough funds for more than a few meals, let alone a tavern. "Consider yourself our guest until a decision is made about your teaching here. I'll inform the other trustees of your presence—unless Mr. Wiggins has already done so," he added wryly. "Perhaps we can hold an interview as soon as tomorrow."

"That would be wonderful. Thank you, sir." Hanlon reached into the front part of his satchel and produced an envelope. "Mr. Kichline asked me to give you this."

Peter turned the envelope in his hands, recognizing Charles's stout handwriting. "Thank you."

"It is I who thank you, sir."

                       ❧ • ☙

Peter sat by the fire puffing his pipe while he opened the letter, as Susannah sat across from him working quietly on a new sampler.

> *My dear Peter,*
>
> *I bring you greetings from Bedminster and hope you are well as we observe the rites of spring and Easter, recently passed. May the hope of the resurrection strengthen you and your children daily in the earthly absence of your dear Margaretta.*
>
> *This letter is coming to you by way of Mr. William Hanlon, who arrived in Bedminster about a week ago, just as I became aware of your school's unfortunate situation. I met Mr. Hanlon at our brother Andrew's tavern and hearing of his desire to teach school on his way to take up his studies at Yale College, I decided to investigate him further.*

That corroborates his story, Peter thought. Not a mistrustful man by nature, he was nevertheless cautious and considered by most to be a good judge of character. He glanced outside. The rain was beginning to slow down.

> *He has been staying with us for several days, and although his condition is rather threadbare, I feel safe in vouching for his character. He is a most earnest young man of orderly habits and a polite nature. In spite of his lack of worldly goods, he never asked for money or material assistance of any kind, only advice about finding a school. While he stayed here, he gladly assisted me with farming labors without being asked to do so. My Susannah also thinks highly of him, especially since he also helped her with household chores. Therefore, I highly commend him to you and to the school in Easton. My only concern is he does not stay long in one place. Nevertheless, his references are excellent, and I believe them to be authentic. Mr. Hanlon will do right by you.*

Trusting his good brother's opinion, Peter settled into the idea of promoting Mr. Hanlon's candidacy to the other trustees. At this point, Charles's letter became more personal.

> *In addition to Mr. Hanlon, I may be able to assist you in another matter. Knowing your servants' indentures are about to expire, I suspect you will require a new housekeeper. Our brother Andrew's wife has a niece who wishes for adventure beyond her home in neighboring Tinicum, and when Catherine mentioned your situation, the young woman expressed a*

deep interest in assisting you. I have met Phoebe Benner a few times at Andrew and Catherine's home, and she strikes me as a responsible young woman of cheerful disposition.

Peter hoped she was also a good cook. He glanced at his daughter, who met his eyes and smiled sweetly. How much she was her mother's daughter with her pink complexion and blue eyes! He wondered if Margaretta had looked like this as a young girl. He returned her smile and resumed reading.

If you would care to take her on, please let Andrew or me know, and we will be happy to make arrangements for her trip to Easton.

He liked the idea of helping someone in the family.

My dear Susannah asks me to send her affections to you and yours. I am happy in this first year of matrimony, perhaps more so since it took me such a long time to tie the knot. Although I am an old man of thirty-nine, my young bride has helped me enjoy a rebirth of my faded youth. I do believe all things happen according to their appointed time.

Please remember me to young Peter, Andrew, Jacob, and my dearest little Susannah, for whom I have an uncle's deepest affections. You are daily in my prayers for your health and well-being.

I am ever your devoted brother,
Charles

Peter folded the letter, then tapped it against his chin, staring into the fire. "Does Uncle Charles send good tidings?" Susannah asked.

"Yes, my dear, very good tidings."

❧ • ☙

CHAPTER TWELVE

The trustees originally wanted to interview William Hanlon at the school house, but so many people showed up they moved to the courthouse instead. Word had spread around town the new teacher was from the southern colonies. It wasn't every day they got to see someone that exotic. The likes of Anthony Esser and Robert Bell openly wondered if anything good could come from North Carolina.

Inside, the women fanned themselves, and the men perspired under their waistcoats. Ziba Wiggins opened the windows, which let in air both fresh and foul when a breeze from the rivers carried in the scent of animal dung, along with the usual sounds of grunting pigs, lowing cows, and baaing sheep. When the seats ran out, and people began leaning against the whitewashed walls, Peter could tell from his constant walking about, the caretaker was becoming panicked, probably thinking about all the dirt and grime they'd brought in with them. Already the floors had taken the brunt of boots and shoes bearing the remains of dusty roads and soggy pastures.

The buzz of voices filled the chamber as the trustees took their places, and William Hanlon sat down before them. Peter thought it remarkable how self-possessed he appeared, how earlier that morning he'd eaten a hearty breakfast and conversed about life in North Carolina as if nothing important were about to happen. Greta had cleaned his clothes the best she could, but Hanlon still looked like a ragamuffin, though he managed to bear the dignity of a minister. If he got the job, the trustees would have to see to a new suit of clothes.

"This meeting please will now come to order," Lewis Gordon announced. Few stopped talking. "We will now begin this interview," he called out, his voice squeaking on the last word. Some stopped talking, but more than a few people continued their conversations.

Seeing his friend in trouble, Peter rose and addressed the crowd. "Ladies and gentleman, Esquire Gordon requires your attention." Quiet fell upon the filled room, and Peter sat down again.

"Thank you, Sheriff Kichline," Gordon said. "Thank you, one and all for coming to this meeting of the school trustees. We are about to make a decision affecting all our children and families. Please understand, however, the questioning will initially be limited to the trustees." He cleared his throat. "I would like to introduce you to Mr. William Hanlon of North Carolina."

At the mention of the colony, the murmurs rose again, although his origins came as no surprise. It was why they'd closed their shops and left fields and houses in the first place.

Gordon turned to the young man. "Mr. Hanlon, thank you for your interest in becoming Easton's school teacher. The purpose of this meeting is to find out more about you so we can make an informed decision. We take the education of our children very seriously."

Peter hoped the young man didn't feel like he was on trial, even if it looked that way.

"Thank you for interviewing me, sir. I also take education seriously."

Gordon nodded, looking surprised by the confident words. "Please tell everyone your name and a little about your background."

"I'm William Farrell Hanlon, and I was born in Dobbs, North Carolina in 1747."

Peter heard Robert Bell whisper loudly, "Nawth Car-o-lie-na," and some of the people around him sniggered. He'd expected as much.

"How did your parents come to live there?" Gordon asked.

"My paternal grandparents came to the colonies from England in the early 1720s. At first, they went to Virginia, then they settled in North Carolina in 1731. My mother's people had been there for five years."

"And where were they from?"

"They were also from England, sir, Warminster to be exact."

"Do you have brothers and sisters?"

"Yes, sir, there are five boys and four girls. I'm the fifth born."

A pig grunted just outside the window near Gordon, then a porcine chorus rose. "Mr. Wiggins, can you do something about that din?" he said.

"Right away, sir!" Wiggins hurried from the room.

Gordon took a deep breath. "Where did you go to school, Mr. Hanlon?"

"There was no school in our community, sir. The closest one was ten miles from our farm, and I only went between harvests."

Robert Traill spoke up. "If I may, I'm wondering how an uneducated farmer from the backwater of North Carolina can teach our children?" Using his best Scottish brogue, he rolled his r's impressively.

Peter could tell his friend harbored no malice toward Hanlon, but he wished Traill had toned down his bluntness.

"Begging your pardon, Mr. Traill," Hanlon said, "I was educated."

Traill folded his arms across his chest and nodded, "Go on, please."

"Whenever I could, I borrowed books from the teachers, and I became friends with the esquire in town, who also let me use his library. I read every book available to me. When I took tests at the school, I always got a near-perfect score."

Peter decided if this young man got the job, he would also open up his library to him, something he didn't do lightly. He might be generous with his newspaper, but books needed to be treated much more carefully.

"Then you are largely self-educated?" Gordon asked.

"You might say so, sir."

"How can we be certain you've had enough training to handle our school?"

"Feel free to test me in any of the subjects, Mr. Gordon."

At first, the trustees quizzed him about history, literature, Bible, and arithmetic. Hanlon didn't miss a question. He also quoted long passages from Virgil, Milton, and Shakespeare.

He's doing well! Peter scanned the approving faces around the packed room.

"Your breadth of literature is deep, Mr. Hanlon," said Gordon. "Now then, what about languages? Most of our students are from German backgrounds, and our teacher needs to understand that tongue." The lawyer looked almost regretful for asking as if he couldn't expect this much even from such an astonishing youth.

"*Ich bin mit der Deutschen Sprache vertraut,*" Hanlon said.

Gordon's eyebrows raised, and half the people began talking at once. Not even he knew what the young man had just said, but Peter understood, and smiled to himself.

"That is most impressive, Mr. Hanlon," Gordon said. "We also require the teaching of Latin. Are you familiar with that language as well?"

"*Ego sum Latine.*"

Robert Bell rose. "Is this some kind of trick? Was he trained to say these things?'

"Do sit down, Mr. Bell! As if the trustees would do such a thing!" Gordon's face was red as he turned to the teacher. "Mr. Hanlon, just how many languages do you know?"

"Sir, I am fluent in German and French, and I understand a good deal of Latin, Greek, and Hebrew."

The lawyer tented his hands, tapping the tips of his fingers against each other. "How did you happen to learn them?"

"Again, sir, I am mostly self-taught," Hanlon said.

Another eruption of voices broke out.

"Order! Please!" Gordon had avoided using the gavel since this wasn't a trial, but at this point, he yielded to instinct. "We cannot learn about Mr. Hanlon with this infernal talking! If you don't desist, I'll have Sheriff Kichline remove everyone except Mr. Hanlon and the trustees."

Like naughty children, the men and women obeyed.

"You seem most remarkable, Mr. Hanlon," Robert Traill said. "Tell me, what are your favorite subjects?"

"Thank you, Mr. Traill. I especially enjoy ancient history, the Bible, and mathematics."

"I understand you've taught before?" Traill said.

"Yes, sir. I've had five schools, in Virginia, Maryland, Delaware, and Pennsylvania."

"Where in Pennsylvania?" Traill asked.

"Norristown, sir."

"I have his references," Gordon said, producing several sheets of paper. "I'll allow the trustees to examine these. These are for the trustees only." He peered over the courtroom, challenging anyone to disagree with him.

The questioning continued as the men took turns reading the papers, except for Peter, who'd already seen them. He felt proud of Hanlon, and if he knew the trustees as well as he thought he did, they'd vote in the young man's favor.

George Taylor looked up from reading. "Mr. Hanlon, I'm duly impressed with your scholarship and your demeanor, but I have one remaining concern. May I inquire as to why you've not stayed at a school longer than a few months? I find it unusual you move from place-to-place as if you were running from something."

A hush fell over the assembly, people leaning forward, ears perked up. Hanlon seemed to be the only person who wasn't sweating.

"Sir, I don't wonder you've asked about that," Hanlon said. "Actually, I'm not running from something, but rather to something. You see, I want very much to become a minister, an educated one because there are so few in North

Carolina. I want to attend Yale College, but my family has no money for it, so I'm working my way north to Connecticut, teaching a term here and there."

Someone called out, "Aren't those circuit riding revivalists good enough for the backwoods of North Carolina?"

"Order!" Gordon said.

Hanlon turned in the direction of the person who'd spoken. "There are many fine men laboring for the Lord in that fashion, sir, but even they need to be educated." His southern drawl may have been slow, but his wits clearly were not.

Taylor smiled. "You're a most extraordinary young man."

When the trustees finished looking over the documents, Gordon dismissed everyone else so they could speak among themselves. Peter considered whether they'd thrown the school teacher to the wolves outside, but he thought most of the people had been charmed by Hanlon.

"I don't know about the rest of you," Gordon said, "but I believe this Mr. Hanlon is an answer to our earnest prayers for a new school master. He's intelligent and learned—albeit in a rather unusual manner—and earnest. I don't think we could go wrong with him."

"I agree with you," George Taylor said. "My only concern is whether he'll stay through the current term."

Peter spoke up. "I discussed this with him last night, and he's in no hurry to leave us. He says he'll serve for as long as we require his services."

A few minutes later, the trustees decided to extend a formal call to the teacher. Next came the matter of where he would live.

"If I may address this issue," Traill said, "Mr. Wiggins told me he and his wife would like to open their home to him."

Heads nodded.

"That was kind of them," Gordon remarked. "I think the matter is settled, then. As for wages, I think we should offer what Mr. Humstead was earning."

Traill said he thought that might be too generous, but the others agreed Hanlon was well worth the price.

"And let's throw in a suit of clothes," Gordon said. No one disagreed.

When all was said and done, George Taylor took Peter aside. "Sheriff, I've heard some talk about those thefts possibly being attributed to Indians."

"Let me guess—Frau Eckert?"

Taylor sniffed, "I think we understand each other. I know, and you know, Tatamy isn't guilty, but maybe you should pay him a visit anyway, just to smooth her ruffled feathers."

It wasn't always easy, or pleasant, being sheriff.

❧ • ❧

That evening, the trustees celebrated William Hanlon's new position with a dinner at the Bachmann Publick House. Peter excused himself a little early so he could write to his brother Charles to let him know what had happened with Hanlon and to instruct him to send Phoebe Benner. He wanted to tell Greta about this development, but she had already retired when he got home. In the morning, after she cleaned up from breakfast, she came to speak with Peter before he left to see Nicholas Tatamy. Peter was determined to make the call as pleasant as possible in spite of Frau Eckert's baseless accusations.

"Sheriff Kichline, I must speak with you about something." Greta twisted her apron.

"What is it, Greta?" he asked.

"Well, you see, the captain just got orders to go to a different fort, further west, and he has to leave in two days. He'll be out there for goodness knows how long and, well, he wants to take me with him. If I don't, we don't know how long it'll be 'til he can return." Her voice trembled. "If ever." More twisting of the apron. She looked like a dam about to break.

Peter took a deep breath, then let it out slowly. He understood her predicament, as well as his own. Phoebe Benner might take two weeks to get to Easton. Technically, Greta was still beholden to him, but the last thing he wanted to do was stand in the way of her marriage. Certainly they could manage without a housekeeper for a few weeks. Susannah could help, but how much could a six-year-old girl do and besides, he wanted her to attend school since a teacher was here. Somehow they would manage.

"Greta, you've served this family, and my wife especially, very well these many years, and I'm truly grateful," he said. "We can't always control the timing of what happens, but Providence has arranged these circumstances, so I give you my blessing to marry your captain now." Tears poured down her cheeks, and he squirmed, remembering how emotional Margaretta used to get and how helpless he felt whenever she did.

"Oh, thank you, sir! You are so good to me."

"Yes, well, all the best to you." He was relieved when she didn't try to hug him.

CHAPTER THIRTEEN

Erin was torn between either opening an email from the DAR or making sure Ethan got to the bus stop on time. After she dropped him off, she'd have to get to her class, but she was dying to know what the message said. Her duties as mother and professor won out, but as soon as she landed in the college's parking lot, she sat in the car and opened the message.

> *Dear Erin—My name is Patty Corcoran, and I'm the PA DAR State Membership Chairman, responsible for routing inquiries to local Chapters. I have forwarded your interest in DAR to the Valley Forge Chapter. A representative from the chapter will be in touch shortly. In the meantime, if you have any questions, please don't hesitate to contact me. Regards, Patty.*

Valley Forge Chapter—what a nice ring. Erin always took out of town visitors to see the Liberty Bell, Independence Hall, and Valley Forge National Park when they came, and over the years, she and Jim had frequently taken Ethan there for bike rides and hikes. They'd seen the Visitors Center film about the 1777–78 winter encampment so many times she knew the dialogue almost by heart. To be part of the Daughters of the American Revolution, Valley Forge Chapter, was more than she'd ever dreamed when she was young and planning a life that would be very different from her parents'.

❧ • ❧

After class, Erin drove home and corrected essays, trying not to shortchange her students, but wanting very much to have at least an hour to herself before Ethan got off the bus. At school, she'd looked up the Valley Forge Chapter on her smartphone during a break, and she wanted to write to Sydney Stordahl, the contact person listed on its website, not knowing how long Patty Corcoran might take to get in touch with her on Erin's behalf. An hour and lots of red ink later, she checked her watch. "At least I have forty-five minutes," she told her dog. Then she wrote:

> *Dear Ms. Stordahl,*
>
> *After discovering information about the Valley Forge Chapter of the DAR on the Internet and hearing from your State Membership Chairman, Patty Corcoran, I'm writing to introduce myself. I'm a historian, and I've been researching my family tree to see if there are any Revolutionary War patriots. Just this week I found some good leads, and I'm interested in pursuing membership in the DAR.*

Erin smiled as she wrote those last words.

> *All of the men are from my mother's side of the family. John Sharp of New Jersey was a corporal in the Continental Army; he's my fifth great-grandfather. Also, another fifth great-grandfather, Jacob Fritz, was a farmer in Bucks County during the war. In <u>A Genealogical and Personal History of Bucks County, Pennsylvania</u>, it says, "When (Jacob's son Abraham) was seventeen years of age, a team and wagon of his father's was impressed with the American army to carry powder and store from Trenton to Boston, and he was placed in charge of the team during this journey, and was present at the battle of Bunker Hill, remaining with the army three months, and he then returned home." Another account mentions he "endured many hardships."*

The thought that one of her ancestors was at such an iconic American battle thrilled Erin. She continued:

> *I also found a document, "U.S. Sons of the American Revolution Membership Applications, 1889–1970, Record for Jacob Fritz."*
>
> *I would love to talk with you about how to pursue membership in the DAR now that I've discovered these men in my family background.*
>
> *Thank you.*
>
> *Sincerely, Erin Miles*

She hit "send" after blind copying herself and creating a new email folder titled "DAR." If only she could be sharing this with Jim. With twenty minutes to go before the bus came, she decided to pay a quick visit to her in-laws so she could tell them instead.

❧ • ❧

The Valley Forge DAR seemed as excited about Erin as she was about them. She checked her email while Ethan did homework after supper, finding a lengthy message from Sydney Stordahl in her inbox.

> *Dear Erin,*
>
> *Congratulations on the discovery of your patriot ancestors! I am available to offer guidance and suggestions. I love this stuff, so if you need to say, "Please, I'd rather do it myself," feel free to ask me to nose out. However, I'd be glad to use my resources to help you get as many of the documents needed for proving your relationships as possible. I am a member of several historical and genealogical societies, as well as <u>ancestry.com</u>. I've shamelessly helped complete four sets of papers. I do a good job, and so far, everyone has flown through the vetting if I do say so myself! Although I'm the chapter's current regent, I'm a closet registrar. LOL*

Erin liked this woman's upbeat attitude, although she wondered what exactly a regent was and what she did.

> *The formalities of membership, aside from the application, are as follows: You are proposed for membership at a DAR meeting by the registrar or a friend in the chapter if appropriate. Usually, this happens at the first meeting you are able to attend. The ladies meet you, and you meet them. Get a feel for us and our chapter. As much as I'd love you to join us, you have to pick the best chapter for you.*
>
> *All things being good, at the next meeting, there is a vote for your acceptance into the chapter. That's an agenda item for me. We may make our summer social, which is held in August, a meeting if we need to accomplish chapter business. These are just formalities, and I've never seen anyone not accepted, but they are in the bylaws, so we do it. Here is what you need to complete your application to the DAR.*

Starting with yourself—your birth certificate—it must name your parents, your marriage certificate or divorce decree if appropriate. Your spouse's birth certificate and death certificate, if appropriate.

Sydney has no idea about Jim, Erin thought. *That part isn't going to be as pleasant as the rest of it.*

You need to prove the relationship child-to-parent for each generation. There are several ways to do this, but vital records are easiest (usually).

Then you need your parents' birth, death, and marriage certificates. If you are the product of a second marriage, we need to know that too. And so on, back to your patriot ancestor. Since you think you have three, pick the easiest one to prove for your initial ancestor. After you are a member, you complete "supplemental" applications for the other ancestors you have. You go through the same work for each supplemental.

Her thoughts shifted into high gear. *I think my birth certificate is in the lock-box in the basement, and probably my marriage certificate as well. Do Mom and Dad have theirs, though?* She smiled. *I can only imagine what they'll say when I tell them I'm applying for membership in the DAR! Won't they be impressed?* She continued reading:

You mentioned an SAR reference, but I have to tell you SAR papers are not approved for application to the DAR. Our genies are super tough.

Erin conjured an image of Barbara Eden in her "I Dream of Jeannie" outfit from the 1960s show, and she laughed out loud.

"What's so funny?" Ethan asked, looking up from his math workbook.

"I think the way words can have different meanings is interesting."

"Oh, okay."

She must mean "genealogist." Erin read on:

SAR only needs to prove the descendant line. In DAR, you need to prove both parents for at least the first three generations. We try to complete the application as much as possible, even if we have to make an educated guess. If you connect to another DAR member, you can just use her National number as proof of relationship. You can find that out by searching the GRS database on the National public website.

That certainly wasn't an option, Erin thought. *No one in my family has ever been remotely connected to the Daughters of the American Revolution.*

The books you quoted "may" be acceptable. The criteria vary for those family books. We can try it, why not? They consider the time when the record was made, distance from the actual events recorded, and other issues. I'm attaching a copy of our application, which you may already have. I can jump in and help if needed. If you send me your info, your parents, and their parents, I can start the search on ancestry.com. If you have their parents, even better—it will help me know I have the right line.

I know it's short notice, but perhaps you can join us for our May meeting tomorrow at the Historical Society in Norristown at 12:30? It is unusual for us to have a program for this particular meeting, but it was the only time the speaker could be with us. As regent, it's up to me (as long as I don't violate the bylaws). It's great to have the power to affect change! Muhahahaha. LOL

Here's hoping to see you tomorrow!
Sydney

Apparently, DAR members aren't above using words like muahahaha, at least not this one. Erin was developing a mental image of Sydney—forty-something, petite, and cute. *She probably has a permanent twinkle in her eye. Hmm, I wonder if Pat and Al can stay with Ethan tomorrow.* She picked up her cell phone.

"Hi, Mom. I have some really good news."

"What's that?" Pat Miles asked.

"Have you heard of Ancestry.com?"

"I've seen their ads on TV." Erin heard what sounded like drawers being pulled open and her mother-in-law saying, "Not that one, Al. No. Yes, that one!" Then, "Sorry, Erin, I'm making a pie crust and asked Al to find my pastry cutter."

Erin's mouth watered. Pat Miles won awards at the county fair for her pies. "No problem. Anyway, I've been on Ancestry looking for my family, and I've discovered my mother's side goes all the way back to before the Revolution, but we just never knew. I'm actually trying to become a DAR."

"What a happy piece of news!"

"Yes, and I've been invited to attend a meeting tomorrow, but Ethan has a game. Do you think you could—"

"That's a wonderful opportunity for you," Pat said before Erin could finish her sentence. "Of course, we'll take care of Ethan."

"You could be a DAR," Erin suggested.

"My mother was, but I just never got involved," Pat said.

"Maybe you will, and we'll both be members together!"

"I'd like that."

After a brief pause, Erin confessed, "I don't know what to wear." She imagined there would be in attendance high-born women in dresses and suits holding out their pinkies while they drank tea from china cups. On the other hand, they might be using words like muahahaha and LOL. She couldn't make those two ideas work together and gave up trying.

"I don't think you could go wrong with a nice spring dress," Pat said.

When Erin went upstairs to check out her closet, she felt like a girl going to her first birthday party, looking forward to presents and cake.

She pulled into the parking lot of the Montgomery County Historical Society at 12:20 and found two open spots behind the brick building. It didn't look like anyone used the front door anymore, so she used the back one, hearing a pleasant ring-buzz when she entered. The small lobby contained several glass cases containing Civil War and other local artifacts, and to the left was a library. An elderly woman wearing a volunteer's tag emerged from the restroom.

"May I help you?" she asked.

"I'm here for the DAR meeting," Erin said.

"You'll find the ladies on the other side of those stairs," she said, pointing.

Erin thanked her and walked up a short flight of stairs to a room where large portraits and pastoral scenes graced the walls, and a regiment of grandfather clocks stood mutely beneath them. The lighting was brighter than in the entry, and the room smelled of old books, leather, and wood but without the usual mustiness. There were five rows of chairs and along the back wall, a table was spread with finger sandwiches, crackers, cheese, fruit, and pastries. She supposed there were twenty women there, most of them wearing dresses or suits, and a few older members in dress slacks and spring blouses. All of them sported blue and white ribbons populated by gold pins of various shapes and sizes. At the center of the room, a woman in her seventies was setting up a projector, her badges so weighty, she actually seemed to list to the left. Erin felt a tad out of place, not because of the way she was dressed, which was perfect, but because of her pinless condition. She was suddenly reminded of her days as a Girl Scout earning merit badges.

A tall woman with a short bob and enough medals to impress a five-star general came over to her. "You must be Erin."

"Yes, and you must be Sydney." They shook hands and smiled at each other.

"I am, and I'm really glad you could come, especially on such short notice."

"I am, too. This is a really nice place," Erin said, looking around.

"We've been meeting here a few years. The location is kind of central for most of our ladies. Here, let me introduce you."

Erin met the vice-regent, chaplain, secretary, and half of the members. There seemed to be a healthy blend of old and middle-aged women, all of them friendly. Then Sydney led her to a woman named Nancy. "Nancy, this is Erin Miles, who's looking into membership. Erin, this is our registrar."

"It's nice to meet you," Nancy said. "If there's anything I can do to help, just let me know. The process can be a little challenging sometimes."

"Thanks," Erin said. "I appreciate that."

A younger woman came up to Sydney. "I think we'd better start. Our speaker's on a tight schedule."

Erin sat toward the back next to Nancy as Sydney called the meeting to order, which was followed by some sort of ritual. Erin would've felt totally lost except Nancy had a copy of the routine printed on a card bearing the DAR symbol. The rite consisted of the Pledge of Allegiance, a responsive greeting like a kind of prayer, and something called the American's Creed, which sounded a little like the Presidential oath of office when Erin recited it—the combination of patriotism and devotion giving her chills. She could hardly believe she was standing here in this august assemblage repeating words that had stood for generations in a place she'd dreamed of, but never thought she'd be.

A few of the women read reports from committees they chaired, including one for veterans and another for "Continental Congress," which made Erin wonder if George Washington and Benjamin Franklin might suddenly show up. Most of the names and terms were unfamiliar, but she figured like anything else, once you got used to them, they would become second nature.

Then, to her horror, her cell phone started ringing in the middle of the treasurer's update, and Erin quickly stifled her latest, "Don't Worry, Be Happy," ringtone. She could've kicked herself for forgetting to put the phone on vibrate. Nancy leaned closer, "Don't worry. It happens." As she attempted to recover her decorum, Erin wasn't sure what to do when a small, lidded basket got passed to her. Again, Nancy came to the rescue. "This is a collection for the Indian schools we support. Feel free to pass."

She got out her wallet and put a five-dollar bill in the container before handing it off.

"Before I introduce our speaker, there's one other item of business," Sydney announced. "We have a prospective member with us today, Erin Miles, who's from, is it Lansdale?"

"Yes," Erin said, suddenly feeling self-conscious.

"Erin is researching her patriot, and I'm giving her a hand. According to our protocol, we need to vote on receiving her into our membership."

One of the ladies passed out pieces of paper so the members could vote "yes" or "no," then a thirty-something woman counted the ballots. Several minutes later she announced, "Erin Miles has been unanimously accepted into the Valley Forge Chapter pending her application to what the woman referred to as "national." No one seemed to question or doubt her announcement.

Erin broke into a smile as the ladies applauded. *Piece of cake.*

CHAPTER FOURTEEN

At breakfast, Ethan slid a carton of milk in her direction and said, "This has an expiration date back in February." Later in class she referred to Kang as "Jacob" and Sarah as "Liz." Then the school secretary called during Erin's break. "Ethan's permission slip for field day was due yesterday, but he still doesn't have it." An hour later her dentist's receptionist phoned—Erin had blown off her teeth cleaning. Her family research had become all consuming.

On the rare occasions when she wasn't thinking about her ancestors, her mind went into a kind of default mode—life after Jim. Life after Hatfield College. *I'm not about to teach freshman comp. Maybe I should just finish my dissertation and be done with it. Maybe some other school will want me to teach history—there are enough of them in the area.* Even the thought of making those things happen overwhelmed her. Thinking and talking about her genealogy was much easier.

Fortunately, people were still listening, and she tried asking about others' ancestors so she didn't become a total bore. Some folks knew a little, others a lot. She'd been rendered speechless once when a neighbor disclosed, "My great-grandfather was a hit man for Jimmy Hoffa."

ᡠ • ᡥ

Shortly before her last class of the semester, Erin's DAR application hit a snag the size of a pothole, a Pennsylvania-sized pothole after a severe winter, a pothole big enough to be named. Sydney notified her of the chasm in an email.

> Hi Erin, I'm digging through some Fritz people, and I've run into a problem. One source says Jacob had only one son, also Jacob, whose daughter Mary married Daniel T. Brotz, your great-grandfather. We have in the DAR database a Jacob, who's a verified patriot ancestor, but none of the names map up to your line. You're related to them, but you have to be a direct descendant for DAR membership. Can you send me your references for the line? I remember you had a book that told a lovely story re. Jacob Jr, but it doesn't look like anyone has used that line to get into the DAR. Do you know who Daniel T Brotz's parents were? Do you have info on John Owen? I'm trying to push these back but don't have much to go on.

The part about "don't have much to go on" sent a chill through Erin. Was Sydney saying she couldn't be a DAR after all because the only patriots in her family were uncles or cousins?

Erin grabbed her notebook and started answering the message, beginning with all the information she had about the Fritzes. Then, thinking Sydney might be trying to steer her in a different ancestral direction added:

> I'll see what I can find, including information about the Owens. You may be interested to know my great-grandmother Smith handed down a story that we had Leni Lenape blood, but so far I've only found Germans! My Owen family is reportedly Welsh, but I don't know how or when they came to America. I hope this is a little helpful. I'll keep looking. This stuff is addicting! Thanks so much for your help.

She decided to message her old friend Jennifer Fritz to see if she knew anything about her family history. Erin didn't have long to wait for an answer.

> Hi, Erin. Great to hear from you! I love seeing you around Facebook. My husband has done a lot of my family research, and I know my ancestors come from Bedminster, too. I'm pretty sure my guy is John Fritz. Wouldn't it be amazing if we ended up related?! Keep me posted.

Sydney also responded in her usual, quick fashion, seeming as enthusiastic about finding a patriot for Erin as Erin herself. Since she was hitting a dead end with Jacob Fritz, she said she was veering off in a different direction.

Specifically, I'm looking for pensioners' records, she wrote.

Thirty minutes later—*Well, that didn't work either. Now it's time for oaths of allegiance.*

Erin was glad Sydney knew what she was talking about because Erin certainly didn't—pensioners and oaths were mystifying terms to her. Her new friend ended her last email on a cautionary note:

> *If I find what I'm looking for, this will be a new ancestor (I'm specializing in those these days <shaking head>) and we have to prove everything to the nth. The genealogists LOVE it when you use an established ancestor. It makes their job very easy, especially since they are only allotted 2 hours per application. New ancestors take a lot of time. If we can't find anything to substantiate the Bucks Co story about Jacob Fritz, we'll have to find a supply tax, pension, or oath. Still plugging away!*

She didn't understand why Sydney was looking under every hill and spreading tree when Erin already had documents showing a direct relationship with Jacob Fritz. She wrote saying so, in a nice way, but still, Sydney wouldn't budge.

> *You see, Erin, there were so many Fritzes in Bucks Co—are you sure you have the correct one? I've come across at least four Jacobs of the correct age in the county before I stopped looking. My concern is the genealogy that listed the three wives of Jacob Jr, one of which your research indicates you are related, claims Jacob had only one son, Jacob Jr. The Jacob Sr that married Catherine Nash did not appear to have a son named Jacob. Have you found something indicating they did?*
>
> *Scratching my head over this one. Remember we have to prove parent-child relationship with a baptismal record listing parents, a will, a land record, or something like that. I was hoping for more low hanging fruit, but you haven't got much on your tree. This will be a fight to the finish. A trip to the Bucks Co Historical Society or the Mennonites might be in order.*

What if Sydney loses interest in helping me if I don't come up with something more promising? Erin picked at the cuticle on her left pinkie. Then she stopped and sat up straighter. *There's no way I'm going to let that happen.*

ॐ • ॐ

After teaching her last class of the semester, Erin grabbed a jelly donut from the leftovers she'd brought to her students and sped from Hatfield to the Bucks County Historical Society at Doylestown's fabled Mercer Museum. She had an hour and fifteen minutes to settle the Jacob Fritz conundrum once and for all. When she reached the austere library of "the Castle," industrialist Henry Mercer's turn-of-the-last-century concrete showplace, she saw a bank of lockers and a sign at the door instructing patrons to leave all their belongings in one. That was strange. How could she find what she needed if she couldn't bring her notes? She dug into her wallet for quarters and stuffed everything inside a locker except her leather portfolio, then she approached the desk staffed by an elderly woman wearing pink Nikes.

"Hi, I'm hoping to use the library to find an ancestor for the DAR," she said.

The woman nodded and pointed to her right, "Through those doors."

"Is it okay if I take my notebook inside?"

"Yes, but no pens."

That statement was like finding out her dentist didn't permit toothbrushes in his office. "But how will I write?"

"You may use a pencil."

"Oh, okay, thanks." Erin wondered what that was all about as she went inside the room containing several wooden tables running down the center and endless rows of bookshelves cradling thousands of volumes about local history. Three other patrons sat at the tables, surrounded on all sides by stacks of books. Erin wasn't sure where to begin, and she didn't like feeling like a rookie. At the far end of the room, a woman sat at what appeared to be an official-looking desk with cubbies, so Erin approached her and repeated what she'd said to the receptionist. Then she admitted, "I'm really not sure where to begin."

"We have a lot of information on the Fritz family." This had had a cheering effect on Erin. "Come along, and I'll show you where to find it."

Ten minutes later, Erin was sitting at a table with a half dozen heavy volumes about both the Fritzes and eighteenth-century Bucks County. She found out her ancestors had lived near here, just to the north, around Tinicum. She'd always loved that area and was beginning to understand why. She waded through hand-written lists of baptisms and marriages, obituary indexes and stories, including one about two brothers, Christian "Tinicum" Fritz and John "Weaver" Fritz, who'd come to America together in the early 1700s—some sources said 1710, others 1720. *Didn't Jennifer Fritz mention this John guy?*

The family seemed to have been given a choice between worshiping God at the German state church, or leaving their country altogether, so they decided to pursue religious freedom in Pennsylvania. Erin had been researching history for most of her life, but she'd never felt such a personal connection before this. All those people whose lives she'd known and taught about, from Pocahontas and John Rolfe to Thomas Jefferson and Paul Revere, had personal lives just like these people, her people. Those lives laid the framework for America. She felt like shouting, but this was no place for such behavior.

"I see you're researching the Fritzes," said the man sitting across from her, fifty-something, bald.

"Yes. Do you know about them?"

He snort-laughed. "You can't know Bucks County history without running into them." He looked pleased with himself for being so clever. "So, what are you looking for?"

"I'm trying to figure out which Jacob I'm connected to."

He wasn't encouraging. "All I can say is good luck. There were so many Fritzes, it's a haul to sort them all out. The family is genealogically complex, to say the least."

As he returned to his own pile of books, Erin felt lost in the maze of family tree branches, wondering how she could ever prove her ancestor Christian had produced a verifiable patriot with enough supportive evidence to get past those formidable DAR "genies." Five minutes later, the librarian came over.

"I'm confused," Erin said.

"Maybe I can help."

She sat down and bent her gray head over first one book, then the next, after which she got up and wordlessly tracked down two other volumes. Erin watched in fascination. This woman was good. Finally, the librarian looked up and delivered the goods.

"What did she tell you?" Melissa asked. She and Erin were at Starbucks sipping something called "shaken" tea, and sharing an iced pound cake. "Did she solve the mystery?"

"Pretty much. She shoved this one book in front of me and amazed me by the way she made sense out of this person connected to that person by a bunch of names and numbers. I've done a lot of research in my time, but this woman had some amazing skills, I tell you." She drank some of her tea, enjoying the coldness slipping down her throat, then continued. "She definitely connected me to the Christian 'Tinicum' Fritz line—he's something like my five times great-grandfather—but there were lots of guys in the family named Jacob—kids, and great grandkids, and nephews …"

"They must've really liked the name Jacob!" Melissa said. "I had an Uncle Jacob. At least my grandmother used to talk about him. He had one of those Civil War-type beards, and one time a sparrow landed on it and did what birds do." She laughed at the memory. "I only met him once, when he was in a nursing home. He asked me if I knew who he was and when I said 'Uncle Jacob,' he said, 'No. I'm Augusta.' 'Augusta?' I asked, and he answered, 'Augusta Wind!'"

Melissa was in fine form this morning.

"That's hysterical," Erin said, laughing. She waited a moment to continue. "Well, my Jacob wasn't the relative who had a son who served in the Revolutionary War. Since that part of the family were mostly Mennonites, they didn't believe in fighting, like the Quakers. I'm probably wasting my time looking for a patriot in that line."

"Oh, what a shame, Erin. I know how much you've been counting on old Jacob."

"At least I found a connection to an old friend I grew up with in P'burg, Jennifer Fritz. She lives in Florida now, and we've reconnected on Facebook,"

"That's a bonus, then." Melissa broke off a piece of cake and starting chewing, appearing deep in thought. "I can't believe how involved this DAR process is. So, what happens next?"

"I'm certainly not giving up, that's for sure." She leaned back into the chair. "I went home and started looking on other sides of my family, and I see two good possibilities. On my Owen side—that's my mom's dad's family—there's a grandmother whose last name was Sharp—originally Scharfenstein—and in the same place they lived, I found a John Sharp, who served in the Revolution. The thing is, there were a bunch of guys named John Sharp in that part of New Jersey. When I look in the records, they remind me of when my necklaces get all tangled." *And Jim always straightened them out for me.* She rallied herself. *I'm not going there now!* Instead, she chose to share some good news. "Then I saw this other guy named Peter Kachlein, who was a colonel in the Revolution from Easton, and there's a Joseph Kachlein in my tree. If he's connected to Peter and Peter's my ancestor, then I'm in!"

"Wow, Erin, a colonel! That would be so cool."

She grinned. "I know. Ethan would love that. It's funny, Melissa, I practically grew up in Easton, and I never knew my family went back so far there. There's so much more to them than I ever knew."

"Those are some really deep roots."

"I know. I always felt, well, second-rate because my parents didn't have important positions in the community, and my dad's parents were immigrants." Erin had just confided something deep and painful, a distant place in herself she didn't often share, or try to think of. "Well, the truth is they certainly made a big noise up there in Easton," Melissa said.

Erin laughed, "You're part German, aren't you?"

"Yes, but as I mentioned before, my family didn't come to America until the 1910s."

"Speaking of noises, they sure came with a bang, though, didn't they?"

"I guess so." She looked down, and Erin could tell Melissa didn't want to boast.

"What exactly did they do again?"

"They supplied manufacturers with different machinery and parts, I forget all which, but at that point with American industries booming, they did well."

How strange that my ancestors go all the way back to the early 1700s and were leading members of their communities, but my parents always seemed so far removed from people who they thought "had money" or were important. On the other hand, Melissa comes from "money," but her family hasn't been in America all that long.

She recalled being a student at Lafayette College, feeling a little less than her classmates whose last names didn't end in vowels or who didn't have to wait tables to pay for room and board. *I don't feel like that anymore, actually haven't for a long time, but not just because of how my life has been as an adult. Now I feel that way because of how my life started—way back at the dawn of American history.*

❧ • ❧

CHAPTER FIFTEEN

Peter dismounted from his white horse as a bevy of chickens clucked around the side of the barn, announcing a visitor.

"Sheriff! How nice to see you!" Nicholas Tatamy leaned his hoe against the fence and wiped his hands with a handkerchief.

"I'm happy to see you too." He finished hitching the reins to a post and strode over to shake Tatamy's hand.

"What a pleasant surprise on a glorious day."

They both stood there surveying the blue sky speckled with white clouds stretching outwards toward the Wind Gap.

"How are your crops?"

"The rains have been good. The corn is growing ahead of schedule this year. Come into the house and sit awhile. My wife will be very happy to see you."

"I don't want to interrupt your work. I just came for a brief visit." The truth was, he did want to stay longer. He liked these good people.

Tatamy gestured toward the fields. "This can wait, Sheriff. I always enjoy having you here, and my wife so enjoys speaking her German with you."

Peter smiled. "I wouldn't dream of denying her that small pleasure. First, however, I need to speak with you alone."

"Why, of course. Is there a problem?" There was concern in his brown eyes.

On the ride out to Tatamy's, Peter had thought through what to say, but the words still didn't come easily. "There have been some recent thefts at the

Easton taverns and Mr. Hart's store. No one knows who's responsible, but I'm wondering if you've seen anyone strange hanging around this area, or during your visits to Easton."

Tatamy wasn't stupid. "Frau Eckert suspects me." His words combined wisdom with a touch of weariness and a generous seasoning of humor, which pretty much summed up his disposition. His father had been a tribal chief who'd converted to Christianity, a man of peace who'd married a white woman and lived to see one of his sons shot because someone thought he looked "suspicious." When Chief Tatamy died, Nicholas took over his three hundred fifteen-acre tract, married a German girl and for the most part, lived comfortably between their two cultures.

"You know Frau Eckert," Peter said. "You also know I don't share her sentiments."

"Yes, I know, Sheriff Kichline." He reached up to put a hand on Peter's shoulder. They'd always understood each other.

"She never liked my father either." He grinned as he removed his hand. "Actually, it's interesting you should ask about thefts because I've had a few of my own."

Peter's eyebrows raised, and he crossed his arms over his chest. "Is that so? What's happened?"

"For the past week, I've been missing things, wondering if I might be losing my faculties. First, there was the matter of a hen and a few dozen eggs. I'm also out a bale of hay from the barn, and oddly, my beaver felt hat."

"Your hat?"

Tatamy nodded. "I hung it on a peg in the barn when I got too warm. Then I heard one of the children screaming and ran to see what was wrong. Our youngest had fallen on a rock and scraped his knee. By the time I returned to the barn, my hat was gone."

Peter leaned against the fence, thinking. "How long were you away?"

"A half hour or so."

"Did you hear any noises coming from the barn while you were in the house?"

Tatamy thought for a moment. "I don't think so."

"Were the chicken and eggs stolen at the same time?"

"No, that happened a few days earlier."

"But this time, only your hat and some hay were taken?" Peter asked.

"Yes."

"Has Mr. Lefevre mentioned anything about thefts at his place?"

"You know, he has," Tatamy said. "Money I believe, also some food and other goods."

"Hullo!" A woman's voice called out, and the men looked toward the house where Mrs. Tatamy filled the doorway. "Herr Kichline! *Wilkommen!*"

"Let's not disappoint her," her husband said, smiling in her direction.

Remembering her good nature, as well as her good cooking, Peter echoed, "Let's not indeed!"

❧ • ❧

Before heading back to Easton, Peter rode his horse to the adjoining property where John and Anna Lefevre kept one of the most renowned taverns in Northampton County. If there was anyone who knew the area's comings and goings as well as Peter, the Lefevres did.

"Sheriff Kichline! How nice to see you! Mama, look who's here!" John Lefevre said.

His missus appeared from a back room, holding a wet rag, her face glistening from hard work. "I'm always pleased to have you put your feet under our table," she said, pointing to a chair. At this time of day, there were only two men in the tavern, and once they looked to see who had entered, nodded greetings to the sheriff and returned to their conversation. "What can I get you? I have some nice rabbit stew and corn bread."

"Oh, no, thank you, Madam. Normally I would love to have some, but you see, I've just had my lunch."

"There's always room for more." She smiled up at him.

Peter felt the weight of Mrs. Tatamy's apple fritters and ham biscuits in his stomach. "Actually, I am quite full."

"Are you certain?" She squinted uncertainly.

"Yes, this time, I'm here on business."

"I'll just get you some apple pie." Before he could dissuade her, she had disappeared.

Lefevre shrugged his shoulders. "What can I say? She likes to feed people."

"Yes, and she's an excellent cook." He changed the subject. "I'm up here looking into some recent thefts in and about Easton. A lot of people come through your tavern, and I'm wondering if you can report anything amiss."

"Honestly, Sheriff, a lot of strangers pass by here every week. I haven't seen anyone I would call suspicious lately." Lefevre laughed, "There are plenty of characters, though."

"Our county does have a fair share of those." Peter smiled.

Mrs. Lefevre returned with coffee and what appeared to be an entire cherry pie. Setting it before the sheriff, she took a seat next to her husband. Peter wasn't sure how he'd be able to get out of eating some, or even if he wanted to.

Her husband spoke. "Mother, do you recall the young couple from a week or so ago? He was a self-described pow-wow doctor selling medicine he made from chicken manure."

Her laughter rumbled like a small earthquake, filling her chest and causing her to cough. "Yes, and he couldn't understand why we weren't interested."

Peter cracked a smile. He hadn't heard of that particular scheme before.

"We've been missing some food here and there, things like ham and biscuits, although I can assure you, my wife runs a tight ship." Lefevre gave her an admiring glance. "I'll send word if I come up with anything else, Sheriff."

When he reached Easton, Peter rode past the courthouse and waved to Mr. Wiggins, who stood on the steps in the bright sun. He noticed Egbert Weed with his pigs and dismounted to see how the novice farmer was getting along.

"Good day, Sheriff."

"Good day," He noticed the man was still dressed more for church than the fields. "How are you?"

"Well, thank you."

Peter surveyed the piglets. "They seem to be growing stouter."

"I've been feeding them just as the Old Pig Drover told me, and they've gained weight. I might just make a go of pig farming after all." He lowered his voice. "If only my good wife would stop losing weight."

A lady walked by and shot Weed a scalding look when one of the pigs brushed up against her skirt, leaving a muck mark. "Really! I wish *someone* would do something about these pigs!" She hurried away before Peter could say anything, the pigs grunting jubilantly.

"I guess not everyone likes having animals around here."

"That would be correct," Peter said.

Many of the townspeople considered the presence of livestock undignified now that Easton had its own courthouse. Not knowing what to say about Mrs. Weed, Peter tried to encourage the man. "I do believe you're getting the hang of farming after all."

He sighed. "I wish my son would."

"He hasn't taken to it, then?" Peter cocked his head to one side, listening.

"He spends a good bit of time in the fields playing his music."

"Music?"

"Yes," Weed said. "He has the best intentions, but he always ends up sitting down and getting out his violin."

"Have you any other sons?"

"Yes, but they're still in the city. They haven't decided whether to join us in Easton or not, being of age. I needed John to come with his mother and me."

"Hopefully, he'll soon learn farming, just as you are. Good day to you, Mr. Weed." He spent a few minutes talking to Ziba Wiggins and a few other men at the courthouse, then decided to stop by the Dolls' for Susannah. Since school wouldn't begin until the following Monday, he'd given her permission to visit them today.

"Oh, Sheriff Kichline, how good it is to see you!" Frau Doll said. "I heard all about Greta, and we simply must do something." Her cap looked like it had been strung up a flagpole, her hair askew under the part it barely covered.

"Susannah told us all about her need to marry so she can follow her captain. Would it be alright with you if some women in town gave Greta and him a supper?"

Susannah clasped her hands in front of her. "Oh, please, Papa, I would help, too."

He was outnumbered, but he didn't mind. In fact, he'd wanted to give Greta and the Captain a wedding supper but had no idea how to make one happen. "Why, yes, of course. That's very kind, Frau Doll. Do you think …"

"I've already spoken with several women, and we know exactly what to do," the woman said. He wondered why she'd bothered to ask in the first place when she was already swirling through preparations with hurricane force.

"We can have the supper right here." She paused for breath, her cheeks glowing from excitement. "I've also been thinking about your tight spot, Herr Kichline, how her leaving will be a burden for you and your family."

"I'm sure we'll be fine." He managed to squeeze into the conversation. "My brother in Bedminster is sending his niece to us, so we shouldn't be without help for very long."

"Ah, that's good news, but what about the meantime?" She paused for just a moment. "Say, Anna, could you help the sheriff's family?"

The young woman smiled from behind her mixing bowl. "Of course, Mama. I'll be happy to give you a hand, Sheriff Kichline."

"Thank you," he said with a slight bow.

Susannah started clapping her hands together. "Oh, Papa! How wonderful! I just love Fräulein Anna, and she's such a wonderful cook!"

Peter had the feeling he'd just been managed by a zealous group of females. Somehow he didn't mind.

He didn't recognize Greta at first, but the lovely form standing beside Captain Hough bore a striking resemblance to her. She looked genteel, poised even, in the light blue brocade dress he'd given her as a wedding gift—one of Margaretta's favorites. When he'd asked his children what they thought of his idea, they agreed the dress would be a nice way for Greta to keep her former mistress's memory alive. With her hair swept up into cascading waves and her countenance a mixture of shyness and conquest, she looked like she was ready to take on the world with her lover, resplendent in his red British uniform. Two of his comrades in arms were in attendance, which led to a general outbreak of swooning among Easton's young ladies.

Peter felt choked up seeing Greta in that dress and to keep from breaking down, he glanced at her father instead. Hans Schmidt looked as comical as a sheep in elephant's clothing. He'd borrowed one of Peter's waistcoats for the occasion, but the sheriff was a good head taller and considerably narrower through the middle. Frau Doll had taken in the arms and pinned up the breeches, but even so, Hans appeared as if he were a cask on the verge of spilling its contents.

Peter surveyed the crowd of well-wishers at the courthouse, which was where the German Reformed congregation worshiped since they didn't have their own church building. He thought the entire town had turned out for the wedding, not because everyone was so well acquainted with Greta or the captain, but because any good excuse for a celebration brought Eastonians together.

At the end of the short ritual when Pastor Henop pronounced them married, the couples' friends gathered at the Dolls', where the ladies of the house and their cohorts had prepared a feast. Not to be robbed of a reason to imbibe or indulge, other villagers took themselves to the public houses to lift a glass—or two—to the newlyweds.

Toward the end of the celebration, Peter saw Hans standing in a corner of the dining room looking more than a little forlorn, so he went over to him. For a moment, they stood in silence watching Greta saying her goodbyes and thanking the Dolls many times over for their kindness.

"I'm going to miss her," Hans finally said. "I don't know when I'll see her again." He cleared his throat.

Peter clapped his hand on the man's shoulder. "This is both a good and a hard thing."

"I do like the captain."

"I do, too, Hans. I think he'll take good care of Greta." *I wonder if Hans regrets his decision to stay at the mill now that Captain Hough and Greta are going further west. This isn't the best time to bring up the subject, though. I'll give Hans time to think about his new circumstances. Naturally, I hope he stays, but if necessary, the boys and I will manage, and I can always get a new indentured servant.* For now, he stood with the father of the bride discussing politics and the weather, until Greta and the Captain came over to them.

"I'm about to go, Papa."

"Please excuse me," Peter said, planning to leave them alone for their farewells. "Before I go, however, I want to thank you for your many kindnesses to my family and me, Greta. I know Frau Kichline would have enjoyed seeing this day." He swallowed around the lump in his throat.

"I felt as if she weren't so far away, wearing her dress. Thank you so much, Sheriff."

"Yes, well, I wish you and the captain every happiness." Peter handed her an envelope, which she accepted with a surprised look. "A token of my gratitude to help you begin life together."

"Thank you, Sheriff," she said, impulsively throwing her arms around the startled man's neck. "You've been the most wonderful person to work for."

To Peter's relief, the captain settled for a handshake. "Thank you, sir. That is very kind."

Peter bowed, then went in search of Anna Doll.

❧ • ☙

CHAPTER SIXTEEN

Although his name suggested otherwise, Peter felt a certain kinship with the Apostle Paul, who'd once urged the faithful to do things decently and in order. This he valued highly and stressed to the members of his household, but since Margaretta's death, his life had been far less orderly, though every bit as decent. Once Greta had been straightened out, and things started running smoothly again, her abrupt departure had brought yet further change. He knew she was about to leave anyway, and help was on the way, but his life still felt like a carriage passing over a series of deep ruts. He dressed that morning, mildly grumpy at the prospect of more adjustments. As he buttoned the front of his best waistcoat, Peter calculated it would be about two weeks before his brother received his letter and the young woman could make it to Easton to assume the Kichline's household duties.

He felt vexed with himself for being irritable, especially because Anna Doll was being kind enough to lend a hand in the meantime. Her mother even offered to do his family's laundry, no small task. He wanted to pay them for their trouble but, knowing the way the Dolls enjoyed helping neighbors, they would likely refuse. He would make it up to them somehow. One thing made him smile as he adjusted his cravat—the look on Frau Eckert's face when she'd scolded him for not asking her to help instead. He remembered how the conversation had taken a different turn once he'd stood firm.

"Ah, well, with the courts in session, I'll be rushed off my feet," she said.

"That you will, Frau Eckert. How will you and Martin manage?" he'd asked.

"I added more help. You know that crazy farmer who dresses like this is Philadelphia and who feeds his pigs with a spoon?"

"Yes, but you know, Mr. Weed is starting to catch on, and—"

She interrupted him. "His son is every bit as useless when it comes to farming. He prefers music." When she'd laughed, a ray of sunlight from an open window had caught one of her remaining teeth. "He's going to play the fiddle here and help with serving. That should bring the customers in."

While she would've kept his family's stomachs full had she ended up being their temporary housekeeper, her fractious tongue and smoldering breath, who could bear? He was glad the Dolls had approached him before Frau Eckert had a chance. Anna was an agreeable young woman, and Susannah adored her, which would make the transition easier for all of them.

He began quietly reciting the twenty-third Psalm as he did every morning in German the way he'd learned it from his mother as a boy. Downstairs, he found the boys freshly turned out for the Lord's Day, hovering by the table, beautifully set not only with china and silverware but a huge platter of breakfast meats.

"Good morning, Father," his oldest son said.

Andrew and Jacob echoed their big brother, "Good morning, Father." Their eyes darted from him to the food.

"Good morning, sons." He drew a kind of cheerfulness from the delicious scents.

"Good morning, Herr Kichline." Anna Doll came from the kitchen with Susannah close behind, the little girl bearing a broad smile and a plate of sweet breads. Anna's face was slightly flushed, highlighting her greenish-blue eyes.

"Good morning, Fräulein Anna. Everything looks delicious," Peter said.

"We've been preparing your favorite breakfast, Papa, haven't we Fräulein Anna?"

The young woman smiled at her as they placed the items at just the right spots on the table. Decently and in order. Anna looked at Peter, waiting for him to take charge.

Funny how Margaretta used to look at me that way. Peter felt a chill run up his right calf. "Let's sit and enjoy this pleasant feast," he said.

When Anna started heading out of the room, apparently unsure of her place, he called her back. "Fräulein, I do hope you will join us for this and every meal. You and your family are part of our own."

"Thank you. I'll do just that after I get the coffee."

"Oh, yes, Fräulein Anna, you are one of us!" Susannah said.

He glanced at Anna Doll, once again grateful for her unselfish gift of time and energy. He was surprised to realize she was easy on the eyes as well.

In the years before the county courthouse was built, quarter sessions were held in the larger rooms of Easton's taverns, for which the owners received three to seven pounds, including candles and firewood. When the public houses were no longer required for the meting out of justice, they didn't exactly get hurt from the loss of court rents, not when Easton swelled with Philadelphia lawyers, litigants, politicians, and the simply curious, all requiring food and lodging. Peter took his place at the front of the courtroom, fondly remembering when he and Margaretta had hosted many quarter sessions in their tavern.

He saw the new school teacher sitting toward the back of the room and nodded in his direction. Classes had been suspended because the children were too distracted to learn with the town brimming with energy. Besides every public building, including the schoolhouse, was being used to accommodate the crowds. Just last night Mr. Hanlon had stopped by to borrow a copy of Pliny's *Epistulae* from Peter and to ask the sheriff if he thought it would be alright to bring the students to hear some of the cases. Peter reviewed the docket which he thought would be suitable for the ears of younger Eastonians, then checked with two other trustees. They all agreed seeing the wheels of justice would help prepare the children for responsible citizenship.

He was glad the cases involving nonpayment of taxes wouldn't be heard until the following day, especially since the Schultz widows hadn't been able to ante up went he saw them a few days earlier. Theirs had been a calm despair, women without money, husbands, or children, but he urged them to put their faith in God, who cares for widows in their distress. He'd been trying to figure out since then some way to help and even now, hoped to come up with a solution to their dilemma.

Court came to order a few minutes later, one of the first cases involving the peevish butcher Anthony Esser, who claimed a local farmer had cheated him. *Court week just wouldn't be court week without Herr Esser bringing charges against someone.*

"He promised me three good sheep two months ago, and he never delivered." Esser was almost shouting.

"You need not raise your voice, Mr. Esser. I am not deaf," the magistrate said.

Esser's face reddened, and Peter marveled he'd never had a heart attack. Actually, he couldn't recall ever seeing the butcher in a good mood; he seemed a man with an inner fire fueling perpetual rage. Peter brushed a fly from his face, then folded his arms across his chest as he listened to the testimony against the farmer, a hearty German, who looked like he could give as good as he took, but whose English was so poor the magistrate couldn't understand him.

"I wonder if you would be so good as to translate for us, Sheriff Kichline?" the magistrate asked.

"Yes, of course." He turned to Farmer Stieff and asked, *"Hast due die versprochenen Schafe zu Herr Esser?"*

The man's face became animated. *"Ja! Ja! Ich gab sie, die Schafe wie versprochen."* He glared in Esser's direction.

Peter turned to the magistrate. "Mister Stieff says he delivered the promised sheep within the allotted time."

Esser stood and shouted. *"Er ist ein lugner!"*

"Order! Order in this courtroom!" The bewigged magistrate brought down his gavel, seeming to know enough German to recognize the butcher was accusing the farmer of lying. "You have had your turn to speak, Mr. Esser."

As Stieff's testimony continued, the magistrate learned while the farmer had delivered the sheep, Anthony Esser hadn't been happy with their weight. When asked what he'd done with the animals, Esser revealed he'd kept them.

"I see no evidence of wrongdoing here," the magistrate said. "You are free to go, Mr. Stieff. As for you, Mr. Esser, I don't want to see you in this courtroom again. If I do, you will spend a day in the stocks. Do you understand?"

The butcher nodded, which didn't satisfy the magistrate. "I asked you a question, and I expect a decent answer."

"Yes, I understand."

As Esser rose and left the courthouse, muttering to himself in German, Peter had a sudden inspiration, which he planned to act upon as quickly as possible.

Peter thought it ironic during a week devoted to the public good, there were always those who pushed the town and its citizens toward their limits of patience. Weren't they concerned about being put in the stocks or receiving twenty-nine lashes for breaking the law? Unfortunately, once they'd absorbed more alcohol than their bodies and minds could handle, prudence and caution were often dispensed with. Three times that Monday night, Peter awoke to residents pounding on his door in tears or anger over the noisy revels at the taverns. Margaretta used to say her husband could've slept through the last trumpet, but other townspeople were being kept from their forty winks. He'd learned in previous years to keep his suit of clothes laid out next to the bed in order to change quickly.

On the third night, he climbed out of a deep sleep, a fog engulfing his brain as he heard his oldest son speaking to someone at the front door. Peter realized, however, he'd been so tired from breaking up a fight near the ferry at one o'clock he'd simply dropped his clothes somewhere on the floor when he got back. Nevertheless, when he ran his right hand over the chair, lo and behold they were there.

That morning he looked up from *The Pennsylvania Gazette* as a smiling Anna Doll served him a liberal portion of creamed beef on toasted bread.

"Good morning, Sheriff Kichline. I hope you are well. You had quite a night."

He creased his brows. "Good morning to you, Fräulein. How did you know?" He gave a small laugh. "Of course, the whole village knows."

"I heard a lot of shouting, Papa," Susannah said.

"I could hardly sleep." Andrew punctuated his comment with a yawn, which he quickly covered with his hand.

"Before we discuss last evening, let's give thanks for this good meal." Everyone's head bowed as Peter prayed simply, "Oh, Lord, our Heavenly Father, we thank Thee for Thy many blessings, including this food which Thou hast supplied for us. Bless the hands that prepared it, and use it to strengthen our devotion and service to Thee. We pray in the name of Thy Son, our Savior Jesus Christ. Amen."

They began eating, and once they'd were sufficiently full, conversation picked up.

"Papa, since there's no school today, I'd like to help Fräulein Anna with the housework. She's going to show me how to make dumplings, too," Susannah said.

The sight of her small face with its glow returning after weeks of gray mourning lifted his own spirits. "I think that's a wonderful plan. You know how much I enjoy dumplings." He winked at his only daughter.

"Oh, Papa, you like everything!" she said, teasing.

"I like dumplings, too," Andrew said. "I like them sweet, and with chicken." He gave Anna a hopeful look.

"I'll make some of both then," she said. Anna turned to the Sheriff. "Herr Kichline, I'll take the family's clothing to my mother today, so if there's anything in particular you need, she and my sisters will take care of it."

"Thank you very much."

"We're pleased to help."

He thought of something she should know. "By the way, Fräulein Doll, I've given permission to Mr. Hanlon to use my library whenever he wishes."

"He seems like a nice person. Earnest."

"Oh, he's the best teacher, Fräulein!" Susannah's face lit up. "I like him so!"

Her brothers exchanged amused glances.

Peter wondered if there was something else he should mention. Then again, he was all about solving mysteries. "The strangest thing happened last night," he said. "I forgot to lay out my clothes after I went out the first time, but they were on the chair just when I needed them later on."

"I hope you didn't mind, Herr Kichline. I noticed how tired you were after the first time you got called away, so I put them there for you just in case." Anna's face took on the colors of a vivid sunset, reflecting her embarrassment over having done a fairly intimate thing.

"I didn't realize you'd stayed last night,"

Jacob piped up. "I asked her to, Papa. If you needed Peter and Andrew's help, Susannah and I wouldn't be alone with all those strangers running around."

He stirred through his thoughts, trying to remove the lumps. *Why didn't I think of that?*

"She stayed in my room," Susannah said, answering another of his questions.

"I trust that was alright?" Anna's eyes had widened.

"Of course. Thank you."

How was it she had suddenly become indispensable?

The previous week had been especially demanding, the worst happening when he had to confiscate a property the belligerent tenants couldn't keep up, ending with the men of the house shouting and cursing, and the women and children sobbing. That people, who couldn't hold on to their homes, broke down when he appeared was pathetic and sometimes downright dangerous when they tried to drive him off at gunpoint, which had been the case this time around. He and his deputy had finally persuaded the man of the house to surrender, along with his tearful, pleading wife. Peter had waited until their wagon rolled down the dirt road with their few possessions before sealing the place. He hadn't gotten back home until nearly nine in the evening, bolted the warmed-up remains of ham, dark bread, and pickled beets, and promptly fallen asleep in his chair by the fire.

Although that wretched scene stayed with him, he tried to focus instead on one far happier ending. After visiting the Schulz widows again, finding they still couldn't meet their taxes, he paid Anthony Esser a call, finding the butcher's shop nearly deserted. Peter waited until the only patron had been waited on, then approached the beefy proprietor.

"How can I help you, Sheriff?"

"Actually, Herr Esser, I may be able to help you."

He grunted. "How is that?" He went to work on a side of beef.

Peter explained the Schulzes' situation.

Esser met the sheriff's eyes for the first time. "I've been eying their property for quite some time."

"I'm aware of that,"

"Are they going to lose it?" Esser seemed glad of the prospect, and Peter tried not to lose his temper.

"Not if I can do anything to help." He leaned closer in spite of the disagreeable blood and meat fragments on the man's apron. "The widows have agreed to make a deal with you. If you will pay their taxes for as long as they need to live in their home, they'll turn the property over to you immediately. Except for their house and small garden, you may use the rest of it, and when they pass away, it will all be yours."

"I'd rather they just sell it all to me."

"They're in no position to move, Herr Esser. They have nowhere else to go." He glanced meaningfully around the vacant shop. "Your standing in this community has suffered, and this would go a long way toward making the village feel better toward you."

"Then people would know?"

"I'll make sure of it,"

"*Ja, ja.* This I can do."

With these things on his mind, Peter had gone to bed late after he woke in his chair, then tossed about for an hour and a half before finally fading into sleep.

Peter, Jr. told the others as they gathered for breakfast. "I looked in on him at six-thirty when he hadn't stirred and decided not to awaken him."

"Maybe we should just let him rest," Andrew said as he and the rest of the family sat down to breakfast.

"He hasn't had much sleep since early last week," Jacob commented, reaching for a sticky bun.

Susannah slapped his hand. "We haven't prayed yet."

Her brother looked up at the ceiling and gave a low whistle.

"Yes, let's all say a prayer," Anna Doll said, and she looked toward Peter, Jr., who cleared his throat.

"Almighty God, we give Thee thanks for this food. Please use it to strengthen our bodies to do Thy service, through Jesus Christ. Amen."

"Peter, you sounded just like Papa," Susannah said.

The sixteen-year-old beamed. Apparently, there was no higher compliment.

Peter slept until almost nine-thirty when he awakened with a start, seeing the sun shining through the windows, hearing the sounds of conversation in the house, the clopping of horses' hooves, and people talking out on the street. He opened his eyes wider to clear them of a thin crust, then reached for his father's ancient pocket watch, startled at the late hour. He sprang from the bed as if called to an alarm and dressed in a hurry. *I need a strong cup of coffee and several pieces of Anna's breakfast breads, if my sons haven't eaten everything in sight. Oh, but that woman can bake.* As he neared the bottom of the stairs, he heard two feminine voices, one of them hers. She was standing in the dining room talking to a diminutive young woman with light brown hair and freckles.

"Good morning, Sheriff Kichline," Anna said. "I'd like to introduce you to Phoebe Benner."

CHAPTER SEVENTEEN

Erin was only going to pop in and out of the drugstore for toothpaste and ibuprofen until she passed the card aisle's splashy ads for Mother's Day, which had not been anywhere near her radar screen. She found a card for her mother fairly quickly, but she was more careful to get just the right sentiment for Pat Miles because this first holiday after Jim's death would probably be emotional for his mom. Instead of bursting into tears herself, Erin actually smiled as she recalled how Jim had treated Mother's Day. "I'm not giving you a present because you're not my mother," he'd say with a laugh. He always made sure Ethan gave her something special, though. She still had the expensive pajamas her toddler had once given her, wrapped clumsily in a grocery store bag with a twist tie at the top. She had a small sadness to think without his dad's guidance, Ethan would probably forget all about the holiday.

As for her mother, Erin decided to pick up a box of her favorite Russell Stover dark chocolates with nuts. She stood there holding the cards, listening to "Caribou Queen" playing in the background, feeling as if she'd forgotten someone. And so she had—her father's wife. The woman had so deeply resented her and her brother when they were growing up, she'd driven a wedge between them and their father. Audrey couldn't even bear to hear Bridget's name spoken. Erin had never thought of her as "stepmother" any more than she would think of Ethan's teacher as a sister. Bridget just happened to be a woman who'd married her father, thus, "my father's wife." She doubted Hallmark had a category for that.

Erin stepped aside to let a man with squeaky shoes pick up a card from the row she'd been blocking, her thoughts bumping into each other like glass in a kaleidoscope. She recalled Bridget had been married once before with no children to show for that marriage or from her relationship with Tony Pelleriti. She'd been nice enough to Erin and Allen in recent years, always looking a tad remorseful, and now Erin had the wild thought she just might like to reach out to Bridget as a woman who could use a warm remembrance on Mother's Day. She found a card for "someone special" with a light verse inside about wishing her a day of gladness. She could do this. As she paid for her items, she felt somehow enriched.

When Erin had taken Pat to lunch the day before, her mother-in-law had suggested she might want to sit this Sunday out and not go to church. "I'll take Ethan to Sunday School if you like, or maybe you want him with you, whatever feels right."

Erin had childless friends who avoided Mother's Day like it was a form of head lice, or because their own mothers were newly dead, and they couldn't face everyone else's happiness. Actually, Erin had skipped church a few other times recently, dropping Ethan off at Sunday School, then heading to Starbucks to read the paper. She wasn't exactly avoiding God, but she wasn't entirely comfortable around Him either. He'd let Jim die, then He'd taken away her dream of teaching history at Hatfield. Jim might've been cured, or had a different kind of cancer, or no cancer at all. How could she trust Him? These things unsettled her. All at once she recalled the scene in the Bible where Lazarus had died, and Jesus took his time going to see the sisters. When Martha first saw Jesus, she said, "Lord, if you had been here, my brother would not have died." And hadn't that turned out well in the end? Hadn't her mourning turned to dancing?

On Sunday morning when she woke up, Erin reached for her cell phone and froze when she saw the date—her wedding anniversary. *Why didn't I realize this before, like when I was buying Mother's Day cards and presents? Then again, I only saw signs for Mother's Day and not the actual date itself.* She shut her eyes and rolled over toward Jim's side, curling into a fetal position, weeping into the pillow so she didn't wake Ethan. When she finished, she lay on her back spent, yet strangely energized, as if the storm had swept away a terrible murkiness. She got up and washed her blotchy face with cool water. *I'm glad I decided last night not to go to church today. I'd be a hot mess if I did.* Downstairs, she let Toby out and stood in the doorway staring at the luxuriant grass and burgeoning leaves in the back yard. Then she noticed her wedding photo hanging on the far wall, and as she stared at the young and expectant faces, Erin recalled the verse from the Song of Songs she and Jim had chosen for one of the readings—*For, lo, the winter is past ... the time of the singing of birds is come*—Now, even in her barest season without the love of her life by her side, new growth was emerging out of the hard ground whether she wanted it to or not. It couldn't be stopped.

❧ • ☙

Her son had slept way past his usual wake-up time, so Erin went upstairs after gulping down a piece of cinnamon raisin toast with last fall's apple butter and a sprinkling of diced jalapenos. She opened the door and allowed the determined sun to enter the room by rolling up the blinds in both windows. Ethan's dark blonde hair lay flat against his head, his right arm extended over it, his face peaceful. He stirred, blinking as his eyes adjusted to the light.

"Mom." He looked up at her and grinned.

"Good morning,"

He rolled over and started pulling his patchwork blanket over his head. It took him awhile to wake up, so Erin started talking about not going to church and driving up to see his grandmother in P'burg instead.

"Wait a minute, what day is this?"

"Sunday."

"I know, but isn't it ..." He hopped out of bed and rushed to his closet where he rummaged around for something. Then, with combined shyness and boldness, he handed Erin a card while holding something behind his back. "Happy Mother's Day!"

"Why, thank you, Ethan!" *He remembered*!

She opened a card made out of green construction paper, folded not quite in the center, with a big pink heart drawn on the front in magic marker. Inside the sentiment read, "Happy Mother's Day, I love you, Ethan."

"Mommy, I didn't know what to get you since, you know, uh, Daddy usually helped me with that." He looked down at his bare feet. "But I'm going to empty the dishwasher every day for a month because I know you hate that job."

"That's really nice of you." Erin pushed away images of glasses crashing to the floor and knives ending up where the spoons belonged.

"There's something else." He handed Erin a professionally wrapped package with a violet colored bow.

She held it in her hands, puzzled. "What's this?"

"He, uh, Daddy, wanted me to make sure I gave you this on Mother's Day."

125

Erin couldn't stop the tears—not wracking sobs but a steady, quieter flow. Her fingers trembled as she unwrapped the paper as carefully as her Grammy Ott always had, not so Erin could reuse it like her grandmother used to do, but to save the paper for posterity. Inside was a Pandora bracelet filled with charms—a heart, no two, wait—several different kinds of hearts, one, Erin discovered, for every year they'd been married, including this one. And there was a card, one she knew she couldn't open until she was alone.

That night, alone in her room, seeing Jim's handwriting moved her to more tears. Someday she might figure out how he'd managed to buy that bracelet, but as for the card, she recognized it from the supply she kept in the kitchen desk. He'd pushed beyond his physical discomfort to find the card there, and to write what followed.

Dear Erin, I wish we could be together for our anniversary and to celebrate Mother's Day. I have loved you with an everlasting love, and although we aren't together, if you're in God's hands, and I'm in His hands, then we really aren't far apart. I've never been much for people saying of the dead, "They're up there looking down on me," but the love I have for you will in some way always be with you, until we see each other on the other side, in Heaven. All my love, Jim

Her classes had ended, final grades were turned in. Ethan still had five weeks of school left, giving Erin all the time she needed to focus on her quest for a patriot ancestor. By Tuesday, she felt as if her latest journey down that road had gone from interstate highway to an unpaved back road. She'd located records for a John Sharp, who'd given the Continental Army use of his cart and contributed food to the troops on two occasions. With four different John Sharps in that area, however, she became hopelessly tangled in the various branches of their family trees.

Sydney wrote after Erin explained the situation:

That's a tough one. You said he was thirty-five, and older men tended to join militias because that was all about protecting their families and communities, but thirty-five isn't really old or young. The records you shared with me, and the ones I've found online about John Sharp, aren't definitive enough to connect you with one of them. I'll check Fold3 and get back to you.

In the meantime, Erin used her research skills as a historian to check the Library of Congress website and some New Jersey state archives, buoyed when she came up with a record appearing to be about her John Sharp, due to his age and location. She wrote to Sydney, who answered within the hour.

Good work, Erin! That record does look like a true connection, but I'm afraid it's not going to help you get into the DAR. It shows John paid a substitute to fight in his place, and unfortunately, the DAR doesn't accept that as service.

Erin couldn't understand it. *Isn't that offering aid to the patriot cause? Isn't getting a substitute similar to paying taxes, which is acceptable?* She wasn't about to challenge the DAR, though, not when their standards were as binding as the laws of the Medes and Persians. *I'll check the Owen line instead since my great-great-grandfather married into the Sharp family.* In a matter of minutes, however, she found herself stuck in yet another ditch. *Too bad Owen and Sharp are both popular names from that time in northwest New Jersey. There's a John T. Owen, then a John Y., and John E., all from Sussex County! I'll try finding information in the censuses.* Unfortunately, New Jersey didn't have those records from 1790, 1800, 1810, or 1820, just the time frame Erin needed to establish who her great-great-grandfather Owen's parents were. *Let's try the family trees.* They also dead-ended with him.

At one o'clock she took a lunch break, throwing together a chunk of leftover French bread, three pieces of shrimp, and a bowl of chocolate granola which she ate in front of the TV. She had the Food Channel on but wasn't really focusing and ended up finishing her meal before the Chopped champion was revealed. She decided to take Toby for a walk around the block.

"Hey, cutie!" a man yelled from a passing car along the main road.

Erin rolled her eyes and picked up her step. Back at the computer, she emailed Sydney about the Owen line and how there certainly wasn't "low lying fruit" there either.

Sydney wrote back, *I'm not giving up! You had lots of relatives during the Revolution, and I'm certain we're going to find one.*

Feeling encouraged, Erin started researching her great-great-grandfather, Daniel T. Brotz, who'd been married to a Fritz. He was born in 1811 and seemed to have lived mostly in Hanover Township, now part of the city of Bethlehem if Erin remembered correctly. It looked like his father's name was Johannes, born in 1780, also around the same area. That meant his father was likely born in the 1750s or 60s, just in time to fight in the Revolution. By the time Erin had to get

Ethan off the bus, she had looked into military records for a Johannes' father, and discovered a hit—he'd served as a drummer boy in the war! Tears trickled down her face as she imagined a bold but tender-hearted young man wanting to serve the Patriot cause, but being too young to fight. The idea of getting into the DAR through a musician touched her—Jim would have loved that. Erin hammered out an email to Sydney with the good news.

Her dad called the next morning to see how she was and to thank her.

"Bridget never had a card for Mother's Day before. That was nice of you."

"I'm glad she liked it." Her mind was elsewhere, somewhere in the far reaches of the mid-eighteenth century looking through online birth, baptism, and marriage records to send in with her application for Martin Brotz. *This is your father. Pay attention.*

"I was just wondering how you were."

Erin could tell he wanted to acknowledge she'd just had her first major holiday without Jim, but in his gruff, ex-GI way, he didn't know how to put it. Still, she appreciated it. Nor did she expect him to mention it had been her anniversary—Tony never remembered those, probably because he hadn't been invited to the wedding. Actually, that was only half true. She'd wanted him to come, although they hadn't spoken for seven years, but there was no way Bridget could be there. Erin never would have done that to her mother. Because Tony wouldn't come without his wife, he'd missed his daughter's big day, and Allen had walked her down the aisle instead.

"I'm doing pretty well, Dad." *Should I tell him about my research, which occupies so much of my time and attention?* She felt shy about telling him. He'd only known the experience of a first-generation Italian family and might think she was being uppity, or "High fallutin'."

"I'm finished with classes for the semester," she said.

"Oh, yeah? When's Ethan done? I'd like to take him fishing."

"He has another five weeks. I'm sure he'd love to go with you."

"So, what are you doing to keep busy?" he asked.

"Actually, I'm working on my ancestry."

"Your ancestry?" His voice carried a whine, as if she'd just said she was going to join a tribe of headhunters in Bora Bora.

"Yes, well, I'm trying to find out more about Mom's side of the family. I know about yours, about Italy and when your parents came here, but I'd like to know where Grammy Ott's people were from." She was stepping onto a rocking boat.

"What do you want to know that for?"

"I'd like to join the Daughters of the American Revolution." The words came out of her mouth before she could decide otherwise.

"I'd save my time and money if I were you," he said. "Those organizations bother me all the time. 'Give us money, and we'll tell you where your family came from.' One group tried to get my money for some kind of family shield, or whatever you call that crap. All they want is money. Well, I'm no sucker."

What was that verse about pearls before swine?

❧ • ☙

"I'm working on the connections between your Martin Brotz and his father," Sydney told her on the phone. "Since Martin is a confirmed patriot with the DAR, I'd really like to make this one work."

"Oh, that would be wonderful," Erin said.

"As with the Fritzes, though, there are some issues. We know all the Brotz's in that area were related to each other through Caspar, who was born in 1695 in Germany, but which of the four brothers who came here was your ancestor? All their names begin with Johannes."

"What's with that, Sydney? I keep bumping up against that sort of thing in my research." She leaned against the wall in her home office.

The DAR regent explained. "It's a custom that goes way back in Germany—all the sons in a family are given a first name to honor someone, usually a favorite saint or a relative, so they go by their middle names instead."

The light dawned. "Oh, that makes sense!"

"The thing is, the middle names weren't exactly original either, plus those four brothers had sons whose names repeated as well. Then you end up with two or three Martins or Georges."

She felt daunted. "What do you think I should do?"

"Since this is promising, and the earliest members of that family lived around Allentown," Sydney said, I'd go to the Lehigh County Historical Society to find out what they have. Good luck to you!"

❦ • ❧

CHAPTER EIGHTEEN

I don't really know Allentown very well. I only came when I was little when Aunt Jane brought us to Hess's Department Store since Mom would never dream of driving twenty miles from home. I remember the restaurant and how I used to get ice cream sundaes decorated like clowns wearing upside-down sugar cones for hats.

She parked two blocks away in the closest spot she could find and walked to the lush campus of the Lehigh Valley Heritage Museum. Inside, she glanced at the exhibit of World War II posters on the main level, then went to the library where an older volunteer greeted her. "I'm trying to find out more about my Brotz family because I'd like to join the DAR. They have a Martin Brotz as a confirmed patriot, and I need records to show we're related." Erin tried not to stare at the woman's curious hairstyle, a poodle/shag/mullet, and her overly-pink lipstick. *How old is she? Sixty? Seventy? Hard to tell.*

"We do have information about the Brotz family. Come with me, and we can take a look."

An hour later, Erin felt like the Phillies on a losing streak. Chances were slim she'd be able to pull this one out. "So, if I'm reading all this correctly, I'm not a direct descendant of this Martin Brotz."

The pink lips pursed. "It doesn't look that way. Sorry."

"At least he was my something-times great-uncle. Maybe there should be an organization for less-than-direct descendants of patriots,"

The woman gave a sympathetic smile.

"And there's no one in my Brotz line who was a patriot?" Erin was falling off a cliff, trying to grasp at a branch to keep her from crashing.

"I'm not entirely sure, but from what I'm finding, the ages don't exactly line up."

"I don't quite understand."

"I think your ancestor would've been an older man at the time of the war. Of course, he might have paid taxes or given aid to the cause so you might want to look into that."

Erin checked her watch. "I need to get home for my son's bus. Thanks for your help."

"My pleasure. If there's anything more I can do, just let me know."

On the way out, Erin put a twenty-dollar bill in the donation jar.

"What are you doing, Ethan?" She pulled herself away from the computer screen to watch her son working with a *Curious George* kit she'd picked up for him a few weeks earlier at Marshalls. She was glad her son didn't think he was too old for the lovable monkey just yet.

"I'm writing a book."

"What about?" She leaned in for a closer look.

"Curious George is trying to find an ancestor who fought in the Revolution."

"Really?" Erin was amused and delighted. Her son was catching the bug, too!

"Uh-huh. He's trying to join the MAR—Monkeys of the American Revolution." His blue eyes danced. "Do you like my story, Mom?"

"I love it! Has he found a patriot ancestor yet?"

"Yup. He just needs his paperwork."

She sent Sydney an email, and when the regent answered, Erin could almost hear her laughing.

Monkeys of the American Revolution! Is nothing sacred? LOL

The following day Erin received an email from a New Jersey state archivist about her Sharp ancestor, but the news wasn't nearly as promising as Curious George's investigation:

There is no way to connect any of these Revolutionary War Records with specific individuals. The records do NOT contain any dates of birth or death, nor do they name their spouses. We did find one record that may be of interest, but again, we cannot prove it is your John Scharfenstein (Sharp).

"Grrrrrr!" Erin got up and made a cup of coffee, then sat down to share the news with Sydney, hating this feeling of banging up against one brick wall after another. "Are you used to having such challenging applications?" she asked in an email.

Yes, some apps are really tough, and some are a breeze. The last few I've done have been a real challenge, but I'm not giving up!

Neither was she.

She moved away from the Fritzes, Brotzes, and Sharps for the time being and steered her search in a different direction, checking with Sydney first to see if she was on the right track. With the regent's sharp eye for clues and documents, Erin figured if there were something promising here, Sydney would find it. She was, after all, the Sherlock Holmes of genealogists. If not, she'd save Erin time and energy.

Sydney,
Can you advise me? There's a Peter Kachlein from Germany, who emigrated to Easton, PA, and became a colonel in the Revolution. I'm trying to see if there's a connection because my grandfather, Thomas Benjamin Owen's mother was Louisa Kichline Owen. Her parents were Joseph and Elmira Kichline. Joseph was born around 1830 in the Easton area, and his father was Samuel, born on December 29, 1798, also in Northampton County, probably Easton like everyone else! Samuel's father was Joseph B. Kachlein, born in 1768, also in Northampton County. I'd love to know if my Kichlines are related to that colonel. I don't quite get the Kachlein-Kichline thing, though. How is it my great-grandmother's last name was Kichline, but her grandfather spelled it Kachlein. Hmmmm....

Erin wasn't sure if Sydney had a regular job since she spent a lot of time helping prospective DAR members do research. Erin could understand why someone would dedicate herself to that kind of work, the excitement of linking a current family with previous generations, putting those people against the backdrop of the history she loved reading about and teaching. As for right now, Erin needed to do some grocery shopping or they'd be eating popcorn for supper.

Sydney responded right after lunch.

> *I wouldn't worry too much about that name thing. A lot of immigrants changed their names when they came to America—thus, Scharfenstein became Sharp, for example—and Kichline/Kachlein are close enough I'm thinking they are from the same family. I'll look into this Kachlein-Kichline family to see if you have a connection to the colonel.*
>
> *Once we beard this dragon, and you have your patriot, we'll need the following documents: for Generation 1, your birth and marriage certs, your husband's birth cert. For Gen 2, your mom and dad's birth cert and marriage. Gen. 3, the same as above for your grandparents. From Gen. 4 on, DAR is not as insistent but requires SOME proof documentation for each person in the generation. More is better. Marriage isn't really necessary, but it often provides information you need anyway, like the names of their parents. Wills, tombstone pics, deeds, church records, vital records (issued by the government), all are good sources of documentation. I can help locate some of these items, but anything less than a hundred years old and a vital record, you have to get yourself because of privacy laws and identity theft issues.*

Erin felt a need to sit down. Joining the DAR took a lot of work, and wasn't just a matter of saying, "Hey, I found a Patriot Ancestor" and having members of a chapter vote whether to accept you at a monthly meeting. A woman needed solid, hands-on evidence officially connecting her to a specific Revolutionary War figure, from which she could trace lineal descent. She needed time to assemble the necessary documents, so while Sydney checked out the Kachleins or Kichlines, or whoever they were, Erin was going to sift through her lock box for the first of those "certs." She knew her mom would gladly let her make a copy of her birth certificate. As for her father, she hoped he'd be willing, minus a lecture about shysters coming after her money. Also, had her parents' marriage certificate survived their cantankerous divorce? She knew her mother had torn her wedding dress to shreds, but what about that "cert?" Surely Sydney would know what to do if the document no longer existed.

❧ • ☙

After Ethan left for school, Erin poured a second cup of coffee and opened up her laptop. A childhood pop song floated around the edges of her mind, and she wondered why since she hadn't heard it in years—"I've got this feeling today's the day." She started guessing who had sung the tune and the year it came out, vaguely associating it with a trip to Easton's old Bushkill Park. She told herself she was getting sidetracked. If questions about the song persisted, she could always do a Google search later. She checked her inbox—Sydney had indeed left her a message. Its exuberant heading read, "Kichline!!!!!! Karl (Charles) Christian Joseph Kuechlein." Catching the excitement, she recognized the name from her research on Louisa Kichline Owen.

> *Erin,*
> *At http://files.usgwarchives.net/pa/bucks/taxlist/1781/bedminster.txt, you will find the list of residents who paid the "Effective Supply Tax." Charles is also listed there. He paid to support the colonial troops, and this alone can get him approved as a patriot ancestor!! I found him in the PA Archives paying in 1779 in addition to 1781. We're good! I'm attaching the documents I found.*
> *I'm double checking the lineage to make sure it all makes sense. This lineage is very well documented and should be reasonably "easy" (I can't believe I just used that word) to prove.*
> *This one we can take to the bank!*
> *Sydney*

She wanted to do a happy dance. She really was happy, but she couldn't help feeling like a twelve-year-old back at the Firth Youth Center waiting for the boy she liked to ask her for a moonlight skate only to have someone she'd never even noticed ask her instead. She got the romantic skate alright, but not with the boy of her dreams. Of all the possible ancestors she'd been researching, including ones at Bunker Hill, a fifer, and a colonel, for Pete's sake, here was a verifiable relative who qualified her for the DAR for *paying a tax*. Erin was actually on her way to becoming a Daughter of the American Revolution—but she also felt slightly let down. For this, she felt a twinge of guilt.

She was about to reply to the email when she noticed another one from Sydney, written an hour after the first.

> *When I was investigating your Karl, I also found this information about him.*

Karl Christian Joseph Kichline, c1726-1788. From Thomas Jefferson Kichline, pp. 10–11. *Charles Keichlein as he spelled the name, second surviving son of Johann Andreas and Anna Margaret (Hahn) Keichlein, was born in the parish of Kuechheim-Bolanden, duchy or principality of Nassau-Weinberg Germany, in the year 1726. He came to Pennsylvania with his mother, stepfather Michael Koppelger, and an elder and younger brother in the ship Francis and Elizabeth, arriving in Philadelphia September 21, 1742.*

That was really early, Erin thought, delighted. She was amused by the variations on the name, including Koechline, and how the author's first and middle names paid obvious homage to the nation's third President. No wonder she'd always cried during "The National Anthem"—patriotism ran deeply in her family. She wanted to find this article and read the whole thing.

Like his younger brother Andrew, being under sixteen years of age, he was not required to take the Oath of Allegiance to the British Crown. Therefore, his name does not appear on the list of passengers so qualified at Philadelphia, as do those of Michael Koppelger and Johann Peter Kuechline, the elder brother then nineteen.

Johann Peter Kuechline—this must be the man who ended up being a colonel in Easton, she thought. The spelling she'd seen for him was Kachlein, or maybe Kachline, but all of these people were linked. She loved having any kind of relationship with him, even as a great-uncle, having felt somehow drawn to him from the beginning of her ancestral journey. Hadn't she felt especially close to her Uncle Thomas after her father left? An uncle was someone important.

She read more about Charles, how his name showed up on a deed in 1763 and that he bought one hundred acres in Bedminster for four hundred pounds. His brother, Andrew, and their stepfather bought adjacent farms, and there was something about a tavern in the family. Funny, though, the story didn't say anything about where Peter settled. She guessed Easton based on the record she'd seen awhile back.

Here Charles lived until his death in 1788. Unlike his brothers Peter and Andrew, he took no part in the Revolutionary struggle so far as can be ascertained. His name appears on the list of "Non-Associators" of Bedminster Township, in 1775. He was apparently loyal in his sentiments to the patriot cause, as in 1781, before independence was achieved, he was elected to represent upper Bucks in the Pennsylvania Assembly and served one term.

Now that was better! Charles had been a political leader, like Samuel Adams or Patrick Henry. That felt better to her than becoming a Daughter of the American Revolution on the coattails of a supply tax. She emailed Sydney who answered, *Since the PA Assembly was Colonial at that time, we have a winner!*

❦ • ❧

CHAPTER NINETEEN

Peter liked having two women in the house again, but once Phoebe Benner learned the Kichline family's routine, Anna wouldn't be around anymore, and he disliked thinking about that. She'd blended in so beautifully, had just taken her place in the family. Part of him even resisted Phoebe's presence, but he quickly squelched that as utterly unfair to her. Her cheerful nature and enthusiasm were undeniable, and besides, he was the one who'd sent for her in the first place. Peter, Jr., Andrew, and Jacob didn't seem to have any issues with her, but he noticed Susannah didn't say much to Phoebe and clung to Anna. Over the next two weeks, as Anna began a gradual withdrawal from their everyday home life, Susannah began slipping off to the Dolls' again.

Anna tried to reassure him. "Please don't worry about that, Sheriff. Of course, she would feel this way. She's lost her mother and Greta, and now someone new is here. My family and I love and enjoy her, so if it doesn't bother you, we're happy to have her around as much as she likes."

"You are most kind," he said, feeling a bit like his daughter himself, and not a little ashamed about it.

"I'm here for you as well, whenever you need me," she said.

Peter wasn't sure what had happened to Fräulein Doll's eyes. He ended up thanking her gruffly.

ஜ • ஜ

He looked up from his writing-table and became aware of Phoebe standing in the doorway watching Mr. Hanlon as he silently read Milton. Peter glanced from her to the teacher, who looked at Phoebe and smiled. His mind wandered back years before to the first time he'd seen Margaretta sitting with her father in church. She made such a pretty sight with her thick brown hair all pulled up and her bright face and colorful dress that he hadn't heard most of the sermon that day. He smiled at the memory. What he didn't feel as happy about was the prospect of Phoebe and Hanlon. He didn't think he could stand anymore change around here if the two of them got together.

"Excuse me, uh, Sheriff, may I ask you a question?" Phoebe said.

He put his quill in the holder and looked up at her, "Of course."

"Fräulein Doll told me about a resident whose wife is quite ill, and I'd like to take her some broth and bread. I don't know where she lives, though."

Out of the corner of his eye, he saw Hanlon perk up. "Who is it?" Peter asked.

"Mrs. Weed."

He was touched that Phoebe wanted to help. Closing his account book, he rose. "It will do me good to take a walk, Phoebe. I'll take you there myself, then I'll show you a little of our village, if that suits."

"Oh, yes, that would be fine! Thank you."

"Mr. Hanlon, take your time," Peter said. "You know you're always welcome."

"Thank you, sir. I believe I will." The teacher glanced at Phoebe again.

The young woman was ready to leave as soon as she filled her basket, and they stepped outside into the enfolding warmth of the early June morning. They headed east down Northampton Street, then south toward the Lehigh River and the Weed's property.

"Um, I hope you don't mind my saying so, but I'm still not sure how you want me to address you," she said.

Peter also realized at just four feet ten, she was having difficulty matching his long-legged strides. He slowed down as he considered her comment. He liked her forthrightness, and he could also understand her confusion—she wouldn't call him "Herr Kichline" because as a first-generation German born in America, she didn't use the old language much. "Mr." would be alright as would "Sheriff," but given she was family, they seemed too formal. She was his brother's niece through marriage, so Peter was something of an uncle to her. He decided to give her the choice. "You may call me Uncle Peter if you like." He hoped she would, especially since he missed his brother's five children.

"Oh, that would be wonderful!"

He smiled down—way down—-at her. "You're my brother Andrew's niece and, therefore, part of my family as well." Her obvious joy filled his spirit.

Mrs. Weed's husband wasn't home, but their son opened the door just as he was saying good-bye to another man, one who didn't seem all pleased to see Peter.

"*Guter tag*, Sheriff." The man tipped his hat to Peter, then Phoebe.

"*Guter tag*, Herr Schonck," Peter nodded curtly.

Schonck looked like he wanted to say something but then left in a hurry. Phoebe looked up at Peter as if she were waiting to be introduced, but instead, he shifted his attention to the young man.

"Good day, Master Weed," Peter said. "I'd like you to meet my niece, Phoebe Benner. We've brought some things for your mother."

John's eyes darted from the sheriff to the young woman. "I, uh, I'm John Weed, Miss Benner. My father's in the fields. Please come in." He stepped aside to let them enter.

The Weed's log cabin had just one window, so although the sun was shining, inside was dark and more than a little depressing, especially with Mrs. Weed lying in her sick bed among the shadows. Peter winced, remembering Margaretta's final days, although hers had been spent in considerably more comfortable surroundings.

"Good morning, Mrs. Weed." He removed his hat and held onto it. He didn't think young John would offer to hang it up for him, and he wasn't disappointed. "I heard you weren't feeling well."

"Oh, hello, Sheriff Kichline." She tried raising herself, but the effort ended in a grimace. "How nice of you to come. I'm sorry I can't offer you anything."

"Don't give it another thought. I've brought my niece, who's just come to us from Bedminster. Miss Phoebe Benner, this is Mrs. Egbert Weed."

"I'm pleased to meet you, Mrs. Weed,"

"The pleasure's mine. Did you meet my son, John?"

"Yes," Phoebe said, looking toward the thin young man standing to the side of a beautifully crafted table which seemed out of place here. "We brought you some beef broth and bread." She lifted the basket for her to see. "May I serve you some?"

"That would be very nice. Thank you."

Phoebe put the basket on the table and began preparing the simple meal.

"Mr. Schonck was just here, Sheriff."

"Yes, I saw him." He paused, feeling sweat trickle down his legs in the heat of the cabin. "Did you send for him, Mrs. Weed?"

"My husband did. When we found out there's no doctor in Easton, someone told my husband about Mr. Schonck, that he's a kind of faith healer. Is that true?"

Peter took a deep breath, punctuated by the smell of burning wood and humidity. "Mr. Schonck is what we Germans refer to as a pow-wow doctor."

"That's the word he used, isn't it John?" Mrs. Weed looked over at her son, who gave a barely perceptible nod. He didn't seem at all interested in the conversation, as if he were trying to shrink himself.

"I'm just not sure what that means." She seemed eager to talk, although it required a good deal of effort. "He said a lot of words I couldn't understand, kept repeating them, you know, and he made signs over me." She shivered under the shawl she wore, one that had seen better days in a much nicer place.

"This practice is widespread among Germans, Mrs. Weed. There are people who believe they have healing powers from God, and they use certain words and symbols to cure sickness."

"Does this thing work?" She wore a combination of hope and skepticism on her lined face.

He noticed Phoebe watching him closely. "I believe God gives the gift of healing to certain people, but a good deal of pow-wowing amounts to little more than superstition." He didn't want to mention Mr. Schonck was among the latter.

"I believe in God, Sheriff Kichline."

"That's good, Mrs. Weed. That's the most important thing."

Phoebe carried a bowl of broth past John to the woman's side, and Peter moved a chair next to the bed so Phoebe could help her eat.

"Oh, you dear girl, this is wonderful. Did you make this?"

"Yes, madam. I'm glad you like it."

They stayed the better part of an hour, watching the woman's pallor lift and her mood lighten. She kept trying to draw John into the conversation, but after twenty minutes he excused himself. Phoebe promised to return the following day to check on the patient.

"Do you think I should allow Mr. Schonck to come again, Sheriff?" Mrs. Weed asked as her visitors stood at the door.

"Perhaps you'd like me to send for the Reverend Henop instead."

"Does he speak English? I don't have much knowledge of German or your customs."

"Yes, he speaks English," he said smiling.

When they emerged into the daylight, his eyes had to adjust to the brightness, and although the temperature was rising, he felt free of the cabin's oppressiveness.

"She's a lovely person, Uncle Peter."

He enjoyed hearing her address him that way. "Yes, she is. I believe your broth and bread helped her, as well as your kind conversation."

"I like helping people."

"I can see that." He smiled at her and said, half teasing, "Perhaps you have a gift of healing?"

"Oh, I don't know about that! You know, I saw pow-wowing once back home, and for some reason, it made me shudder. It seems a good idea on the one hand, yet on the other, there's something dark there."

He nodded. "There's a fine line between doing it according to God's Word and drifting into magic and superstition. Some people stay within the framework of Holy Scripture while others wander off into spiritual darkness."

"What about Mr. Schonck?"

He pushed his lips together. "Let's just say I have my suspicions."

They neared the Great Square where half the townspeople had turned out, tending their noisy flocks, buying and selling, seeing and being seen.

"I like Easton," Phoebe said, her eyes searching the throng.

"I'm glad. Do you miss your family?"

"A little, but I was ready for adventure." She looked up at him. "Do you understand?"

"Perfectly. Adventure brought me here as well, rather than stay in Bedminster myself."

"How wonderful we're alike in that way!" She popped her hand over her mouth. "Please forgive me for being so familiar, Uncle Peter."

"That's quite alright," he said. He appreciated people who said what was really on their minds. "Have you been to Mr. Hart's establishment? He has a store the ladies in town enjoy."

"Oh, yes. Anna Doll took me there."

"Do you need anything today?" He knew she had the money he gave her to run the household, as well as an allowance, and according to his brother, Charles, Phoebe wasn't exactly poor to begin with.

She laughed. "Uncle Peter, I always want to go to a store!"

They walked up the wooden steps and entered the cool interior where Meyer Hart welcomed them. His son was with another customer, but he nodded and smiled at Peter, then cast an admiring glance at Phoebe.

"Well, well, if it isn't our good sheriff." Hart spoke his usual, genial greeting, but Peter sensed anxiety behind it.

"Good morning, Herr Hart. This is my niece, Phoebe Benner, but perhaps you've met already."

She gave a small curtsy, and he smiled. "Yes, we have. The women in your family sure do run to good-looking," the proprietor said with a wink. As Phoebe blushed, he asked if he could help her find anything.

"I believe I'll just look around."

"Yes, yes, child. Help yourself. I would like a word with you, Sheriff, if you please." Hart motioned for Peter to follow him to the side of the counter while Phoebe walked over to a shelf with containers of tea. "I was hoping to see you today, Herr Kichline." He lowered his voice. "There's been more stealing."

"When?"

"Within the last two days. During court week, a few items were stolen, but that isn't unusual with so many different elements coming to town. But now I am down two pairs of men's stockings, as many women's caps, and a copper porringer."

The sheriff took a deep breath and slowly exhaled.

"I believe you'll hear similar accounts from other proprietors."

"Do you suspect anyone?" Peter asked.

Hart shook his head. "You know Frau Eckert believes Nicholas Tatamy is guilty, but I think he's a fine man."

"Was he in town recently?"

"Yes, come to think of it, he was." Hart's face clouded. "Surely, you don't believe …"

"No, but maybe the thief times his stealing with Tatamy's visits to cast suspicion on him. How does he know, though, when Tatamy is around?" As Peter considered how that might be, he saw Phoebe talking with Lewis Gordon's sister. It was nice to see his niece taking her place in the community. An idea suddenly occurred to him, and he discussed it with the proprietor.

"Yes, yes, I like that," Hart said, nodding. "That might just work. Let me know if there's anything I can do."

"Keep an especially sharp lookout."

"Hopefully, I can manage to do that without making my customers feel uncomfortable." He leaned closer. "I don't want to chase anyone away."

Peter smiled. "I don't think you could ever do that. Well, now, I think I'll go speak with Frau Eckert. Will you excuse me?"

"Yes, of course."

He walked over to the ladies and exchanged pleasantries, then he told Phoebe, "I need to visit Frau Eckert. Would you like to come with me, or do you still have some shopping to do?"

"I'm just finishing, Uncle Peter. If you don't mind, I'd like to go with you."

"Certainly." He waited while young Hart added up her purchases.

A few doors down, Peter noticed the unmistakable charm in the shape of a star Frau Eckert had placed over the front door of her tavern. His glance naturally shifted to the area under the threshold where he saw the other one. He sniffed and shook his head.

"What are those?" Phoebe asked, following his movements.

"Charms, part of an old German custom, yet another superstition, I'm afraid."

"What do they mean?" She leaned closer for a better look.

"Someone has stolen something she highly values," Peter said. "The belief is if you place these charms just so, the thief will return them on the third day."

Frau Eckert opened the door and, looking about to explode, cried out, "Herr Kichline! *Gott sei Dank!* There's been another theft!" Peter opened his mouth to respond, but she cut him off.

"That *indisch* has taken my bridal box!"

❧ • ☙

CHAPTER TWENTY

He sat with Elena Eckert, Martin Lutz, and John Weed in a quiet corner of the tavern while Phoebe volunteered to wait on two local farmers who looked like they'd won a lottery when they saw her.

"I'm telling you, Sheriff Kichline, Tatamy stole my bridal box! I feel it right here." Frau Eckert thumped her right hand against her bosom.

"Suppose you tell me why you think so."

She leaned closer, her breath the murky blast he always expected but never got used to. "He was in here the day I missed it. I never go to bed without looking at the box and that night, I saw it was gone." She sniffled. "Eduard gave that box to me when we married." She wiped her tears with an edge of her apron, then became fierce again. "This was on one of the tables that night." She thrust a felt beaver hat toward his chest.

He recognized the small tear on the crown. Although his stomach knotted, he told himself this didn't prove anything. The two young men sat there looking puzzled and not a little frightened of this formidable female. "Are you familiar with this bridal box?" he questioned them.

Martin spoke up. "Ja, Herr Kichline. When I clean her room, I see the box. She insists I dust it carefully."

"And he does," she said with a satisfied nod.

"When did you last see it?" Peter asked.

"I, uh, believe the day before yesterday when I cleaned her chamber."

"And after that?"

"I haven't been in her room since then, sir."

"Master Weed, are you familiar with this box?" Peter looked over at him.

The thin youth shook his head without making eye contact with the sheriff. "I just work downstairs."

"He never goes to the rooms," Frau Eckert said. "That is Martin's job. John plays music and sweeps the tavern. That is all."

"I see." Peter gazed at Weed, who was watching Phoebe, which greatly annoyed him. "Did you fellows see Mr. Tatamy?"

"Not here, I only saw him at Mr. Hart's store when I was running an errand," Martin said.

Frau Eckert looked like she wanted to argue, but Peter spoke up. "And what about you, young man? Did you see Mr. Tatamy in here?"

"Uh, yes, sir. He came in while Frau Eckert was in the back room and Martin was away."

"And you waited on him?"

"Yes, I did. He had a mug of ale."

Peter wanted John Weed to look at him, willed him to do so, but he would not. "Did you only see him in this room?"

"Yes, sir."

"Was he ever out of your sight?"

Apparently Weed needed to think about this. "Yes, sir. Frau Eckert called me to the back room while he was here."

"Did you see him, Frau Eckert?"

She didn't seem to hear the question. "I want you to arrest that savage!"

"And I need you to slow down," Peter said, placing his hands palms down. "This isn't a court of law. I'm simply gathering evidence. In our system, Mr. Tatamy has the presumption of innocence until he is proven guilty—if he is proven guilty."

She jumped to her feet. "He will be!"

When he left fifteen minutes later with his niece, Peter knew one thing for certain—John Weed was lying. Nicholas Tatamy never drank alcohol, probably because it had been his father's ruination.

Back at the house, he told Phoebe, "I need to go to Bethlehem to continue my investigation. I'll stop by the mill to let my sons know, and I'll make sure they stay at home this evening. If there's anything you need, they or the Dolls will help. Will you be alright?"

"Oh yes, Uncle Peter. We'll be fine. I'll prepare food and drink for your journey."

"Thank you, Phoebe. I'd appreciate it." He was pleased she'd anticipated his needs without being told, and any reluctance he had to leave dissipated. She could be relied upon.

He had a plan, but to put it into motion, he needed further evidence, so he stopped first at the Seipsville Inn on the road leading from Easton to Nazareth. He was there by mid-afternoon. Yes, Peter Seip told him, he'd been missing some things.

"About how many?" Peter asked, "And of what nature?"

Seip scratched his gray and white bearded chin. "Oh, I'd say a handful, mostly cooking items, including a copper kettle. I'll tell you, my woman was none too pleased."

"Have you noticed any suspicious patrons?"

"Nobody I'd willingly throw out of my inn if that's what you mean."

"Has there been anyone you haven't seen before?"

More scratching. "You know, Sheriff, there are plenty of those kind around. Could've been any one of them young whippersnappers with their scheming heads."

He visited all the taverns between Easton and the Moravian community of Bethlehem, where he finally stopped at the Sun Inn at eight o'clock. At this crossroads, a stagecoach ran daily between Bethlehem and Philadelphia, and Peter would spend the night, gathering information from locals and travelers. He enjoyed the tavern's fine fare, which the energetic owner, Jost Hellerich, was always eager to share with the county sheriff. This time, he also showed Peter how he'd just managed to bring water from the Monocacy Creek into the building using wooden pipes.

"That's amazing, Herr Hellerich." He could've spent hours examining the fascinating system, but there wasn't time. He stated his purpose after they sat down to dinner together.

"I've been missing a number of linens in the last two weeks," young Hellerich said. "I have difficulty operating a public house properly without ample linens."

Peter swallowed a bite of perfectly seasoned trout, letting it dissolve on his tongue before asking, "What would you say their value was?"

"About fifteen pounds. I don't know how the thief got away with taking linens of all things."

"How many servants do you have?"

"Three just now, and all of them have been upstanding. I don't doubt them at all."

"I'm glad you have people you can rely on." He took another bite of the fish. "This is very good."

Hellerich smiled. "We take pride in our trout, the right kind of pride, that is."

"Do you mind if I question your servants?"

"Go right ahead, anything to find the thief, but like I said, I have faith in their honesty."

After the supper rush ended, Peter gathered the servants into an upstairs room, a woman in her twenties wearing a Moravian-style white cap and plain dress, and two teenage boys, all wide-eyed about being questioned by the Northampton County sheriff. The darker haired boy reminded him very much of John Weed because he wouldn't look at Peter, and his leg started pumping when he mentioned seeing an Indian hanging around the tavern on the day of the theft.

"Do you know who the Indian was?"

"Well, sir, I heard some folks say he lives around these parts, but I don't know for sure." He also began tapping his right hand fingers on his knee.

"Look at me, son. Why would you be suspicious of him?"

He glanced briefly at Peter then looked away as if he'd been scalded. "They aren't to be trusted."

"Hans!" the woman said. "You know better! There are many fine Indians. God made them just as he made us."

The young man shrugged as he stared at his feet, which had stilled.

"And how about you, young man?" Peter asked the other fellow. "Did you see anyone suspicious?"

"Just some light-haired man I'd never seen before."

Peter saw Hans's head whip up quickly, a startled expression on his smooth face. "And why was he suspicious?"

"I'd, uh, I'd rather not say."

When he could get nothing more out of them, he dismissed them, but the following morning when he found himself alone with one of the boys at breakfast, he brought up the matter again.

"Is there anything you'd like to say to me while the others aren't around?"

The servant stood there with a pewter pitcher of water, sweat beads rolling down its sides, clinging to the bottom. "I don't know, sir." He looked over his shoulder.

"Are you afraid of what might happen if you do?"

"I, I don't know." He looked at Peter. "I'm sorry, Sheriff. I want to, uh, help."

"Do you suspect Hans of being involved in the thefts?"

"I can't say for sure, sir. I, uh, I saw him talking to that light-haired man I told you about. It, it gave me a funny feeling." Again, the glance over his shoulder.

"Had you ever seen him before?"

"A few times, sir. He uses the stage coach."

"How old would you say he was?"

"Maybe his twenties, sir."

"Can you describe his appearance?"

He paused. "He was medium tall and thickly built. His hair was the color of straw, and the face was sort of pocked."

Peter made a mental note. "Did he wear any clothes that made him stand out?"

"Not really, sir. Just regular clothes and a hat."

Some instinct made him ask, "What kind of hat?"

"You know, the beaver felt kind a lot of the farmers wear."

His heart rate sped up. "What about Hans? How long have you known him?"

"We came together from Germany three years ago with other Moravians."

"Do you consider him trustworthy?"

"He's always been honest and hard working."

Peter looked out the window, watching the creek flow placidly, mourning doves skittering on its banks. Another patron came downstairs.

"Is there anything else you need, sir?" the young man asked.

"Not now, but perhaps later. Thank you."

"Yes, sir."

❧ • ❧

On the way back to Easton, Peter stopped at John Lefevre's public house and told him the robberies had been taking place throughout the county's taverns.

"Do you have a suspect, Sheriff?"

"I do. I wonder if you've seen a man in his twenties of medium height and blonde hair with a broad build?"

"There was a fellow like that here a few days ago, and his face looked sort of, well, it had marks on it ..."

Mrs. Lefevre had swished into the room. "Pockmarks, dear, like he'd had a sickness."

"Did you notice anything missing after he was here?"

151

"I most certainly did!" She placed her hands astride her ample hips. "Two good loaves of my rye *brot*. Wheat doesn't grow on trees you, know."

Peter gave a smile and looked at the freshly swept floor. This woman ran a tight establishment. "Have you ever seen this man before?"

"A few months back. I never liked his looks neither," she said. "The pocks I can live with, but it was his surliness, his bossiness. That one wasn't raised right, I tell you!"

"Do you have any idea what his name was?" They both looked at each other and shook their heads. "Please let me know if you see him again. If you do, send word to me right away."

"We will, Sheriff."

❧ • ❧

"Mr. Tatamy, I think this man may be setting up the robberies and spreading rumors you were involved. Would you be willing to help me catch this thief?"

Nicholas pressed his lips together as he leaned on the fence looking toward the hills to the north. "You know, I make it a point not to hold against white men any troubles my family has known." He gave a small laugh. "I am, after all, half white myself. But when someone tries to dishonor me because of my ancestors, that I cannot abide." He turned toward the sheriff. "What do you want me to do?"

"Let it be known to as many people and as publicly as possible, you'll be going to Easton next Thursday. I want that to get back to my suspect."

"Do you think the plan will work?"

"That's my sincere hope, Mr. Tatamy."

CHAPTER TWENTY-ONE

Two weeks and counting before the end of Ethan's school year, and Erin planned to use them to travel hither and yon for documents and proofs to support her application. Sydney had sent her a sample one to fill in, and Erin found the form intimidating, to say the least with its minute requirements about names, dates, and places of relatives she'd never even heard of until recently. Every statement required the necessary "verification," and when she had them all lined up, the final record had to be recorded on acid-free, 24 pound, 25% rag cotton paper. *When we're ready for it,* Sydney had emailed her, *I have an abundant supply, so no need to buy any.* Without her, Erin would be toast.

Thankfully, she'd gathered a great deal of information already from Ancestry.com, so she didn't think there would be all that much left to formally link her to Charles Kichline. On the other hand, she didn't think she'd be anywhere near ready to send her application to DAR headquarters in fourteen days. That particular thought led in the direction of the coming months of vacation and what she was going to do with them. During all the summers of his life, Ethan had enjoyed traveling to the beach and the mountains, to his dad's family reunions, and one or two site seeing trips, often by plane. Jim had been the consummate vacation planner, leaving Erin only to pack. She remembered the way he effortlessly hoisted suitcases, duffle bags, boxes, bikes, and kayaks into and on top of their vehicle, then undid it all when they reached their destination.

A wave of anxiety swept over her as she developed a mental picture of herself doing that on her own. What would this first summer without Jim be like for her and her son? She knew she didn't want to sit around moping, that he needed to have fun. Maybe they could do day trips or brief overnight ones that didn't require a lot of luggage, like to Gettysburg or Baltimore, or perhaps they could team up with her in-laws. Then again, why not go on ancestry trips? They could visit some of the places their long lost relatives had lived, and a good one to begin would be Bedminster, where most of the first Kichlines in America had lived. Maybe they could find Charles's homestead, if it still existed, and locate his grave. One thing was sure, she was going to have to do some summer planning in the next two weeks if she wasn't going to make a huge mess of her son's vacation.

When she wasn't securing documents, Erin was searching for anything she could find on the Internet about the Kichline family. She'd emailed a Bedminster Township employee and received a lovely email with attachments. *Wow! Your family indeed lived in Bedminster, in fact, the town of Keelersville was named after your family. Keelersville is located on Ridge Road on the boundary line of Bedminster and East Rockhill.*

Erin couldn't make a connection between all the random spellings of Kichline and Keelersville, but she figured this woman must know what she was talking about. She referenced a map she attached, and when Erin examined it, she realized with not a little excitement the Kichlines and Fritzes lived in the same general area.

> *Your family donated land to build the first Tohickon Church (now Saint Peter's), originally called "Keichlines Church." The cemetery had many Revolutionary soldiers buried there. The family opened a public house next to the Tohickon Church, and you have a family connection through a marriage to the daughter of Colonel George Piper. The Piper Tavern has an excellent menu and is worth the trip if you find yourself in the area. All this information and MORE are contained in the attachments from the pages of the History of Bedminster book, written by Pauline Cassel and printed by the Bedminster Bicentennial Committee in 1976 making reference to your family name as Keichline and Kelin. I hope the information provided will add to and/or verify your family tree.*

Erin read the documents, marveling at the leadership Colonel Andrew Kichline had shown in that part of Bucks County during the American

Revolution in both the militia and Continental Army also, and how her Charles had been in the Pennsylvania Assembly. She emailed the pastor of the church to see if he had additional information and mentioned she'd be visiting Bedminster in a few days. Then she eagerly reported what she'd found to Sydney, who wrote back in a rather wistful tone:

> *You're lucky you live so close to where your ancestors settled. Many people don't have that luxury and have to either travel great distances, do everything by snail and email, or have someone else do it for them. Those can all get expensive. There's another thing about it—few people live in the same area their ancestors came to hundreds of years ago.*

She considered that last line, sipping iced coffee and looking out the back windows of the sunroom. She remembered how eager she'd been to see the wider world as a teenager, to go way beyond Phillipsburg, Easton, and Allentown; how thrilled she was when her Aunt Barbara had invited her to spend the summer with her in California when Erin was sixteen. Something had completely surprised her there, however. While she had loved seeing the iconic Golden Gate Bridge, Dodger Stadium, Disneyland and the San Diego Zoo, she'd kept a calendar in her diary, crossing off each day as a reminder she'd be back home soon.

Then in college, she'd first gone away to Boston for the thrill of the adventure, but then she'd become so homesick after the first semester she ended up transferring to Lafayette back in Easton. And when she traveled abroad as a senior, she kept another calendar inside her trip journal and kept telling herself she only had a short time to enjoy this experience and then she'd be home.

When she applied to graduate schools, Erin decided on Villanova so she wouldn't be more than an hour's drive from her family, yet not so close she'd be directly enmeshed in their woes and intrigues. Marrying Jim had been a blessing to her with his family concentrated around Lansdale and other parts of Montgomery County, all of them an hour away as well. Experience had taught her she couldn't handle more, and now she understood why. *My ancestors settled in, and occupied, a big swathe of Northampton and Bucks counties for many generations. My roots there go very deep. I belong there.*

"Where is Grandfather Charles's house, Mommy?"

"As far as I've been able to tell, neither his or Great-Uncle Andrew's house is still there," Erin said.

She drove like a snail along the country road flanking her ancestor's property, checking the rearview mirror to make sure she wasn't slowing anyone else down. "I suppose if I dug deeper, I could find out for sure."

"Would you?" His blue eyes lit up, and he smiled. How she loved seeing that.

"I'd like to know, too. But see all that land?" She pointed out the window, and he nodded. "Your seven times great-grandfather owned all of that."

"Wow! So it belongs to us now, too?"

She chuckled. "Not exactly. Over the years, other people have owned it, and I'm not sure whose it is now."

They drove a mile up the road and turned left toward St. Peter's Tohickon Church, a stately colonial building with rounded arch windows and a bright red front door. She read the signage, "Est. 1743," and added, "By my Great-Uncle Andrew." Cemeteries flanked both sides of the road, each of them dappled with flaming azaleas and trees in the prime of their spring finery. Erin parked in the gravel-paved lot, and when they got out of the car, a chorus of crickets and robins chirped their welcome. She stood for a moment to get her bearings, feeling the peacefulness of the quiet country setting, letting the reality soak in that she was a descendant of the people who'd settled this place, who'd laughed, loved, had babies, fought wars and disease, and who now slept in their graves. Erin knew from an email the church secretary had sent that Andrew and his wife, Catherine Benner Kichline, were interred behind the church, but there was no record of burial for Charles or his wife, the former Susannah Bopp.

Many people back then were interred on their property, and there weren't always headstones. That's likely what happened with them.

Erin pushed away disappointment over not being able to visit their graves and pay her respects in favor of the thrill of being in the same place Charles and the rest of her family had lived nearly three hundred years ago. Her thoughts turned back to Ethan and the conversation they'd had at breakfast about visiting a cemetery and her concern it might be upsetting for him so soon after Jim's death. It was hard to know sometimes what would plunge Ethan into sadness—things she could never have anticipated, like going to the produce section of the grocery store one day. Ethan had burst into tears when they were picking out sweet potatoes of all things. "Daddy hated sweet potatoes," he'd said with a sob. Since she'd done the same thing weeks earlier in the cereal aisle, she understood.

"Ethan, are you okay with this?" she asked now, standing there with reminders of death behind and before them.

He scrunched his eyebrows. "Why wouldn't I be?" He didn't wait for an answer. "Those gravestones are so cool, but I have a hard time reading them."

Alright then. He's okay, and I'm okay. Let's do this.

They started looking for Andrew and Catherine's markers among the flat, slab-style markers of the eighteenth century, many with curving curlicues on the top. Time and the elements had worn away a good deal of the lettering, and some were so smooth there wasn't any way to tell whose they were. The cemetery was obviously well cared for, with all of the standing stones upright, although many of them couldn't help but lean. There were no weeds, just freshly cut grass and sprinklings of flowers planted by loved ones. The very day with its mellow warmth and blueness of sky bore witness to hope beyond the grave.

She and Erin found the gravestones a third of the way back, inscribed in German, Andrew's bearing a Revolutionary War marker and an American flag.

"This is it, Ethan!"

They stood before the monuments straining to read the inscriptions, but beyond their names and dates, the rest was too difficult to make out. She wished she'd brought paper and crayons to do a marking, but she wouldn't let Ethan keep crayons in the car when it got hot out. How many of these graves belonged to her long ago family?

As she started considering how she could find out, Ethan spoke.

"Just think, Mommy, we're related to them even though they lived a really, really long time ago. These stones are so old." He ran a hand over his many times great-uncle's marker.

"I think being related like that is pretty neat, huh?" she asked. Although interesting, she still found herself swallowing regret this wasn't Charles's grave, nor was she directly descended from Andrew or Peter, the dashing colonels in the family. Reality chased the feeling away, like Toby going after the neighborhood's stray cat. What did she have to complain about? Charles had been a good man, a quieter man, who'd supported the cause as a member of the Pennsylvania Assembly, for goodness' sake.

She took a lot of pictures including a selfie, which she texted to Melissa.

"What did Uncle Andrew do in the war?" he asked.

"He was a colonel, and he went to Canada on an expedition really early on. I'm trying to find out more."

"Was he killed?"

"Not that I know of." *He did die young, though, about fifty-two. Back then people didn't live nearly as long as they do now. I wonder if widows grieved the same then, or maybe the shock and surprise of losing someone didn't happen as much, or not at all because life was so much harder, more uncertain.*

"Mommy, I wish we'd brought flowers."

"Me too." She wondered why she hadn't thought of that.

"There are some dandelions over there. I'll get a few for their graves." Ethan went off on his mission, then he tenderly draped the yellow weeds over Andrew and Catherine's stones, a gesture whose sweetness brought tears to her eyes. They walked around for several minutes, and on the way back to the car, Ethan picked up a fallen branch and began carrying it as if it were a rifle and he a valiant soldier. She was walking taller herself.

CHAPTER TWENTY-TWO

Grammy Ott's baptismal certificate was as large as Ethan's Pokemon poster, but in far worse shape, having been folded several times. When Erin first unwrapped it, she feared the fragile paper would tear into several pieces, or be stuck together. She took her time and managed to open the document, relieved to find the writing still plainly visible. One thing she knew, she wouldn't put this precious certificate into the plastic folder with her other DAR documents, including her personal records and amazingly, a copy of her parents' marriage certificate, which had somehow survived her mother's wrath. Audrey told Erin to keep the thing, holding it out as if it were going to bite her. Erin still needed "docs" for the previous generations, but at least she was finding most of that on Ancestry.com. When she told Sydney, the regent's response startled her.

Some records from Ancestry are okay; that is if they're official. You can't use anything from family trees—unless there are actual documents to back up the information—because anyone can say anything they want, and inaccuracies get passed along to other members' trees. It doesn't really count unless there is documentation to prove dates, events and relationships.

Although Sydney made sense, Erin regarded the news as a boulder in her path. How in the world she'd ever thought this would be easy! Sydney advised Erin to visit the Easton Area Public Library and any cemeteries for proofs of dates and relationships.

For a price, you can get docs through local, county, and state offices, but I would try going the hands-on route first, though. Since you live so close to Easton, where most of those relatives were from, try their library and local history organizations, which have copies of church records, births, baptisms, marriages, and deaths, especially from the distant past.

She dared herself to pick up the phone. Erin needed her father's birth certificate, and she had never in her life asked him for anything so personal. After their falling out during college and grad school, they'd danced around the edges of politeness, then slowly began a more sustained dance of greater intimacy after Ethan was born. She still couldn't believe her dad hadn't told her until a year after the fact he'd had a heart attack. At this point, their relationship was still a work in progress and asking him for his baptism record felt like she might be getting ahead of things. She also knew how he felt about the DAR. She sat down with a bowl of peanut butter ice cream mixed with jarred pesto to mull it over, Toby sniffing almost disdainfully. "What?" she asked, sounding something like Nicholas Cage. It was time to ask Sydney's advice, although it left her feeling vulnerable.

I understand what you're saying, Erin. I deal with a lot of applications in which first-generation people have serious issues, some where they haven't spoken to a relative in years and aren't about to begin now! If you possibly can, if you think it's worth it, it might not hurt to ask, and if he refuses or you can't bring yourself to do it, then just spend $25 to request a copy from the county courthouse. It will take a little longer to get, that's all. I really do sympathize. Good luck!

"What should I do, Toby?" She scratched behind his voluminous ears. He regarded her soulfully, but then he always looked like that. "My father doesn't even know you, doggie. In fact, he's never visited any home I've lived in as an adult, and now I'm supposed to ask for a copy of his *birth certificate?*" Maybe, *I don't have to call. I could write him a letter first and not worry about getting tongue-tied. He'll have to pay attention, something he usually has trouble doing when I see him, or we talk on the phone. Then I'll call a few days later. Yes, that might just work.*

160

Memories poured through Erin as she drove down Northampton Street toward the library. She remembered her little girl self walking hand-in-hand with her mother and grandmother to Orr's and Pomeroys' Department Stores, and to Farr's for back-to-school Weejuns and Easter patent leather shoes, always with a matching handbag. She recalled hot dog lunches at Woolworths and sweet treats from the Carmelcorn Shop with its sugary aromas that pulled her inside and forced open her relatives' wallets. As a teenager, she'd cruised up and down "the strip" on Saturday nights flirting with local boys in low riders. And what about the endless matinees she and her friends had sat through?

By the time she'd entered Lafayette College, the town's luster had dulled to a tarnish, a casualty of the glitzy Palmer Park and Lehigh Valley Malls. One-by-one the stalwart department stores had fallen like tin soldiers until downtown became a succession of boarded-up store fronts, drug dealers, and the down-and-outs. The more elegant stores like Lenny's, Bixler's, and the London Shop hung on, trying valiantly to keep the city's head above water. It was around that time Erin had decided to live somewhere else, somewhere brighter, where nobody knew her family secrets and not to visit more than necessary.

Erin waited at the light on Sixth Street happy to see the place going through a renaissance. The eateries weren't just restaurants, they were destinations, and although the gaudy Dollar Store still cluttered up the Circle, distinctive shops, renovated historic buildings, the Sigal Museum, and the Crayola Experience dominated it, rather than the other way around. Even the old State Theater had become a spiffed up "center for the performing arts," its current marquee announcing Tony Bennett—*the* Tony Bennett—would be appearing in a few weeks. Back in the day, nobody famous hung around Easton, although a high school friend claimed he'd once seen Billy Joel ordering a Quarter Pounder at McDonald's.

The light turned green, and she drove a block past row houses to the library, perched on a bluff overlooking Route 22. She parked in the lot and walked up to the front entrance, past the imposing sepulcher of Easton's founder, William Parsons. Even as a child, she thought it was more than a little weird to have someone buried in front of a library. Past the circulation and reading areas, Erin found the Marx Room of local history, a glass-enclosed space with long wooden tables and stacks of books lending a gentle scent of paper and bindings. The place was quiet, almost reverent.

Five other people, mostly middle-aged and up, sat at the tables with books and papers fanning around them, reading and copying information. A man stood at the desk talking to the librarian, and Erin figured it might be awhile before she could ask for help. She chose a corner of one table to put her purse and tote bag, and the woman across from her looked up and smiled. She wandered over to a row of green-bound volumes along one wall bearing the names of local churches.

She didn't know where to begin finding her ancestors because she wasn't sure where they'd worshiped, except for her Grammy Ott, who'd been raised Lutheran. Fortunately, there was an index which led her to the books with last names ending in "K." Erin brought it to the table and started looking for her great-grandmother's parents and grandparents, trying to connect the dots with those generations. Right away, she located several entries for Joseph and Samuel Kichline, along with letters and numbers attached to their names, each representing one of Easton's churches, mostly the German Reformed congregation on North Third Street, the one her mother had belonged to as a child.

"My parents never went," Audrey had told Erin more than once, "but my father saw to it we were there every Sunday. He even ironed our dresses and suits."

"Why didn't Grammy do that?"

"I don't know. My dad mostly looked after us. I guess she was busy working."

Like every local child, Erin also knew the church was famous for having served as a hospital during the Revolutionary War. She sometimes had walked past it and imagined the groans of wounded soldiers and their gratitude for a warm place to sleep and a hot meal. She found the church's book and a few minutes later, references for Joseph and his wife, Anna Elizabeth, then his father, Samuel. She returned to the indexes to look up Samuel's father, Joseph, whose own father was Karl, or Charles, her patriot ancestor. There they were! As she filled her notebook with their names and dates, slipping bookmarks between pages she needed to copy, she wondered what kind of lives they'd led, about their work and their homes, their loves and losses. As she sat there, she felt her roots reaching down through the floor, into Easton's very soil.

An hour later she could feel someone standing over her—the librarian, tall, forty-something, with medium length blonde hair, and a pleasant smile. "You look like you're finding what you need. Is there anything I can help you with?"

"I'm doing really well," Erin said. "I'm trying to find birth, marriage, and death documents—I'm applying for membership in the DAR."

"What name are you looking for?"

"Kichline, but there are a lot of different spellings."

The woman laughed. "Don't I know it!"

Erin narrowed her eyes. "You know the name?"

"Why, of course. That's one of Easton's most prominent old families."

Erin felt her chest swell.

"By the way, I'm Sandy."

"Hi, Sandy. Erin Miles." They shook hands.

"Suppose you show me what you found."

Erin took five minutes to share her needs and discoveries. When she finished, she asked, "Do you know where I can find information about my three times great-grandfather's death?"

"I guess you didn't find anything in the church book?"

"Not that one. I'm having some trouble with that record."

"We can take another look," Sandy said, "but we also have obituaries from the local papers going pretty far back. Some are also indexed on our website. By the way, did you know this was once a cemetery?"

A man interrupted them as he walked toward the door. "Bye, Sandy. Thanks for the help."

"You're welcome. Tell your aunt I said hello." She back turned to Erin. "So, the library stands on the site of the German Reformed Church burial ground."

Could that be why Williams Parsons was buried near the entrance? "I grew up here, but I never knew about that." She paused. "So, my ancestors were buried here?"

"Most likely, yes."

"How did a cemetery ever become a library?" She was incredulous.

"In the early 1900s, Andrew Carnegie started giving money to communities to start or expand their libraries, and for some reason this spot had to be used for the new library."

"What about the cemetery, though?"

"The graves were dug up and reinterred, many of them just up the road at the Easton Cemetery." She pointed in that direction.

"I thought they might still be under here," she said.

"Actually, there still are about thirty people buried here in a mass vault, ones that couldn't be identified or claimed by their families."

"They're under the building?" Erin's skin tingled.

"Yes, and the parking lots."

The subject of dead bodies was still raw. "Do you know what happened to my Kichline family?"

"They're up in the Easton Cemetery," Sandy said. "All you have to do is go there and ask at the office right outside the gates. We also have a chart in the back of where everyone was buried on this site. Would you like to see it?"

"Uh, sure." She followed Sandy past several rows of books to a back wall with maps and antique photos adorning it. The librarian pointed to one of them toward the bottom that listed the names and burial locations of people.

Erin moved closer to find Kichline or Kachlein, and there were, in fact, several names, but the tiny print hindered her ability to tell who was who.

"I guess you know about Colonel Kichline, right? He was an important leader in the Revolution, and he was buried here."

"Yes, I know. He's actually my six times great-uncle," Erin said.

"Nice! I've had a lot of people come in here looking for information about him." Sandy leaned closer. "You know, some people say this place is haunted because the dead didn't like to have their graves disturbed."

Erin shivered. "Really?"

"I remember working at my desk once when I was alone, and I felt a cold presence." A chill shot up Erin's right calf. When she didn't respond, Sandy dropped the subject and offered to make copies of the records Erin needed. "I'll be sure to include the front matter—the DAR's a stickler about that. Several minutes later, Erin paid for the copies.

"Thanks so much for your time and help," she said. "I've really enjoyed getting to know more about my family and how far back they go in Easton's history. I never knew this until now."

"Do you still live here?" Sandy asked.

"No. I've lived in Lansdale since I was married. My family is still up here, though."

"Not everyone can get away from a job to do this kind of research."

"Actually, I'm off for the summer. I'm a professor."

"Where?"

"Hatfield College. I teach history." She felt dishonest saying that, but she didn't want to tell Sandy the whole story.

"History seems to be in your DNA," the librarian said. "Well, I look forward to seeing you again sometime."

Erin suddenly remembered something. "Oh, I do have one more question. There's a document of some kind about the Kichline family."

"I think you mean 'The Kichlines in America.' We have a copy here but …" She looked at other patrons lined up at her desk.

"No problem. I can find it another time."

"You can find the text online. Just Google the document."

Erin drove down Northampton Street looking for a place to have lunch, identifying at least three restaurants she would've loved eating at with Jim. Tears began streaking down her cheeks, and she reached into the box of tissues in the center console. *It must've been all that talk about cemeteries and corpses.* She wasn't in the mood for a sit-down lunch now. Instead, she found a parking spot in the Circle and walked across North Third Street to the Dunkin' Donuts where she got a toasted garlic and onion bagel with strawberry cream cheese and an iced latte. She ate them on a bench outside the Crayola Experience watching young families coming in and out of the vibrant building. *The next time I bring Ethan to town, we'll go there. That will get this summer off to a good start. It's time to begin making new family memories, even though I wish the three of us were making them.*

❦ • ❦

CHAPTER TWENTY-THREE

He wasn't entirely unhappy to find Anna Doll standing in his kitchen, but at the same time, he felt baffled by the sight of her. Where was Phoebe, and why was Anna looking so grim, so unlike her usual, pleasant self? He recovered his wits and greeted her with a slight bow. "Good day, Fräulein Doll."

"Good day, Sheriff Kichline."

Has something happened to Susannah? He felt his gut wrench at the thought.

"I hope you're not upset to see me here, I mean so unexpectedly, that is." This frazzled young woman was normally the soul of calm.

"You're always welcome here, but where are Susannah and my niece?"

She shook her head, looking at the floor. "Susannah's with my sister." She paused. "I hate to tell you this, Herr Kichline, but Phoebe's gone."

"Gone? Where has she gone?"

Anna reached into her pocket and produced a smeared note, scrawled in what appeared to have been great haste. "Susannah says she woke up about five o'clock this morning and found this outside your door. She brought it to me, and when we returned, Phoebe was gone."

"May I see it?" He reached out for the paper, feeling annoyed his daughter hadn't come to him first. The message was written on a corner of *The Pennsylvania* Gazette, which he slid a little further from his eyes to read: *Dear Uncle Peter, I am sorry, but I must leave. It's for everyone's good. Please don't try to find me. Yours, Phoebe Benner*

He knew instinctively she was in trouble. Big trouble. *She left us in a tight spot, something she wouldn't have done without a very good reason. I know that much about her. Something frightened her badly, and I need to find out what happened, and where she is. If only this hadn't occurred when I'm about to break this other case open.* He let out a long breath and shook his head. He noticed Anna's hands trembling.

"I'm very much afraid for her," she said. "Do you have any idea what might have happened?"

"No, but I'm going to find out."

"I'll stay here again if you like." Her eyes met his, then quickly lowered.

"How can I ever express my gratitude?"

"You just did."

He bowed from his waist. "I thank you sincerely."

"I'm only too happy to help."

He looked around, snapping into investigative mode.

"Papa, I didn't know she was leaving." Susannah buried her small face in his chest.

He patted her back. "There, there, no one is blaming you." He felt her body shaking, and although he was in a hurry to get information, he knew better than to rush her. A few minutes later he took her by the shoulders, smiled, and kissed her cheek. "My dear girl, I need to ask you some questions. Do you think you can answer them now?"

She closed her eyes and nodded resolutely. Anna smiled encouragement from the chair she sat in nearby.

"Do you know where Phoebe was during the day yesterday?"

"She was here mostly," Susannah said.

"Did anyone come to visit?"

"Yes. Mr. Hanlon." She smiled as if she were privy to a secret. "I think he's sweet on Phoebe."

"Yes, well, was there anyone else?"

"No, Papa."

"Where were your brothers?"

"Peter worked at your desk while Mr. Hanlon was here, then he went to the mill after my teacher left."

"What about Andrew and Jacob?"

"They were already at the mill."

"After Mr. Hanlon left and Peter went to the mill, were you alone with Phoebe?"

"Yes, Papa."

How could he ask this? "What was she like?"

"We laughed about some things, things that, well, you might not understand." She colored slightly.

"I see. Were you together all day?"

Susannah looked up at the ceiling and gave a start. "There's a spider up there!"

Peter looked up and saw the black insect dangling in the corner. "I'll take care of it when we finish talking. Please try to answer my question, *liebling*."

"Um, we were together most of the day, except for right after supper. I was playing with my doll, and Peter was reading in your chair. She said she was going out for a little while."

"Do you know where she went?" *Now we're were getting somewhere.*

"I wasn't paying much attention, Papa."

"Think as hard as you can about it."

A horse whinnied outside the windows, followed by a man shouting in German, then it quieted to the usual background hum of Northampton Street.

"Well, she did say something about taking food to someone."

Anna broke in. "Phoebe has mentioned to me she goes to the Weeds to help out."

"I see." He turned to his daughter. "Is that where she went, Susannah, to see Mrs. Weed?"

She lit up with excitement. "I'm sure of it, Papa!"

"How long was she gone?"

"Let me think." She scrunched her eyebrows and pulled at her chin. "Not too long."

"What happened when she returned?"

"Oh, Papa, she was as white as a ghost. It was like she saw me, but she didn't really see me." Susannah waved her hands, flustered. "I mean, she looked past me."

"Did she say anything?"

"No, she just went right to her room."

"Were your brothers here then?"

"Andrew was upstairs," Susannah said. "I don't know where Peter and Jacob were."

"Where did you find Phoebe's note?"

"It was on the floor by your door when I woke up this morning. I couldn't sleep, so I got up early."

He leaned closer, putting his hands on her shoulders. "Why didn't you show it to me?"

"Because, Papa, you needed your sleep and besides, Anna Doll understands things. And, well, she's part of our family now."

He collected his thoughts, willing them into submission.

Anna spoke up. "When we went to her room, Miss Benner's satchel was gone and all of her clothes."

This is not good. Not good at all.

He tried to reassure Susannah with a pat on her shoulder then headed out for the Weed cabin, relieved Anna was helping his daughter deal with her emotions. Margaretta had always been so capable when it came to making the rough places smooth in their children's lives while he usually just felt clunky. A man needed a good wife for so many reasons.

A striped gray and black cat followed him as he walked down Julianna Street toward the Weeds' cabin and stood at a respectable distance while Peter looked around their barn for Weed and his son. Clouds hovered low in the sky, pressing moisture through the air. Once they lifted, he thought, it was going to be a very hot day. He found the meager animal shelter empty except for some stacks of hay. The pigs were gone and with them, their owners, likely out to pond or pasture, although he hadn't seen them in the Great Square as he passed by. Something didn't feel right, but he couldn't put his finger on it. Inside, he found Mrs. Weed alone in her bed coughing, her face the color of day-old bread.

"Why, S-sheriff, welcome," she said, which set off another coughing spell.

He reminded himself to be gentle with her. "Good day, madam."

"P-please, h-have a seat."

He picked up a chair with one hand and set it close enough to talk, but not to catch her sickness. She looked much more frail than on his last visit.

"W-where is M-miss B-Benner?" Her faded blue eyes looked past him.

"She is elsewhere today. How are you?"

"W-weaker, I'm afraid," she said, then stopped to cough again. "I was glad to see her y-yesterday. She is d-dear."

"Yes, she is."

More coughing.

"She brought pudding. And br-bread."

She looked eager to talk but quite incapable. He knew he couldn't stay long, or he'd wear her out, but he needed information and hoped he'd be able to get as much from her as he could.

"Yes, she is quite the cook. Did anyone else get to enjoy the food?" he asked.

"Husband. Son, too, before he left."

His pulse quickened. "He probably was going to work, then?"

"Yes. Fr-frau Eckert."

"Does anyone else look in on you?"

"M-Miss Doll. Sometimes her s-sisters."

"Then you have made some friends in our little village since coming here. That's good." He'd chosen his words carefully, hoping she'd take the bait.

She nodded. "The Dolls, P-pow-wow, and another young man."

Peter leaned closer, his pulse quickening. "He's a friend of your son, then?"

"Yes. B-brings flowers and f-food." She coughed more quietly this time.

He took a chance. "I'm having another strong man like that around is helpful."

"D-Duncan is v-very strong."

Duncan.

When Mrs. Weed broke into a deep coughing spell, he went outside to get cold water from the well and after giving it to her stayed a few more minutes, eager to get on with his investigation. Something told him to go inside the barn once more. As he approached the building, he noticed a pile of hay lying there haphazardly, and he went over and began kicking at it until his boot struck a clump of dirt underneath. The cat that had followed him slunk over and stood watching as Peter bent down and started digging with his hands. In less than a minute, he uncovered the work of many days: an assortment of cookware, bowls, and silver.

The star charm was no longer at the entrance to Frau Eckert's establishment, and when he went inside, she was laughing with customers near the main fireplace. When she saw him, she broke into a broad grin. "Oh, Herr Kichline! I'm very glad to see you!" She came flying at him and for a moment, he was afraid she was actually going to throw her arms around him. "It's back! My bridal box is back!" She clapped like Susannah whenever the little girl was especially excited.

He frowned, wondering how this had come about.

"The charm worked! Oh, I'm so happy!"

He nodded slowly. "I'm very pleased for you, Frau Eckert. When did this happen?" *Does this have anything to do with John Weed or that Duncan fellow? Could John have stolen the box and for some reason, returned it?*

"Yesterday afternoon I went to my chamber, and there it was, sitting on my bed just as you please!"

"Do you have any idea how the box got there?"

"Why, of course, Herr Kichline." She regarded him as if to say, "Are you so thick?" She said, "The charm did it!"

He ignored that bit of information. "Were the contents intact?"

A cloud suddenly darkened her face. "No, sir, and I can't say I'm happy about losing the spices I kept in it, but they're nothing compared to the box itself."

He looked over at the bar where Martin stood wiping it down, and their eyes met. The young man smiled and nodded, appearing relieved. No, that was not a guilty face, not that he ever thought so. As for John Weed and Duncan …

❧ • ❧

He found the school teacher talking to Mr. Wiggins in the Great Square and after greeting them, noticed his tag-along cat had slipped into the wider world of townspeople and animals.

"I wonder if I might have a private word with you, Mr. Hanlon," he said.

"Why certainly. Excuse me, Mr. Wiggins."

They walked a few paces away from the building. "I wonder if you're especially busy today," Peter asked, his hand on the young man's right shoulder. He knew the teacher would help. Hanlon and Phoebe had met in Bedminster, and it was obvious there was a spark between the two young people.

"Not today, sir. Is there something I can do for you?"

"As a matter of fact, there is. I could use your confidence in a matter."

"Yes, of course."

He steered Hanlon further away from people, and he quietly and quickly told him about Phoebe's disappearance. Predictably, the teacher's expression mirrored what was going on in his mid-section.

"What do you think happened?" Hanlon asked.

"I don't exactly know, but I'm torn between two urgent matters: her disappearance and a case I'm this close to resolving, which may actually be related." He held his right forefinger and thumb an inch apart. "I'm being pulled in two different directions."

"What would you like me to do?"

"Go to the livery and tell Mr. Armstrong to let you borrow one of my horses. Then go to the mill and get Peter or Andrew to help you search for Phoebe. They have their own horses and can saddle up quickly. Jacob will need to stay close to home. I'm guessing she's started for Bedminster, down the river road."

"Yes, of course, right away, sir. What should we do if, uh, *when* we find her?"

"Bring her back to Easton. Doing so is a matter of the utmost urgency, Mr. Hanlon. Do everything you can to reassure her."

"How should I do that, Sheriff?"

He grinned. "I don't think you'll have any trouble figuring it out."

❧ • ☙

CHAPTER TWENTY-FOUR

As desperately as he wanted to look for Phoebe himself, something said "stay put," the thief might just be showing himself in town, and Peter would need to be there. He trusted young Hanlon, an experienced traveler who knew the way to Bedminster, and Peter, Jr. would be a capable companion, who also was familiar with the route. If anyone could find Phoebe, those two could. He prayed they'd do it quickly—a young woman wandering about in the woods in a poor mental state would make an easy target. He suspected she'd stumbled onto something sinister during her visit to the Weed cabin, and as an image of John Weed appeared in his mind's eye, he clenched his hands. He wanted to wring that young man's neck. God help him if he had hurt or threatened his niece. He walked briskly to the Bachmann Publick House to tell the Taylors he was close to making an arrest, to keep especially alert.

"And I'll bet that thief isn't Nicholas Tatamy," Ann Taylor said with a huff. She obviously didn't share Frau Eckert's sentiments.

Peter decided not to let even these good people know what he knew and remained silent.

"At any rate, Sheriff, I'm ready for him." She patted the keys at her side, the ones securing padlocks on the grill that came down every night to guard the bar's valuables.

"Good thinking, Mrs. Taylor," he said. "I don't mean to alarm you, just to give fair warning."

He stopped at the other taverns, as well as Meyer Hart's store, to encourage their vigilance, then he walked toward home. Just past the courthouse, he saw Egbert Weed and his son with their pigs, and the father saluted him with a wave. John, on the other hand, barely nodded and looked away. This fellow was likely hiding more than just the stolen items he'd so poorly buried. Anger swelled in his gut, and Peter drew upon deep reserves of self-restraint to keep from grabbing the fellow by the collar and dragging him off to jail. The site of John's forlorn-looking father and the belief that acting nonchalant was best helped him keep his hands at his side and his temper in check.

"Good day, Sheriff," Egbert said.

"Good day, Mr. Weed." He turned to the son. "John."

"Hello, Sheriff." He sounded like he had a wad of linen stuffed in his mouth.

"How is your dear wife, sir?"

"Bad off." Egbert shook his head. "I don't know what to do. I pray all the time for her to get well."

"Prayer is always a good idea," Peter said.

"Thank you for sending your housekeeper to us. She's been so kind. She's also quite charming, isn't she, John?"

Peter shot a glance at the son, whose eyes bore the look of a cornered rabbit. The young man coughed into his closed hand and looked away.

"Let me know if there's anything I can do for you, Mr. Weed." Peter touched the corner of his hat and said, "Good day." He was so into his thoughts on the way home he blew right past Robert Traill, who looked after him with his mouth hanging open and his hand half raised.

Peter nearly collided with his daughter when they rushed to the front door as William Hanlon carried Phoebe inside, Peter, Jr. following just behind. Anna Doll came around the corner and led the teacher to the back chamber near the kitchen, fluffing the pillow and pulling the covers down. Hanlon laid her the young woman on the bed, and Anna removed Phoebe's soiled white cap, then her muddy shoes. Dirt and blood smudged the young woman's face, and Peter saw she'd been scratched several times on her cheeks and arms. Her eyes were closed, but she was moaning and shivering.

"Does she have fever?" he asked.

Anna put the palm of her hand against Phoebe's brow. She looked into his blue eyes, filled with concern and anger. "No, Herr Kichline, she's in a stupor."

"Is she going to be alright?" Susannah asked through trembling lips.

Anna answered for him. "She'll be fine once we clean her up and feed her." He remembered how Margaretta used to complete him like that.

"Would you please get some clean cloths and a basin, Susannah?" Anna asked.

The little girl flew from the room.

Phoebe's eyes opened a little, and she smiled weakly at Anna, then Hanlon. When she noticed Peter, however, she sat straight up and screamed, "Get me out of here!"

Peter gave a start. *What in the world?*

"All is well, dear Phoebe." Anna's voice was soothing as she pushed her gently back on the bed. "You've had a fright. You need to rest."

"I have to leave!" She started sobbing.

He wanted to do something, anything to relieve her fears. Peter, Jr. came up next to him and whispered, "She's been like this on and off."

He motioned to his son and Hanlon to follow him out of the room and, catching Anna's eye, he inclined his head toward the door. "I'll be back when she's calmed down." The men gathered in the parlor where he took note of their wrinkled, dirty clothes and disheveled hair. He guessed they must be hungry and thirsty, so he went to the kitchen and found a pitcher of water and some mugs, as well as a cake of cornbread. They drank thirstily, then started telling what happened while they ate.

"We found her halfway between Easton and Bedminster," his son said, wiping crumbs from his lips with his fingers. "She'd been following the river road."

"She was hiding in some holly bushes, but her scarlet cape gave her away," Hanlon added.

Peter, Jr. nodded. "She was all huddled up in a little ball, shaking, and when she saw us, she started crying."

"She seemed happy at first, but then she got like she was just now," Hanlon said.

"She kept saying we were in danger, we had to go back, but we made her come," young Peter said. "That wasn't very pleasant. Fortunately, she didn't have much fight left."

"Did she give any reason why she thought you'd be in danger?" his father asked.

"No, sir."

"We couldn't get it out of her." Hanlon was pale, his hands trembling from the experience. "We just kept trying to reassure her we wouldn't let anything bad happen. She wasn't worried about herself—just us." He paused for a long drink of cider. "Something is terrifying her, Sheriff, that's for sure. Do you have any idea what it is?"

"I believe I do."

❧ • ☙

He waited to gain entrance to Phoebe's sick room, remembering how he'd felt this way before, actually four other times when Margaretta was delivering their children. He disliked feeling helpless and anxious like he wanted to jump right out of his skin but couldn't figure out how. Apparently his son and William Hanlon were going through the same thing, the three of them pacing like bobcats. Finally, Peter, Jr. could take it no more. "I'll be at the mill checking on Andrew and Jacob," he said, heading out the door.

He knew he could check on things in town, but there was only one thing on his mind, and he didn't feel like discussing anything else with anyone else. He picked up a volume of Bede and found himself reading the same paragraph three times before the words registered. Hanlon appeared to be going through the same thing with his beloved Milton. Four hours later, as the sun drifted toward the west, Anna entered the parlor, her skin pale against her blonde hair, which had escaped from her cap in several places. Peter and Hanlon jumped from their chairs and dropped their books in tandem.

"How is she?" the sheriff blurted.

"She woke up a little while ago and sipped some broth. Then she said she was hungry, so I gave her bread."

"Is her mind clear?"

She frowned. "Yes, but she's still terribly afraid."

"Has she said why?"

Anna shook her head.

"When may I see her? I think I can help," he said.

"How about if I make supper for you while Susannah stays with her, then you can go in? I think she just needs a little more time."

He didn't want to wait. He wanted to go. Now. An hour ago. Two hours ago. "Alright," he said.

❧ • ☙

After a light meal, he visited Phoebe's room by himself thinking she'd be more willing to talk openly one-on-one. He hoped he was right. Candlelight bathed the room as night fell, and in spite of her earlier agitation, Peter thought Anna and Susannah had brought her a measure of peace. "I'm glad to see you're doing better, Phoebe. We've all been very concerned."

"I'm sorry I made such trouble."

"You mustn't think of that." He sat across from her. "My dear niece, you need to tell me what happened."

Tears rolled down her cheeks. "I, I can't, Uncle Peter. I just can't."

He chose his words carefully and deliberately softened his tone. He didn't want her going off again. "He has no power over you."

She turned her head and stared at him as if he'd unlocked some truth. "Oh, but he does!"

This was progress. "What has he told you he'll do?" He wasn't sure if "he" was John Weed or Duncan.

She looked down at the sheets covering her. "He said … oh, please don't make me, Uncle Peter! Please!"

She was shaking and, praying for wisdom, he took a chance. "Duncan is a weak man."

Her eyes flew open, and she finally looked into his. "He doesn't seem that way to me!"

Good. "That's just his image. I know differently."

"You do?"

"Yes, and he can't hurt you, Phoebe. I won't let him."

"Oh, but Uncle Peter, I'm not worried about myself. It's, it's—you!"

"Me?" He felt the wind go out of him.

"He said if I told you, he knew where you lived, and he would … Oh, I can't tell you!"

Deep breath. "He's lying, Phoebe. Men like him are cowards."

"Please don't make me." Her voice was that of a child.

He covered her trembling hand with his, finding it almost as small as Susannah's. "Tell me what happened. Telling me will help a lot of people."

She inhaled sharply and appeared to be wavering. Finally, she relented. "Mrs. Weed is so nice, and she's so sick. I took her food, and her son, John, was there. He got up and went outside like he'd remembered something he had to do. I didn't think anything of it and stayed awhile longer. When I left their cabin, I sort of got turned around. I mean, I forgot how to get back home." Her slight body trembled under the covers. "I walked by that sort of barn they have, and John was standing there with someone, a thick sort of man with reddish-blonde hair and, and cruel eyes." Tears rolled down her cheeks.

"His name is Duncan," Peter said.

She stared at him for a moment, then continued talking, "I hid behind a barrel while they were talking about things they'd stolen. John was handing him a copper porringer, and the man yelled at him because he expected more. Then John said, 'There is more,' Then the man—Duncan—said something about a, I think it was that woman's bridal box, and how John was a fool, and he'd better not try anything like that again, or he'd, he'd … Oh, Uncle Peter—he'd make sure Mrs. Weed didn't get better!" She covered her face with her scratched hands shimmering slightly from Anna's ointment.

An unholy urge rose in him to take Duncan by the throat. *If he touched my niece. . .*

She went on with the story. "John was upset, trying to smooth things over. He seemed like he didn't want Duncan to be there but couldn't do anything about it. He said he'd steal more to make up for it, but taking a bridal box wasn't right. I suddenly sneezed, and that's when they found me. Duncan yanked me by my arm and demanded to know who I was, but I was too scared to say anything. When he asked John, he said I was the sheriff's niece. I was so scared, Uncle Peter."

She surprised him by sitting up with a show of strength, yet managed to look strangely vulnerable, her eyes wide. He instinctively leaned closer.

"That horrible man asked me what I'd heard them talking about, but I was too afraid to speak. He knew, though. That's when he said if I told anyone, especially you, he would kill me and then he'd find you alone, then my cousins, and … I had to run away. What else could I do?" She started sobbing, which brought Anna to the door. A look of understanding passed between them.

He sat on the edge of the bed and held Phoebe, feeling her tears dampening his waistcoat. Nothing was going to happen to her, his children, or himself. As for Duncan …!

CHAPTER TWENTY-FIVE

He needed help, but he couldn't spread the alarm too generally, or Duncan might disappear only to resurface and cause havoc somewhere else. Peter had seen that pile of goods hidden on the Weed property, and Duncan would be around to collect before long. Just how long, Peter didn't know, and that's why he had to step carefully and lay a foolproof trap. He considered bringing John Weed on board, but he didn't want to scare him off, or compromise his family's safety. Besides, he didn't really know the youth's motives in all of this, whether he'd been strong-armed into stealing, or was a willing participant, although he suspected the former. For now, he wouldn't let on to Weed that he knew anything.

He went to Robert Traill, a physically strong man who could be counted upon for discretion, and shared his idea.

"Count me in," Traill said, his broad chest appearing even more expansive, his ruddy face full of conviction. "I'd like to see the back of that reprobate."

Peter also sought out his boys at the mill, asking one of them to volunteer their help. His namesake was quickest to respond.

"I'll stay home with the women," Andrew said.

"Me, too," Jacob said.

Back at the house, he found William Hanlon in the parlor, his face tight with worry. Peter sat him down and told him what was going on.

"What can I do? Please let me do something to help," Hanlon said.

"Would you be willing to assist Mr. Traill?"

"I'm in, sir, anything you need."

Finally, Peter rode out to Nicholas Tatamy's farm to tell him about Duncan and John Weed.

"Well, that's a relief," the still hatless man said, passing a red handkerchief across his brow. "I'll come to town as soon as I finish up here."

"I'll help you here." Peter removed his outer coat and rolled up his sleeves, feeling the relief of their absence in the early summer heat. Less than an hour later, they started heading back to Easton, Mrs. Tatamy and the children waving from the house.

The place was busy—conversation, cards, beer and rum flowing freely, along with lively fiddle music.

"Sheriff Kichline!" She broke away from her other customers.

He removed his hat and stepped toward her. "*Guten abend*, Frau Eckert. I'm happy to see your establishment so busy."

She took him by the arm. "And I'm happy to see you. Actually, I've been seeing a lot of you recently," she said not a little coquettishly.

An uncustomary screech from the fiddle made him wince, and when he looked over at John Weed standing by the fireplace, their eyes met. The young man blanched, glanced at his instrument, and began playing "Pop Goes the Weasel" in earnest as patrons tapped their feet.

Pace yourself, Peter told himself. Take whatever time is needed.

Frau Eckert steered him toward the only empty table, in a side room where she pointed to a chair and, hovering over him, pressed her bosom against his shoulder. He instinctively moved out of range, scraping the chair against the wide floor boards.

"What can I get you, Sheriff? The drink will be on the house."

"*Danke*. I'll have an ale," he said.

"Anything for you. I know just the kind you like." She hurried off on her mission.

He preferred sitting in the main room so he could observe the crowd, especially to see if Duncan might be hanging around. It seemed as if the fellow preferred lurking among the shadows, but he might show his face at some point, especially if he'd been imbibing. Moments later, the tavern keeper returned with his drink.

"Here you go, Sheriff." She placed the pewter mug on the table. "Is there anything else I can get you?" She cocked her head.

"Ah, no, thank you very much. This will be fine."

"I'll keep you company shortly, but there are so many customers tonight." She waved her arm toward them.

"I'm fine."

She winked and swished out of the room. What was it with her? Disliking the isolation, he rose with his ale and moved toward the main room where he stood in the doorway nodding to several men. Mr. Chatterfield motioned for him to join him and two others, so Peter walked over and spoke for several minutes, mostly about the good effect on the village of the Stamp Act's repeal. At just the right moment, Nicholas Tatamy walked through the door.

"Gentlemen, would you allow my friend Mr. Tatamy to join us?" Peter asked.

"Why, yes, of course," Chatterfield said. His companions looked like they wanted to say otherwise but not in the Sheriff's presence.

Peter waved Tatamy over. "I believe you and Mr. Chatterfield are acquainted, and these are …"

"Yes, I know them as well," Tatamy said. "Good evening."

"Good evening, Mr. Tatamy," the tailor said, and his friends muttered their greetings.

Martin came heading toward their table until Frau Eckert bumped him out of the way with her left hip. "Sheriff, I couldn't find you …" She stopped abruptly. "If it isn't Mr. Tatamy." Ice coursed through her remark.

"He's my guest this evening, Frau Eckert," Peter said lightly, yet in such a way as not to be disputed.

"What can I get you?" she asked.

"Do you have cider?" Tatamy asked.

"Of course. And what about the rest of you?"

"We're good for now, Frau Eckert," Chatterfield said, speaking for his companions.

The men made small talk, which Peter always found difficult, preferring to get straight to a point and quickly. Small talk had its advantages on a night like this, however, so he played the game. When John Weed laid his fiddle aside to take a break, Peter excused himself a few moments later and found the youth standing behind the tavern in the dark, looking from side to side. Conversations from inside mingled with the energetic chirping of invisible crickets.

"Good evening, Mr. Weed,"

The young man did a great imitation of a frog jumping. "Oh, uh, good evening, Sheriff."

Light spilled onto them from the windows, and Peter saw the tavern keeper's ample silhouette. She was probably wondering where he went.

"I'm enjoying your fiddle playing."

"Uh, thank you, sir."

Peter saw him stuff something into his waist coast. "Will you be playing more?"

"Uh, yes, sir. Frau Eckert gives me a five-minute break every hour."

"That should be just long enough to steal something," he said casually.

"Wh-what?"

"I know what's going on, Mr. Weed. In fact, I'm ready to haul you to prison over what you've stolen, as well as how you've stirred up the entire village against Mr. Tatamy." He moved closer, chest-to-chest, or more like his chest to Weed's forehead. "Not to mention how you frightened my niece so badly she found it necessary to run away, which greatly endangered her."

"That wasn't me, sir!" His voice was a shout-whisper.

"Oh, so you didn't steal anything?"

"No, I mean, yes, sir, I did, but I didn't want to. I, uh, I got caught up in ..." He looked past Peter, his eyes growing wilder by the second.

"Mr. Weed, I'm not feeling very charitable toward you right now," Peter said.

"Nor am I toward you, Sheriff," came a voice from the darkness.

Duncan's muscular figure hovered into their circle, and in the glow from the windows, Peter saw the flash of a pistol aiming straight at his head.

"You seem to be at the wrong place at the wrong time, Sheriff, or maybe this is the right place and time, at least for me." Sneering lips framed his tobacco-stained teeth, the pale, pocked face full of insolence. "I'd like to know what you're doing out here with the sheriff of all people, Weed." He waved the gun at the young man. "I'm beginning not to trust you. First, you return my stuff, now you're cavorting with the law."

Weed was shaking so hard Peter thought he might faint.

"He came out here on his own," Weed said. "I have nothing to do with him. Honest."

"Honest!" Duncan mimicked him. "You know what's going to happen for snitching."

"I didn't snitch!"

"Well, did he or didn't he, Sheriff?" Duncan moved the gun back toward Peter's face.

The thief revolted him. "You're in no position to speak to me that way."

"Oh, but I am. Put down your weapon, Sheriff."

"What makes you think I have a weapon, Duncan?" he asked.

The broad-chested youth started, surprised to hear his name. "You're the law. You carry a weapon." He spat a wad of brown juice onto the ground between them.

Peter wasn't about to hand his flintlock over.

"Are you deaf, Sheriff? Give me your weapon, now! Otherwise, I blow you, and this here snitch to pieces. After that, his pathetic mother and father. Your choice."

Peter's mind filled with the image of Phoebe shivering in terror because of this miserable excuse of a human being.

"Just throw it on the ground," Duncan said.

Peter produced the firearm and just as he was about to fire at Duncan, another weapon discharged. Seeing the startled look on the thief's face, Peter lunged forward and kicked Duncan in the chest with his foot, sending him reeling. As he was falling, Duncan pointed his gun at Peter's head and fired, missing by the length of a small fingernail. At that, Peter and the hidden gunman shot Duncan simultaneously, and he thudded to the ground, blood oozing from his right temple and chest. He died more quietly than he'd ever lived.

Nicholas Tatamy came up beside Peter. John Weed was on his knees, overcome.

"You have excellent timing, Mr. Tatamy,"

"And you have excellent instincts, Sheriff."

Frau Eckert's voice rose above the shouts and calls of men who'd rushed toward the windows and outside to see what was happening. "What's going on out there?"

"We caught your thief, madam," Peter said, his voice rising above the din.

"I told you about that Indian!"

Peter's blood stirred. "That Indian just saved my life. Your thief is here on the ground."

∽ • ∾

In a back room of the tavern, Peter sat at a table questioning a pale and shaking Weed while Tatamy stood by the door making sure no one entered. "How did you get involved with him?"

"I didn't want to, Sheriff. I was just so afraid of him."

"Why?"

"He found me one night after I started playing here. I was on my way home, and he told me to steal things from Frau Eckert. He'd give me a share of what he took."

"And you did."

"I didn't think I had much of a choice, sir. He was so cruel and threatening if I didn't."

"Why didn't you inform me?" Peter asked.

"That was part of his ul, ul ..."

"Ultimatum."

"Yes, his ultimatum. If I refused to steal, and if I reported him, he said he would, he would kill my m ..."

Peter took a deep breath, guessing this was what Duncan had done at the Sun Inn in Bethlehem, too.

"I didn't want to do it, sir. I even returned Frau Eckert's box because that especially wasn't right. There was never any question of any of it being right, and I'm so sorry your niece stumbled into this."

"You'll have to stand before the judge," Peter said. "In the meantime, you'll be in jail."

"B-but what about my mother? My parents? You're right of course, sir, but I'm afraid for my mother."

"I'll walk home with you and tell them what happened." That was something he didn't look forward to.

They reached the Weed's cabin at almost ten o'clock where Peter told his look-outs what had transpired.

"We'll wait outside while you speak to Mr. and Mrs. Weed," young Peter said.

"Thank you, son." Peter could see the concern in his eyes. As they went through the door to the cabin, he knew in his gut something was wrong. Egbert Weed, hunched over his wife's bed, didn't hear them come in. In that moment, Peter saw himself four months ago at another bedside. Mrs. Weed was dead.

അ • ഇ

Justice came swiftly to John Weed, but not until he'd had an opportunity to bury his mother, who never knew of his troubles with Duncan, whose last name had been Draper. The thief had come from Norristown near Philadelphia, terrifying young people into assisting him, never paying them more than a pittance, while constantly threatening them. Fortunately, he hadn't made good on any of his threats to kill people, although he'd come mighty close the other night. The judge had brought Weed and three others like him into the courtroom, deciding their punishment would be a day in the stocks. Peter considered this fair—these weren't willful thieves, but they had participated in Draper's crimes. Nor had they reported him as they should've done, although they'd been living under the threat of violence to their families and themselves.

Late in June, Peter found Egbert Weed near his cabin feeding his pigs under a blazing sun.

"Sheriff." Weed nodded from under the brim of his hat.

"Mr. Weed. How are you and your son faring? I haven't seen you in the Great Square."

"I haven't felt welcome." He paused. "Nor should I be." The grunting pigs filled the silence. "My son isn't a criminal, Sheriff."

Peter sensed he had more to say, so he waited.

"Neither is he a farmer. He wants to play music." He took off his hat and wiped a handkerchief across his perspiring forehead. "Actually, sir, I am not much for farming myself."

"Your pigs are looking well."

"I plan to sell them once the Old Pig Drover shows up again, then we'll move back to Philadelphia. My son would like to make violins, and perhaps we can open a shop together. We can put Easton behind us."

"I wish it had turned out differently for you, Mr. Weed." Peter became thoughtful. "Sometimes we take risks because we wonder what's out there and what we might be able to do, just as my mother and stepfather did when they brought my family to America many years ago. It was what I did when I left them in Bedminster to start my own life in Easton. Sometimes our risks pay off, but at times, they don't." He paused. "I wish you and your son God's peace."

After checking in at the courthouse, he walked up Northampton Street to his home finding Phoebe in the kitchen chopping carrots and leeks. They smiled at each other, enjoying an unspoken joy over her recovered health and spirits.

"Is it alright if Mr. Hanlon dines with us this evening?" she asked, blushing.

"Of course. He's always welcome here."

"Thank you, Uncle Peter."

He playfully snatched a piece of carrot from the table and walked to the parlor, chewing thoughtfully. He was glad Phoebe was well, and things were running smoothly at home again, but how he missed his Margaretta. He paused at the front windows and looked onto Northampton Street where ordinary life flowed before him like the two rivers that bordered and nurtured Easton. Anna Doll suddenly appeared in the crowd walking toward his house with a basket on her arm. When she saw him, she smiled and waved.

CHAPTER TWENTY-SIX

The Easton Cemetery's gothic entrance appeared more suited to horses and carriages than cars, and Erin sat there for a moment getting her bearings, figuring out where the office was and where to park. She pulled "Mr. Scott," the minivan, into a spot in front of the "gatehouse." When she opened the door, the large room she entered was cool and bore the metallic smell of air conditioning. A forty-something woman in a sundress and low-heeled sandals entered from a back room where she'd been talking with someone.

"Good morning. How can I help you?"

"Good morning. My name is Erin Miles, and I'm doing an application for the DAR. I need to locate some of my family members' plots so I can take pictures of their headstones."

"Sure, I can help with that." She smiled as warmly as the June morning. "What are the names?" She went to her desk and reached for a cardboard box.

Erin had written them down, including their death dates, and she handed the paper to the woman.

"Just give me a moment to look them up."

Erin stood there looking around while the woman went back and forth between her computer and the old-fashioned card file. "Kichline is a name I see a lot here." She looked at Erin over a pair of red reading glasses.

"Really?"

"Yes, there are quite a few Kichlines buried here. If you like—if you have time—I can make a copy of all their records so you have them for future reference. Did you know Colonel Kichline is buried here?"

Erin perked up. "He is? He's my lots of times great-uncle," she said.

"Is he now? That's nice."

"That would be great if you could copy those records for me—if it wouldn't take too much of your time."

She shrugged. "No more than ten minutes."

"I didn't mean to rush you. I just wondered."

"No problem. Have a seat."

Erin sat in an old chair reviewing her information about her second and third great-grandparents, hoping they really had been buried in this cemetery so she didn't have to jump through any more hoops. Fortunately, they were. The woman handed Erin a photocopied map of the cemetery with red X's showing where her relatives were buried. There were three, two fairly close together, the other at the far left.

"Here's where Joseph and Ann are," the woman said, "then over here, Samuel and Sarah. I think both of them are close to the road and not hard to find."

"What's this one for?" Erin asked.

"Oh, that's the colonel's grave. I thought you might like to see it."

"Thanks. That was nice of you."

She got back into "Scotty" and drove down the narrow main road hemmed in by lofty trees and granite angels presiding over the stories and secrets of generations. When she saw the mossy gray stone chapel looking like something out of Robin Hood, she parked on the right and got out, hearing the roar of concealed traffic on Route 22's "Cemetery Curve" below. Although she'd been born and raised in this community, she'd never been to this place which dated back to Easton's pre–Civil War days. With obelisks and mausoleums, along with headstones embellished with crosses, doves, harps, Stars of David, lambs, and urns, the graveyard bore little resemblance to Jim's final resting place in a modern cemetery where all the markers were in-ground, and the trees were planted far apart to give an airier feeling. This place bore mute testimony to life's brevity and the fervent hope of the afterlife those people had.

On this nearly cloudless day, Erin didn't feel overwhelmed by the stolid reminders of human mortality, but she wouldn't want to have been walking around there at night. A young man with tattooed arms zipped along on a riding mower several rows away. Except for a few headstones, most appeared to be in good repair, many graced with American flags, military markers, and perennial flowers.

She made her way around several tombstones searching for Joseph and Sarah Kichline, her great-great-great grandparents and almost walked right past them. There the markers were, lying flat on the ground, something she hadn't been expecting. She knelt down and could barely make out the carved letters and numbers. Then she remembered something Sydney had suggested—*Wet the stones before you take pictures. That makes them easier to read.* Erin returned to the car for a bottle of water bearing her lipstick around the rim and dumped the contents over the two stones, watching as Samuel and Sarah's names and dates appeared like one of her son's invisible ink tablets. She shot several photos from different angles, then lovingly rubbed her hand over the aged markers. If only she'd brought flowers. She wanted to honor them, to pay tribute somehow. *Next time.*

She hopped back into her vehicle and went in search of their son and daughter-in-law's graves, finding Joseph and Ann Elizabeth's plots easier to find and read. Their simple reddish stones featured upraised lettering, his from 1900, hers from 1904. When she finished taking pictures, Erin bent down and whispered, "I'm so glad to be getting to know you. I'm proud to be part of this family."

She stood up and brushed dirt from her knees, feeling the solemnity of the old cemetery, breathing in its scent of mowed grass. She smiled down, her heart filling with love for these ancestors, strengthened by their silent witness of having fought the good fight. Erin checked her watch. There was just enough time to visit her many times Great-Uncle Peter's grave. Once again, she followed the office manager's map, over hill and dale, coming to a fence separating this graveyard from the Easton Heights Cemetery. She thought the spot should be around a bend and to the right and parked across from a series of small mausoleums, making sure to engage Mr. Scott's emergency brake. She wondered if such a noteworthy person as the colonel might be interred in one of those crypts, but there were none of them by the area where the X was on the map. For several minutes she wandered around, careful not to trip over heavy tree roots embedded in the ground.

"Excuse me, do you need help finding someone?"

She looked up to see a man of later middle age wearing a yellow Polo shirt and pleated khakis without a trace of a wrinkle. Her instincts told her to be on guard, but his friendly smile informed her otherwise. "I'm having a little trouble finding a relative's grave."

"I work here. Maybe I can help."

Feeling calmer, she wondered if he might be a manager. "His name was Peter Kichline."

Another smile. "The Colonel! He's a relative of yours?"

"Yes, my many times great-uncle."

He nodded. "Now there was a great man. Just follow me. The grave is right over there."

Erin was looking for a significant stone marker with "Colonel Peter Kichline" emblazoned on it, but it wasn't what she found.

"There he is." The man pointed to a flat slab of either marble or granite, she couldn't tell which, with a rounded top, lying on the ground. At the top was an American flag in a holder bearing a Revolutionary War emblem and the outline of a Continental soldier. Erin crouched down to read the epitaph, written in German. His name was spelled Koechlein. She thought she should say something to the man. "This is amazing. Here he is, then." She paused. "The marker is so dignified and simple."

"I think that describes him pretty well."

How did everyone in Easton know about this man except for me? How did my family miss this? Well, she knew now, and she couldn't have been more thrilled.

She'd planned to call her dad about the birth certificate once she got home, but Ethan had homework and baseball practice, then a science project about solar energy to finish. By the time she was ready for bed, she was worn out. She didn't feel like watching TV, or having what might end up being an uncomfortable conversation with her dad, so she went online to find the document the librarian had told her about instead—one she'd already seen parts of when she'd discovered her connection to Charles Kichline. She typed "Kichlines in America" and found the article, which was several pages long. Erin padded down the hall to her office to make a paper copy, which she'd read in bed. Normally when she opened a book late at night, reading helped her wind down and she'd nod off after a few pages. Not this time.

Back in 1926, a Kichline descendant had presented this as a paper to the Northampton County Historical and Genealogical Society. The author, Thomas Jefferson Kichline, whose name she'd seen before, identified himself as Clerk of the Orphan's Court of Northampton County and President of the Kichline Society. Erin wondered which brother he was descended from, Peter, Charles, or Andrew, and how he might be related to her. Had her grandmother known of him? They were alive in Easton at the same time, but to Erin's knowledge, none of her relatives had known anything about their connection to the Kichlines.

After a flowery introduction about the importance of honoring our ances-tors, "to keep green their memory and show ourselves worthy of and grateful for them," he traced the immigrant brothers' heritage back to the mid-1500s in Switzerland. *I have Swiss blood!* Erin felt her left calf tingle. She had loved watching an old TV show about the legendary hero, William Tell, which had sent her on a journey researching the history of the Swiss Confederation. She'd even toyed with the idea of focusing her history major on the Middle Ages, but then her love of America's past won out. Like the people on "Who Do You Think You Are," she was having one of those "aha" moments about why she felt connected to certain people, places, and events—the blood of those who had lived in and through them ran through her veins.

Thomas Kichline told the story of the family patriarch's move to Germany in the early eighteenth century so his children would have better educational opportunities. Then his wife had died, and after he remarried, they had first Johann Peter, then Karl Christian Joseph, and a few months after the father's death, Johann Andreas.

Erin spoke aloud to Toby. "That's sad, isn't it, old boy? Andrew never knew his father. Never had a chance. At least Ethan grew up with Jim and will always remember him." She wiped a tear away.

The Kichline boys' mother had remarried, and they all came to America in 1742, arriving in Philadelphia and settling in Bedminster. At this point in the document, Thomas Kichline broke his narrative into individual stories of the three brothers, starting with Andrew. *That was strange since he was the youngest. Maybe that was Thomas Jefferson's Kichline's ancestor.* Andrew became a tavern keeper and contributed some of his land for a Reformed church to be built, which she already knew about. In 1775, he was selected by the Committee of Safety to be a captain of a local militia company, followed by his commission as a lieutenant in early 1776 in the Continental Army.

"Wow," Erin said, "he served in the Battle of Quebec. That was a cold, nasty affair. This says the Continental Army sustained heavy losses. I wonder what the experience was like for Great-Uncle Andrew. He was right there at the begin-ning of the Revolution!"

The next story, which she'd seen in part earlier, was about Charles, the qui-etest of the three brothers, who didn't marry until his forties. Erin imagined a distinguished figure who moved about his farm and the community dispensing wisdom and pleasantness. In her mind, all the brothers had dark blonde hair and blue eyes. As she already knew, during the Revolution her ancestor had supported the cause with his taxes and sworn allegiance to the Patriots, and in

1781 was elected to the Pennsylvania Assembly for Upper Bucks County. He served one term.

"He must've been really well respected, Toby, I mean for other people in the county to have recognized him like that." She scratched his right ear and smiled when her dog thumped his right rear leg. "I'm really proud of these guys!"

The oldest brother, Peter, had left the family circle early on "to shift for himself," according to Thomas Kichline, showing up in Easton in its earliest days. The town was founded in 1752, but the author maintained Peter was there even before. He'd owned a tavern, become Sheriff of Northampton County, was a mill owner, and had taken part in the French and Indian War. He'd had various roles in the town government, and became a colonel during the Revolution, leading Northampton County's "Flying Camp" at the Battle of Brooklyn in 1776. He was wounded, captured, and later released.

She knew the British hadn't acted humanely toward the "rebel" POWs. She was glad he'd lived to tell about it. After his return, he became a judge, as well as Easton's "First Chief Burgess," whatever that was. *No wonder he is still so well-known there!*

"Imagine, Toby. I never even knew he existed until a few weeks ago, but he left his mark all over Easton, actually all over the county. I wonder why no one in my family knew this stuff." What a difference knowing where she came from would've made to her sense of identity when she was growing up.

"Then again, Peter wasn't my direct ancestor, but an uncle. I really do wish it were the other way around, even though I think very highly of Grandfather Charles." She sighed. "Peter was such a romantic, heroic figure."

Who had his wife been? She examined the document and found her name, Margaretta Umbehenden, who was born in Germany in 1719 and died in March 1766 in Easton.

"That would have made her, let's see … forty-seven when she died." Erin felt a familiar chill in her left calf. "The same age as Jim." Great-Uncle Peter had lost a spouse at a young age, just like her. *I wonder what Margaretta died from? Childbirth maybe? She might have been too old, though. More importantly, how had he coped? Had he ever felt as alone and afraid of the future as I do, or forget things or get distracted because his mind and emotions were on overload? No won-der I feel so close to this man.*

She immersed herself in Kichline history until one-thirty in the morning, saving the end of the lengthy story for the next day. When the alarm went off at six, she hit the snooze button, slept through the next buzzer, then rushed like a madwoman to get Ethan dressed and fed—a chocolate Pop Tart and four grapes—almost shouting commands. "Brush your teeth!" "Brush your hair!"

"Grab your backpack!" They showed up at the bus stop, panting, just as the driver started pulling away. Erin ran after him, waving like a windmill in a typhoon.

"Man, that was close," she told the only mom left after the bus drove away with her son.

"Well, you made it anyway!"

Erin wondered why Robin had such a strange look on her face. Just as she was admiring how put together her neighbor looked with her gleaming white teeth, jeans that fit just right, and jewelry sparkling in the sun against a trim tee shirt, Erin looked down at her own feet. Yup. Bright aqua slippers with the blow dryer motif. Embarrassed, she walked with Robin toward their houses at a swift clip, wanting to bolt inside her front door and put something decent on. When she saw her reflection in the hall mirror, she couldn't blame Toby for looking up and howling at full blast. She was wearing Jim's bright orange Flyers' hoodie over the pink maternity pajama bottoms she still loved but never wanted anyone other than Jim and Ethan to see, and sometimes not even them. She had paraded herself like a circus freak in front of God and everybody. After she went upstairs and changed, Erin ate a bowl of Froot Loops with hot sauce and cottage cheese for breakfast.

◊ • ◊

She finished "The Kichlines in America" before running errands, decently clothed and in her right mind. If Peter, Andrew, and Charles could pledge everything dear to them for the sake of freedom, she could beard her own dragon, to use Sydney's expression. Erin would hunker down and call her dad about that birth certificate.

"My birth certificate?" he asked over the phone. "Oh, yeah, you wrote me about that."

Erin's pulse thumped in her right ear. "So, would that be okay, I mean you sending me a copy?"

"I have a small copy machine right here. Sure. When do you need it by?" he asked.

Did I hear him right? "As soon as you can send it."

"I'll get it in today's mail. So, how's Ethan doing at third base? I'd like to see him play sometime."

She started talking baseball before he could change his mind.

❧ • ❧

CHAPTER TWENTY-SEVEN

Erin didn't check her email until late that night while Ethan took his bath after baseball practice and ice cream at Merrymead Farm. Messages between her and Sydney had been flying back and forth as they headed down the homestretch with the application, and here was another one now.

> *I have the copies of all the docs we need for your app, and as I review everything with the proverbial fine tooth comb, I see we're missing your great-great-grandmother's death info. Dang. I thought we had that covered! We have her birth, and marriage, and her date of death, but no doc to support it. Maybe you could zip up to Easton and get a photocopy of a church or newspaper or cemetery record. Sorry for the hassle, but can you do this ASAP? If we get this app in by the end of the week, it will likely hit the next cycle for review in DC.*

She didn't understand. She'd taken a photo at the cemetery. Erin went downstairs, found her camera on her desk, and started scrolling through the pictures until she found the shot of her great-great-grandmother's marker. To her annoyance, the picture was out of focus. Just when she thought she was finished, there was another hurdle. Tomorrow was going to be pretty light during the day and a good thing, too—there were only two days left before school let out for the summer. She'd planned to do some laundry and clean the bathrooms, but that would have to wait. To Easton, she would go.

❧ • ❧

Erin felt more familiar with Easton Cemetery now and found the grave with no problems. She shot several photos from different angles and various settings to make sure the "genies" in Washington could read them clearly. Then to make doubly sure she had met the DAR's rigorous standards, she drove to the Marx Room at the library to find and copy a corresponding record of her great-great-grandmother's death. She found several researchers there and Sandy in their midst. She wrote her name on the sign-in sheet and found a place to sit near the church records. As Sandy transitioned between patrons, she noticed Erin and smiled.

"Hello! I'm happy to see you again. Erin, right?"

"I can't believe you remembered my name, Sandy." She liked having a new friend in Easton.

While Sandy helped someone else, Erin checked the most obvious place for her ancestor's record, the book for the old German Reformed Church, but after searching every which way, she couldn't find anything. She checked the index book for all of Easton's congregations and finally found her listed under Drylands Reformed. Unfortunately, someone else was using that volume.

To pass the time, Erin logged on to Ancestry.com to see if there were any new waving leaves bearing new hints. To find information about her ancestors through other people's family trees, through census records, graves, and tax records intrigued her. This time, she found two, for her Grammy Owen's mother. Aside from the connection to the Ritters and Fritzes, her great-grandmother's past remained something of a mystery to Erin, and she looked forward to knowing more about the woman who always dressed with dignity, but sometimes spoke like a sailor on shore leave. Her great-grandmother Smith was born and died in Easton, like so many of Erin's maternal ancestors. Her father's name was Edward, and she wondered if he'd fought in the Civil War since he would've been the right age. She clicked on the military records. Yes, he had. Following a few other links, Erin found his father, Tobias Schmidt. Tobias? *Now, that's was a name you don't hear every day! Interesting, He died in Easton in 1878, but he was born in Bucks County.* The family tree she was looking at didn't say exactly where. The record did, however, point to his wife, whose name was Anna Elizabeth Ackerman, from Easton. She figured they must've met after Tobias moved there, and at some point he'd started going by "Smith."

Erin wanted to know more about this Anna Elizabeth, who would've been her three times great-grandmother. Who were her parents? With a few clicks she found her father, Jacob Ackerman, and then Anna Elizabeth's mother was—

Elizabeth *Kichline*! *What in the world!* The Kichlines were on her mother's father's side. What were they doing in the maternal family tree? More clicks led her to find out who Elizabeth Kichline's parents were and—Erin pressed her hand to her chest—her father was Peter Kichline! *Peter Kichline!*

She was more shocked than Captain Renault when he found out there was gambling going on in Rick's establishment. It just couldn't be right, though—or could it, she wondered. The dates were off—Colonel Peter Kichline was born in the early 1720s, and this Elizabeth was born in, let's see, 1792. More searching led her to the answer—Elizabeth's father was Peter Kichline, *Jr.* If all of this was accurate, Erin Pelleriti Miles's six times great-grandfather was none other than *Colonel Peter Kichline!*

She gasped, and a few people turned toward her. Sandy came right over. "Are you alright?"

"I just found something completely incredible,"

"People often do here."

"While I've been waiting for a book I need, I decided to go on Ancestry. com." Erin pointed to her tablet's screen. "I started following hints for my maternal great-grandmother, and there's something completely unexpected here." She paused for a breath. "You probably don't remember this, but when I was here before getting documents for my DAR application, it was for Charles Kichline, my six times great-grandfather on my mother's father's side."

Actually," Sandy said, sitting next to her, "I do remember."

"Well, today I followed some hints about my grandmother's mother's parents, and when I went back a few generations, I found an Elizabeth Kichline, and I when I looked to see who her parents were, I discovered she was the daughter of Peter Kichline, Jr. That means Peter Kichline, Sr. was her grandfather and my six times great-grandfather!"

"The colonel?"

"Yes." Erin was trembling. "How is it possible that of three brothers who came to America in the 1740s, I'm a descendant of two of them? I mean, Charles is now my uncle and grandfather, and the same with Peter." She was jazzed. She was a direct descendant of Colonel Peter Kichline, war hero, sheriff, judge, mill owner, and all-around good guy!

"Actually, that family was all over the place around here, so the connections make perfect sense to me. Where did your grandparents live—in Easton?"

Erin wasn't exactly sure which ones Sandy meant. "My mother's dad's folks were from Stewartsville, but a lot of them had lived in Easton initially. My mother's family was mostly from Easton."

"So, we're talking about the same general area."

Erin noticed there was one crooked tooth on the top row behind Sandy's easy smile, which gave her a gamine charm.

"This really isn't all that unusual," Sandy added. "Did you ever get to read that paper about the Kichlines in America?"

"Yes, and it was so fascinating." A sudden rain storm threatened her parade. "What if these family trees on Ancestry aren't reliable?"

"Sometimes they are, and sometimes they're not, but I have an accurate book about Kichline genealogy. I'll go get it, and we'll see if all the dots connect." Sandy rose to get the volume, and after several minutes of searching discovered they did.

This was Christmas, New Year's, and definitely the Fourth of July for Erin. It was Gene Kelly and Debbie Reynolds breaking into song and dance. She'd hit the genealogy jackpot.

"You're lucky to be part of that distinguished family," Sandy said. Then she suddenly shot up. "Wait right here!" She returned a few minutes later with a tall, middle-aged man with dark blonde hair and a welcoming smile. He strongly reminded Erin of someone, but she couldn't put her finger on it. "Erin, this is Paul Bassett. He's a local historian who's written some books about Easton. I can't believe he just so happens to be here now." Sandy was gushing. "I thought I saw him come in earlier. Paul, this is Erin, uh ..."

"Miles."

"Erin Miles, and she just discovered her ancestor is Colonel Peter Kichline."

His raised eyebrows and the set of his mouth communicated, "How nice!" They shook hands, but Erin wasn't expecting how rough his was. How did a polished preppy-type get rough hands? Maybe his parents had been poor, and he'd worked digging ditches to get through college.

"That's quite an ancestor you have there," he said.

"Thank you." She was ready to start dancing herself, right on top of this table.

"I thought Paul could tell you more about him," Sandy said. When someone called her name, she excused herself.

Paul continued to stand, so Erin waved to the chair across the table, and he sat down. "So, you know a lot about Easton history?" she asked.

"I like to think so," he said, laughing. "What would you like to know about the Colonel?"

"Anything. Everything, actually! I still can't believe he's my ancestor." She briefly explained about him and Charles being brothers.

"Is that so?" He looked under the table for a long moment, and she wondered what in the world he was doing. When he came back up, he asked, "Do you happen to have six toes on one of your feet?"

"Do I ...? Oh!" This was exactly the sort of thing Jim would've said, and she took a moment to find her focus again, swallowing hard to keep tears away. "Uh, no, but it could explain a lot of other things," she quipped, trying to keep the conversation light.

"So, what do you know already?" He folded his hands on the table, ready to listen.

"Well, he was a colonel, and he fought in the Revolution in New York, and he was a leader in Northampton County."

Paul nodded. "Yes to all those things. Your Peter Kichline showed up in Easton in the early days, around the time of its founding in 1752."

She loved the way he said "your Peter Kichline."

"He was a well-educated man, having gone to Heidelberg University, which was a very big deal back then, especially because most of the Germans in Easton were poor and uneducated. They really looked up to him as a protector. He was also one of the trustees of the first school here."

She remembered seeing that early on in her family research. She started taking notes but knew all of this was making an indelible impression on her heart. The sounds of other patrons talking, making copies, getting up and down, faded. There was only this man and her Grandfather Peter's story.

"He owned one of the first taverns in town," Paul said, "but when he was elected Sheriff of Northampton County, he had to sell it because he couldn't do that and sell spirits. He ended up building a grist mill, just over the hill from where we're sitting."

Erin tried to picture the location. "Do you mean along Cemetery Curve?"

"Just below that highway, next to the Bushkill Creek by what's called Mount Jefferson. The library sits on top of it." He paused and looked at her more closely. "Are you from around here?"

"Born and raised. I've been living in Montgomery County since I was married, though, but most of my family is still up here."

"Well, after Kichline built that one, he set up a sawmill on the other side, just below the base of Lafayette College. He was a very wealthy man. When the Revolution broke out, he was elected as a member of the Committee of Safety, and he was in Philadelphia for meetings that led to the Declaration of Independence."

"Wow."

"When the Continental Congress called for the formation of Flying Camps—kind of like the Minutemen, but from all the colonies—one began forming in Northampton County," Paul said. "The Committee chose someone to lead it, a guy named Sidman, but he proved to be the wrong choice. Probably just too young and inexperienced." He leaned back, folding his arms across his chest. "They needed someone and quickly, so guess who they got?" He didn't wait for her answer. "Old reliable—your ancestor. The people of this county knew if anything needed to be done and done well, Peter Kichline was the go-to guy."

"I know I keep saying 'wow,' but this is all so amazing," she said.

"That's okay. He was pretty amazing." He continued. "After he became colonel of our Flying Camp, he led the men to New York at the end of August 1776 in the first major battle after the Declaration. It was the Battle of Brooklyn, also known as the Battle of Long Island, and our forces were clearly routed."

As a historian, Erin knew all this and considered telling Paul, but she didn't want to miss anything about her ancestor.

"The Americans were badly outnumbered, and he ended up losing most of his men. He was also wounded and captured. Later, he was exchanged and returned to Easton after promising not to take up arms against the King again." Paul gave a laugh. "There's some debate whether he actually did or not. That's something for you to look into. After the war, he became a judge, and then Easton's first Chief Burgess."

"I was just reading about that. What exactly is a Chief Burgess?"

"In that system of local government, a Chief Burgess was like a mayor. He didn't get to serve for long, though. He died just a few months later."

"What a life he had!" Erin said.

"Yes, and I've only given you a thumbnail sketch. There's so much more to it. Maybe you should check out the Jane Moyer Library in the Sigal Museum. They have a lot of Easton history resources, and I know they have information about your ancestor."

"I'll do that." She checked her watch and sighed. "I have to leave soon, but I'm up here a lot lately."

"Do you have today off?" he asked.

"Actually, I'm a history professor, and we've finished the semester." She wondered what kind of job allowed him to be in a library in the middle of the day. She doubted writing local history books made much money.

He reached into a pocket and handed her a business card. "Feel free to contact me anytime with questions."

"Thank you." She gave him her card in return.

He examined it and looked up at her. "Miles. Are you related to the Philadelphia Miles family?"

"Yes, they're my husband's. He always took pride in them."

He cocked his head, no doubt wondering about the "was."

"He died in March."

Paul pressed his lips together. "Oh, that's tough. I'm sorry to hear that. Do you have children?"

"One son, who's eight."

He paused, then said, "Of course the Miles family was noteworthy, but the Kichlines—you have a lot to be proud of yourself. You're very lucky. I'd love to have Kichline ancestors."

Erin wondered about his own story. The name Bassett didn't strike her as a local one, but then she hadn't been around for twenty years. He did remind her of someone, though.

An older man wearing blue glasses and baggy khakis came over. "Excuse me, but might I speak with you, Paul."

"Sure, Ron. I'll be with you in a minute."

"I'm just leaving," she said, gathering her things and putting them in her tote bag. "I enjoyed hearing your stories about my Grandfather Peter." *Grandfather Peter*. It had a nice ring.

Paul rose and stood. "You know, uh, Erin?" She nodded. "A lot of men were on the make during the Revolution, politicians looking to pad their wallets or gain power, just like today. But not Peter Kichline. If ever there was an honest man, he was one."

She couldn't help but beam. "Thank you for that."

"Contact me anytime. I love talking about him."

"Me too."

❦ • ❧

CHAPTER TWENTY-EIGHT

"History Here" read the Sigal Museum banner at a building Erin remembered very differently from her youth. Years ago, it had been a women's clothing store, one her mom didn't shop in because it was "beyond our means," but when it morphed into a bridal gallery, Erin had purchased her wedding gown there, with her own money. Sigal's had closed altogether during Easton's challenging period, and she exulted to see the place thriving again. She entered through a set of glass doors into a lobby featuring a welcome station. To the right, an antique film featured firefighters marching in a parade, moving in that choppy, quick way of silent films. Erin stood watching it for a minute, then looked at a sign pointing to a Leni Lenape Exhibit toward the back. To the left was a book and gift shop she knew she'd want to visit. She wondered who had turned this once vacant store into a museum, the city? Maybe the historical society or the Sigal family?

"May I help you?" An elegant, silver-haired woman two inches shorter and considerably wider than Erin greeted her.

"Hi, this is my first time in here, with it as a museum, that is."

"Did you used to shop at Sigal's?" the woman asked.

"Uh, yes, when I grew up here. I live in Lansdale now, but my family is still in Easton and Phillipsburg."

"Oh, what's the name?"

Erin skipped a few generations. "My family goes back to Easton's founding, to Colonel Peter Kichline." She had a hard time saying this humbly.

"Oh! Well, how wonderful! He really is something of a local hero."

"I'm just learning about him," Erin said.

"So much of our history gets lost through the generations. That's one reason we have this beautiful new museum here."

"What exactly is this place?" Erin's gaze wandered to a display case featuring local products, including Moravian Stars, glassware, and books. She always found it hard to talk to someone in a gift shop when all her impulses urged her to hunt and gather.

"This is a museum of Easton and Northampton County history, and it houses the Northampton County Historical and Genealogical Society. There's a research library upstairs, named for our Jane Moyer."

"I've heard that name," Erin said.

"Oh, she's quite famous for her knowledge of local history. She ran the Easton Library for years. She's over a hundred years old now and still comes here several times a week to work in our library. Do you have time to go through the museum? We have some wonderful exhibits, and upstairs they can help with any family research."

Erin wanted to do everything, but there just wasn't enough time. For now, she'd have to settle for a brief shopping experience, hoping to buy books about Easton history and pick up something for Ethan. Then she'd grab a quick lunch before heading back to Lansdale.

"I'll have to come back another time," she said.

"I understand. Is there anything I can help you find?"

"I'm looking for information about my Grandfather Peter." How she loved saying that!

The woman led Erin to five different volumes, including one about Easton during the Revolution, another about its pre-Revolutionary War era, a brochure about the courthouse, and a book about Easton's mills, whose author was none other than Paul Bassett. Erin also bought a children's book for Ethan about George Washington by another local author, a poster of the early courthouse, a paisley scarf that reminded her of Pat Miles, and several chocolate bars featuring Easton's Soldiers and Sailors Monument.

As the woman rang up Erin's purchases, she sang Paul Bassett's praises. "His books are so interesting and well written. Each one seems to uncover things none of us knew before. We're lucky to have him in Easton."

"Then he's not from here?"

She swiped Erin's credit card and handed it back to her. "No. He moved here, oh, about five years ago. He was a lawyer, or maybe it was a doctor, before, from the city."

Erin wondered which city, and why Paul had come to Easton of all places. Was he was still practicing his profession? If so, how did he have the liberty of writing books and doing library research in the middle of a work day?

"He's become such a fixture here it just seems like he's always been around."

"There certainly is a different vibe here than when I grew up," Erin said. "Everything seems so new and welcoming, and so many of the old buildings are being used again."

"I think so, too. I'm from Tatamy, and not even ten years ago, you constantly had to look over your shoulder walking around downtown because of all the drug dealers. We still have our problems, but there's more good than bad now, lots of new stores, restaurants, and art galleries. Of course, there's the famous Crayola Experience, and now our museum. There are other people like Paul Bassett, who've moved here from the city looking for a hometown to love. They've had a big part in bringing the town back. Some of them have become a group of actors who do historic dinner theater productions at the Bachman Publick House."

"How wonderful!" Erin said. "I feel like I'm getting to know Easton all over again, almost like I'm seeing my hometown for the first time."

"I never moved away, but I have similar feelings." She bagged the items, then picked up a brochure. "I'm going to put this in with your things. Easton Heritage Day is in a few weeks, and you'll want to bring your family. Did you know on July 8, 1776, the Declaration of Independence was read in our Great Square?"

"Yes, I remember when Heritage Day first started, when I was a girl in the late 70s."

"Then you know Easton was one of the first two communities to read it publicly. Heritage Day has become quite a production," the woman said. "On the Sunday closest to July 8th, we have a worship service, parade, a public reading by a man in costume, lots of reenactors from different wars, a play about the Indian treaties, concerts, and of course food. The festival is a destination now."

"Then I'll come and bring my son." If only she could bring Jim as well.

As soon as she got home, she emailed Sydney to tell her about Peter Kichline, asking if she could come into the DAR through him instead of Charles. She did love Charles, but she felt such a strong connection to Peter—they had lived in the same place, he cut such a dashing, honorable figure, and he knew what it was to lose a spouse young. She really knew so little about Charles.

Sydney was quick to respond.

> *I checked the database and discovered there were some problems with a recent app through his line. There are a lot of Elizabeth Kichlines! First, let's make sure this really is your ancestor. Then again, we already have the docs prepared for Charles. If you don't mind waiting, and if everything adds up with Peter being your ancestor, it could take several more weeks, maybe even months, to get a new app together with all the supporting documents. My recommendation is you go through Charles as planned, and then I can help you fill out an app for a Supplemental Patriot. That way you can honor both. Imagine, being related like that to two brothers! I haven't run into this one before!*

She called Melissa to get her opinion.

"I say, go with Charles," her friend said, "then go for Peter as whatever it was she called it."

"A supplemental."

"That's the word. That is some story, Erin!"

"Wouldn't Jim have gotten a kick out of it?"

"He would have teased you mercilessly. Remember the time we got locked inside Marshall's because we were still in the dressing rooms when they closed the store?"

She laughed. "He never let me live that one down." After she hung up, took only a few minutes to decide to go with Charles as her patriot. *He was no slouch after all, and besides, I want to get into the DAR sooner, rather than later.*

Ethan came into the room, and Erin tried explaining the ancestral relationships to him, but his blank expression never filled. "Let's just say you're related to an amazing colonel who fought in a big Revolutionary War battle."

"Wow! That is so cool." Now he looked impressed.

Ethan wanted a Revolutionary War costume, which she found on the Internet. On Heritage Day, he tried it on and gazed at himself in his bedroom mirror. "Do you think Grandfather Peter would have liked me?"

"I have no doubt he would've loved you very much," Erin said, her eyes misty.

"Would Daddy have liked to see me in this outfit?"

"I'm sure of that, too."

He turned toward her. "Let's go then!"

They drove to Easton for the first of the events, an ecumenical worship service at Riverside Park's band shell, a place that hadn't existed when Erin was young. There'd been a playground then, as there was now, but this newer model was ten times better. The minister who spoke was fairly interesting, but Erin's eyes and mind kept drifting toward the compelling scenery at the forks of the Delaware, where it met the Lehigh. These rivers didn't frighten her anymore, as they had when she was young. There was so much more to them than floods. She looked over at the dam near the point and wondered how long the concrete structure had been there, probably well before her grandparents' time. Aged houses perched across the water in Phillipsburg, having born witness to generations of families coming and going, to floods, patriotic parades, and wars.

A slight breeze helped her bear the intense July heat, and she smiled over at her little patriot with his eyes straight ahead, appearing deep in thought. She was glad he was growing up with a sense of who her family was, a family that, like the rivers, there was so much more to than she'd ever dreamed. She felt like Cinderella, coming up hard only to discover she was actually aristocratic.

As a tenor sang "America, the Beautiful," her emotions swelled over the words about heroes being proved in liberating strife, "who more than self their country loved." She thought of her own patriot ancestor, Charles, and his celebrated brothers.

She felt a little guilty she hadn't invited her mother to share this, or even told her she'd be in town for Heritage Day. Something in Erin just wanted this to be for her and Ethan as they bonded with Easton and their own heritage on their own terms.

She scanned the crowd and saw Paul Bassett on the other side. He looked back and caught her eye, breaking into a smile. *Who does he remind me of anyway?*

The service ended at eleven, and she and Ethan walked across Larry Holmes Drive, up Northampton Street to the place everyone was referring to as "The Great Square," but which she had always called "The Circle." As she walked the streets of her youth, she kept thinking about her Grandfather Peter, how he had walked these same places and breathed the same air, known the gentle grandeur of these rivers and the sweeping expanses of the hills. He helped build this town out of the wilderness and supported its baby steps before marching stalwartly toward Independence. He'd married and had children here, and like Erin, he'd walked in the footsteps of grief. She felt as if she'd really known him, as if he were alive in some manner, that something of his spirit lingered and was resting on her, not in any "Long Island Medium" way, but more as a sweet legacy. She wondered whether the "the communion of the saints" might just have something to do with it.

CHAPTER TWENTY-NINE

Civil War Reenactors were stationed beside the Soldiers and Sailors Monument, men in beards who looked terribly uncomfortable in heavy blue uniforms with suspicious stains under their arms.

"Is that a real gun?" Ethan asked a narrow-faced man with a nice smile.

"It sure is, son. Would you like to hold it?"

"You bet! Can I, Mom?"

"Of course." She loved seeing his boyish excitement. Someone came up beside her.

"Hello again,"

Paul Bassett. "Well, hello," she said. "What a great day this is!"

"The best Heritage Day yet." He looked at Ethan and grinned. "Is this your son?"

"Yes, this is Ethan. Ethan, this is Mr. Bassett."

The boy seemed much too excited about handling an actual rifle to be impressed with meeting someone. "Hi," He quickly turned back to the "soldier" and asked, "Does this have real bullets?"

"It does not."

Although Ethan frowned, Erin felt relieved. She could just imagine her inexperienced son firing the weapon into the crowd while a SWAT team descended upon screaming men, women, and children.

Paul started chatting with a woman who carried a clipboard and a walkie-talkie.

"Mom, can we get some cotton candy?" her son asked a few minutes later after another boy had come over to handle the gun, and Ethan had reluctantly handed it over.

"Maybe after lunch," she said.

"When will that be?"

"After the reading of the Declaration of Independence."

"When's that?"

"After the town criers."

He moaned. "That's too long!"

The clipboard lady had left, and Paul was paying attention to them again. "If you go now, there are still some good seats in the shade."

"What's a town crier?" Ethan asked him.

"Well, back in the days before cell phones, TV, radio, and the Internet, people got their news in the streets from men who could yell loud enough so everyone could hear them."

"That sounds neat."

"Go see for yourself," Paul said.

"What will they be crying about now?" Ethan asked. A bell clanged, and someone called out "Oyez, oyez, oyez!" more than a few times. "What in the world was that?"

"The town crier," Paul said with a laugh. "He's calling for our attention. Actually, today there's a competition. Some of the criers will argue we should declare independence from Great Britain, and others will say we should stay loyal to the King."

"And what do you think?" Erin asked playfully.

Paul smiled. "Independence of course!"

"Me too!" Ethan said.

She felt warmed by their friendly banter.

"Well, I hope you have a great day," Paul said, but he didn't budge.

"You, too." She led Ethan toward the stage facing South Third Street, passing a Johnny Depp look-alike in full pirate regalia, a man who looked like he took his role a little too seriously. Before Ethan could comment, they saw another strange sight—an older man wearing a Revolutionary War uniform while riding a Segway.

Ethan giggled. "Did that guy lose his horse?"

A young woman with blonde and pink hair came over to them. "Excuse me. Is this your son?" She looked at Erin and pointed to Ethan.

"Yes."

"May I take a picture of him in his uniform for the paper?"

"Is that okay, Ethan?" she asked her son.

"Sure." He stood at attention next to the Segway soldier, who the photographer had brought over to them. After the woman took a few photos, she wrote down Ethan's name and where he lived on a small tablet.

"We live in Lansdale, but I'm from here," Erin said. "In fact, my six times great-grandfather was Colonel of the Northampton County militia."

The woman jerked back her head and said, "That's pretty cool."

Afterward, they found two of the last chairs in the shade as, one-by-one, town criers took to the stage dressed in elaborate, eighteenth-century costumes. There were hearty cheers and applause for the Patriots and sound booing for the Loyalists. Ethan put his heart into the shouting. Erin wished Jim could see him now.

∾ • ∿

Just before noon, the argument for independence was a done deal. The sun beat down upon the canopy, and the sound of fifers drifted toward the stage. Ethan jumped up to see what was happening, and she found her own pulse quickening as a fellow carrying a walking stick and calling out, "I have a declaration!" led a group of costumed men, women, and children to the Great Square. They looked like they'd just stepped out of a history book.

"What's that guy saying?" Ethan asked above the music and crowd.

"He's calling the citizens to listen to a declaration."

"The Declaration of Independence, right?"

She wanted to tousle his hair, but it was covered by a tricorn hat. "Good job!" she said, looking at her program as the reenactors spread out in a line on both sides of the stage. The man identified as "Robert Levers" stepped onto the platform. But what was this? Erin gazed more closely at one of the "soldiers." Why, he looked just like Sean O'Malley, her old high school crush. *That couldn't be him, could it?* He turned his head to say something to a man at his left, and when Erin saw his profile, she knew. *It is him.* She couldn't tell what his hair was like under the hat, but the rest of him looked the same, his face still boyish and nearly free of wrinkles, his figure cutting a handsome silhouette in that uniform.

"Levers" pointed with his stick to the parchment he held. "I have in my hand a declaration! It has just come to us from the delegates of all thirteen colonies meeting in Philadelphia." He began reading, "When in the course of human events it becomes necessary for one people to dissolve the political bands which have connected them to another, and to assume among the powers of the earth, the separate and equal station to which the laws of nature and of nature's God entitle them, a decent respect to the opinions of mankind requires that they should declare the causes which impel them to the separation."

Booing commenced as "Levers" recited one-by-one the Founding Fathers' charges against King George III. The one about imposing taxes without the colonists' consent got an especially rousing response.

Erin felt a rush of chills to think she was sitting on the same spot where history had taken place, wondering if her ancestor had been there. By the time the actor got to the last lines, she was in tears.

"And for the support of this Declaration, with a firm reliance upon the protection of Divine Providence, we mutually pledge to each other our lives, our fortunes, and our sacred honor."

"Huzzah! Huzzah!" There were loud whistles and the pressing boom of a cannon whose concussion Erin felt in her feet. The fifers moved past, leading a company of soldiers, including Sean O'Malley, in a march toward the German Reformed Church, aka First United Church of Christ. Erin glanced over to see Ethan's expression, but he wasn't there. Her heart racing wildly, she sprang into motion, pushing past several people, trying to find him in the dense crowd with all that noise. In less than a minute she spotted him, marching with the soldiers toward the church, his face serious, chest puffed out, looking very much as if he belonged right there among them. Erin grabbed her camera to take a few shots, but she was having trouble focusing.

She took a few minutes to catch up, but there her son was, standing in the churchyard talking to Sean O'Malley of all people. "Ethan!"

"Mom!" He was wearing his Christmas morning expression.

Sean cocked his head and narrowed his eyes. "Is this your son?"

"Yes."

He squinted at her. "Erin?"

She smiled. "Yes, Sean O'Malley, I'm Erin."

Of course, he would have laugh lines around his eyes and mouth, and while he still had a certain flair for the dramatic, the years had removed some of the old, careless swagger. And what was this she thought—he was short! He couldn't have been more than five-six or five-seven, something she'd never noticed in high school. This was like seeing the house you'd grown up in, the one you'd always pictured as being huge, but then as adult, you saw how small the place really was.

First, he bowed, then he bear-hugged her. "Imagine that! Erin Pelleriti!"

"Actually, my last name is Miles now."

Sean looked past her, perhaps looking for her husband.

"This is my son, Ethan."

"I've made this fine young man's acquaintance. He's a great addition to our company," Sean said.

Ethan practically shouted, "My grandfather was a colonel!"

"Was he now?"

Erin hastened to explain. "Actually, his seven times great-grandfather was Peter Kichline, who served as a colonel during the …"

"Your ancestor is *Peter Kichline*?" Sean's eyes bugged out. "You are one lucky fellow, Mr. Ethan, to have such a distinguished gentleman in your family."

The Sean O'Malley knew about *her* ancestor. This was incredible.

"I suppose you're a Daughter of the American Revolution then?"

"I'm in the process of becoming one," she said. "You certainly look like you're a Son of the American Revolution."

"Don't I wish! My ancestors were Irish and didn't get off the boat until a hundred years after the Revolution, but I love this stuff." He waved at the men in their woolen uniforms standing under the spreading limbs of an ancient tree. "I've been doing reenacting for a few years now."

Imagine having a social advantage over Dr. O'Malley's son!

"So, where do you live now?" Sean asked her.

"Lansdale, but my family is still up here."

"I always liked your mother," he said.

That was nice. A lot of Erin's friends had liked Audrey, who'd always taken an interest in them.

He motioned to a quietly pretty woman about his height, smiling under a colonial bonnet. "Erin, uh …"

"Miles."

"Erin Miles, I'd like you to meet Gail. Gail, this is a dear friend from high school."

"I'm glad to meet you." She held out a small hand.

"Same here." She smiled to cover her confusion. This wasn't Pamela Case, but Sean had married Pamela. She remembered seeing the announcement in *The Express Times*. This woman must be his second wife. She recovered her manners. "This is my son, Ethan."

Sean elbowed Gail and joked, "This is the one who got away."

Huh? She wondered why he would say such a thing and to his wife, or whatever she was. There was no mistaking the plaintive note in his quip. She'd always thought once he'd started dating Pamela, he hadn't given Erin another thought. Here he was twenty-some years later telling her not only did he envy her about Peter Kichline, but he'd felt far more for her than she'd ever imagined. She was actually glad when Ethan's whining covered her own speechlessness.

"Ah, Mom, can't we stop talking about grown-up stuff? I want to ask him about his uniform."

Sean gave a laugh and bent down. "Well, young man, what would you like to know?"

"That gun is so cool."

"Would you like to hold it?"

Here we go again, Erin thought. What was it with boys and guns, including these big boys?

"Would I!"

"This is a Pennsylvania Rifle, which has an especially long barrel." He handed the weapon to Ethan, who nearly sank under its weight.

"This is heavy!"

"You bet. These were used from the French and Indian War up until the Revolution."

As Sean prattled on about muzzles, spiraling, and bores, Erin figured she'd better engage his wife, or whoever she was, in conversation. "Your dress is so beautiful."

"Thank you."

"Where did you ever find something like that?"

She dipped her chin. "I made it."

"I'm impressed! I have trouble sewing buttons." Before she realized what she was saying she blurted, "My husband always ended up doing that job."

Gail looked into Erin's eyes. "Is he here today?"

She looked up at the church's distinctive spire and said, "He died in April."

"I'm sorry." She squeezed Erin's hand for a long moment.

There was no awkwardness in the words or the silence that lay between them. After the moment passed Erin, feeling strangely comforted, was able to speak again. "Are you from Easton or Phillipsburg?"

"Morristown, New Jersey."

"How did you meet Sean?" she asked.

"At an encampment in Morristown. We were both reenactors."

"How nice." Erin wondered how long ago that had been. "I'm admiring your basket. What do you keep in it?"

Gail removed a white linen cloth from the top to reveal a small wallet, a package of tissues, hand sanitizer, and a Revlon lipstick. "This is my purse," she said in a whisper.

"Well, you look amazing, but I'm guessing it must be really hot for you. I know I'm melting."

"You get used to it. The church's hall is air-conditioned, and there's food in there."

"That sounds wonderful," Erin said. Ethan was now wearing a sword that went all the way down to his feet. "I wonder if I'll be able to pull him away." She wanted to know more about Gail and Sean, but their relationship really wasn't any of her business. She waited a few minutes before signaling her son. "We need to go, Ethan. We're going inside the church to cool off and get some lunch."

"Aw, Mom, this is so fun!"

"Maybe you can join us again, Ethan," Sean said. "We're always looking for new people to join our group." He produced a business card from inside his coat for Erin.

"That would be so cool!" There was no mistaking the boy's enthusiasm.

Sean gazed at Erin, and she felt heat flow to her cheeks. "I am really happy to see you again. Hopefully, it won't be such a long time before we meet again." He bowed in the manner of a colonial soldier. "And you, young man. Stay in touch. Any grandson of Colonel Kichline is a friend of mine."

❦ • ❧

CHAPTER THIRTY

"He is just adorable!" An elderly woman with bright hazel eyes handed Ethan a second ice cream cone. "Obviously, this soldier has been working hard to defend our liberty. This one's on me."

Ladies who seemed like they knew their way around a kitchen served cold drinks, hot dogs, and ice cream in the church's fellowship hall. *I've never been inside before, but I never walked or drove past here when I was young without a kind of awe in my spirit. This place feels like a part of me. I wonder why my mom stopped coming here after she grew up and why she took Allen and me to a different church.*

The woman spoke again. "I like to see a boy eat. My grandkids live in Montana, so I don't get to see them very much. Your son reminds me of the youngest. By the way, I'm Betty."

"Hi, Betty. I'm Erin, and this is Ethan."

"Hello there, Mr. Ethan. I'm glad to see such young men protecting our country from those British scoundrels."

Ethan's small chest puffed out, not for the first time that day.

"Are you from Easton?"

Erin studied her face, thinking Betty might have been some kind of beauty when she was young. "I grew up across the river, but I spent a huge part of my time in Easton, including going to Lafayette. I live in Lansdale now. Actually, my mother went to this church when she was young, but I've never been in here before."

Betty's eyes kindled. "She might be about my age, then. What was her maiden name?"

"Owen, Audrey Owen."

"Oh, my stars! I knew Audrey Owen! We went through Sunday School together. How is she?"

Erin couldn't help but smile at the connection. "She's doing well. Still living in P'burg."

"Well, you tell her Betty Munley asked about her. She wouldn't know me by my married names."

She wondered how many times the woman had been married.

"As soon as you finish eating, I'll show you our sanctuary. This used to be a hospital for Revolutionary War soldiers."

"My mother told me about that. Of course, growing up here, I couldn't help but hear about that from other people, too."

Ethan gulped down the bottom part of his sugar cone and mumbled, "Let's go see it!"

"Wipe your mouth." Erin handed him a napkin. "And you'll need to take your hat off."

"A gentleman never wears a hat in a church sanctuary," Betty said.

The church was decorated in the simple, classic style of early America that Erin had always been drawn to, mostly white woodwork with slim, yet stately columns and flashes of red on the altar and the pew cushions. A tulip-styled pulpit rose from floor almost to ceiling on the left. How many people had walked these marble floors over the years—over the centuries—members of her own family, names tucked away in books at the Marx Room, people who had lived, and moved, and had their being in this place. Baptisms, marriages, Holy Communion. Funerals. The stained glass windows along the sides were propped open to allow fresh air into the sultry sanctuary. Standing by the piano at the front left, a stout man with hair like Richard Nixon's was talking to a handful of tourists fanning themselves with brochures about the church's history.

Betty led them to the opposite side, near a case containing an ancient Bible written in German. "This church was built in 1775, and when it was completed, it was first used as a hospital for soldiers returning from the fighting in New York."

"The Battle of Brooklyn. My six times great-grandfather was there," Erin said.

Ethan spoke up. "He was a colonel!"

"Well, how about that! The story I'm about to tell you may involve him, then. The Easton soldiers' commander was imprisoned, and he lost most of his men."

"That was him, Peter Kichline," Erin said, her heart thumping at the prospect of learning something new about him.

"Well, he was quite a man," Betty said. "The soldiers in his company who lived through the battle either managed to escape to other units or also became POWs. When the Colonel was released months later, he led a group of his remaining men back to Easton. Those poor men were starving." She shook her head. "The women of the church started baking right away—you know we still love to feed people—but the men were so hungry they couldn't wait. They scooped up the raw dough and ate it."

Erin was speechless, but she felt admiration. Gratitude. Sadness. Those men—her Grandfather Peter—had sacrificed so much.

Betty told other stories, about the historic church's origins, its pastors, the symbolism on the windows, including an unusual one featuring a Star of David. "That was in honor of Meyer Hart, a Jewish merchant in town who donated nails for this building," she said. "You might not think that's such a big deal, Mr. Ethan, not when you and your dad can just buy them off the shelf at Home Depot, but back then, making nails was painstaking work."

Erin's emotions went from sixty miles per hour back down to zero in two seconds as her son's eyes met Betty's faded blues. "My daddy is dead." The room closed in. Other people's voices sounded like they'd been forced into a blender. *What do I say, or do, for Ethan?*

Betty did it for her. "That makes me sad, honey."

Erin thought the woman would be tactful and drop the subject.

"When did he pass?" Her arm went around Ethan's slumping shoulders.

"A few months ago."

Betty pressed her lips together and shook her head. "My son lost his dad when he was about your age."

"He did?"

"Yes."

"How did he die?"

Erin cut in. "Ethan, maybe she doesn't want to talk about it, honey."

"No, no, that's alright. It happened a long time ago, during another war. Our country certainly has had its share of wars." Betty paused. "Ned was a career Marine when he went to Vietnam." She seemed to be absent from her body, transported to another time, another place. "He was with the Second

Battalion at the Battle of Khe Sahn in 1967, and while his men were trying to take an observation post, they were ambushed."

After a respectful pause, Erin said something she hoped didn't sound trite. "That must've been terribly difficult for you." She hated it when people said banal things, especially "Time heals all wounds." There were times when she didn't want her wounds to be healed because that would mean putting Jim further behind her. He was already much too far away.

"It was difficult," Betty said. "I hadn't been going to church for a while, just laziness on my part, I suppose, but after he died, I wanted to come back to this place, but I was afraid."

"Really? Why?" Erin felt sweat trickling down her back in the heat.

"This may sound funny, but I was afraid to trust God. I wanted to, needed to, but if God had taken Ned, how could I be sure he'd take care of my son and me?"

Erin felt like yelling "Bingo!" That's exactly what she'd been going through but hadn't quite known how to put it. Instead, she whispered, "I know just how that feels."

Betty reached out and squeezed her right hand, a firm, cool squeeze. "Do it anyway. Even when you doubt. There's no one more trustworthy or reliable than God, no other place to go that offers what we so deeply need. This I promise you." The old woman gazed into the choir loft at the back of the church and began to recite something she'd obviously committed to memory years before and had probably repeated often: "Do not be deceived, Wormwood. Our cause is never more in danger than when a human, no longer desiring, but intending, to do our Enemy's will, looks round upon a universe from which every trace of Him seems to have vanished, and asks why he has been forsaken, and still obeys."

She couldn't stop the flow. Erin reached for a tissue in her overstuffed purse. "C.S. Lewis, right?"

"Yup. *The Screwtape Letters*. But there's a Bible verse that kind of goes along with it, from the Book of Job."

As Erin wiped her eyes, she and Betty recited, in tandem, "Though He slay me, yet will I trust Him."

❧ • ☙

She was too tired to sleep. She closed her eyes and found herself imagining she was sitting in the band shell along the Delaware, standing in the church, walking up Northampton Street. There were reenactors. The Declaration of

Independence. Huzzahs and the canon. Sean. Betty. Even Paul Bassett made an appearance. Past. Present. Back then—way back then. And now. She finally turned on the lamp and noticed on her nightstand one of many books she'd purchased at the Sigal Museum. *Northampton County in the American Revolution* by Dr. Richmond E. Myers. On the cover was a depiction of Robert Levers holding the Declaration as two men in uniform listened atop their horses.

Erin read several pages before coming to the part about July 8, 1776. *The Colonel and all other field officers of the First Battalion, repaired to the Court House, the Light Infantry Company marching with drums beating, fifes playing, and the standard which was ordered to be displayed.* She stopped. Read the words again. This was about her Grandfather Peter. Chills raced up her left leg as she "saw" Ethan falling in step with the soldiers, tracing Peter Kichline's very footsteps. Ethan had marched with them as if he belonged, *knowing* he belonged. This was his rightful place. It was hers, too. She was being drawn back to Easton at the Forks, to the past, yes, but also to a future, and a hope.

❧ • ❧

About the Author

At fifteen, Rebecca Price Janney faced-off with the editor of her local newspaper. She wanted to write for the paper; he nearly laughed her out of the office. Then she displayed her ace—a portfolio of celebrity interviews she'd written for a bigger paper's teen supplement. By the next month she was covering the Philadelphia Phillies.

During Rebecca's senior year in high school, *Seventeen* published her first magazine article and in conjunction with the Columbia Scholastic Press Association, named her a runner-up in their teen-of-the-year contest. She's now the author of nineteen published books including two mystery series, as well as hundreds of magazine and newspaper articles. Her other books include: *Great Women in American History*, *Great Stories in American History*, *Great Events in American History*, and *Great Letters in American History*, along with *Harriet Tubman*, *Then Comes Marriage?* and *Who Goes There?*

A popular speaker, Rebecca also appears on radio and TV shows. She's a graduate of Lafayette College and Princeton Theological Seminary, and she received her doctorate from Biblical Seminary where she focused on the role of women in American history. She lives with her husband and son in suburban Philadelphia.